FEETS

FEETS
A CIVIL WAR NOVEL

JAMES GHOLSON, JR.

Outskirts Press, Inc.
Denver, Colorado

Feets
A Civil War Novel

Outskirts Press, Inc.
http://www.outskirtspress.com

ISBN: 978-1-4327-4126-6

Outskirts Press and the "OP" logo are trademarks belonging to Outskirts Press, Inc.

PRINTED IN THE UNITED STATES OF AMERICA

Table of Contents

PART I

I

Memphis

For my father, G. James, Sr.

Steam rose from the slick, macadamized, earthen roads that began at the Mississippi River's edge and led eastward towards Nashville. The shower had come quickly, dumped its brief rain near the riverbank, lowering torrid temperatures generated by the scarlet shock of sunlight peeping from behind the clouds covering the fiery red ball glued to the steel blue sky. A few blocks beyond Auction Square slouched an unmarked pen for slaves. Its pugnacity rebelled against the stolid aristocratic building that bore the name Calvary Episcopal Church. The six-foot tall wooden slats framing the fence blistered from the punishing beams of sunlight cracked and peeled in response to successive days of ninety-degree heat. Unlike Calvary's cross that wore four points, the geographical map of Memphis bore only three: one that pointed north, one that pointed south, another pointing east, and none that arched westward. The right arm of the cross at Memphis was missing, as was its Christian potency in the lives of slaves from Africa.

The polished brass of Posse's rifle sent sun sparks across the gleaming cobblestones that led downward into swirls of muddy water and a beach of stone forming an embankment for boats. The shower had been anticipated by the pin oaks and weeping willows located higher on the Memphis bluff. A chorus of their branches wrenched their leaves back and upward, frolicking gaily to absorb as much rainwater as possible. Sound moved slowly so as not to strain against the merciless combination of humidity and sunlight. Even human speech was slow and deliberate with the overbearing sun smashing the snap of consonants into the vowel sounds that immersed them. Sparrows, redwing blackbirds, and the occasional mockingbird danced along the river's edge, sampling the mosquitoes and other insects still bold enough to challenge their feathered quickness in a transparent atmosphere of molasses.

Midday humidity and the boiling temperatures of 1863 Memphis slowed even the flight of flies. Instead of the zingy whistle that usually accompanied their movement, one heard a long, rumbling groan that announced their presence. Seeming to know this, the birds fed upon them and strutted about with a corpulence that renounced flight. The eddies and rivulets which formed in the Mississippi fractured the river's surface, leaving veined fissures on those portions of the river not engaged in the merry reflections and twinkles that trapped sparkles of sunlight.

Periodically, the bloodhounds of Posse Raiford got in their minds to chase the pigeons, themselves focused on the litter in which could be found the occasional peanut. Notably slow afoot, the dogs were regularly out sped and reluctantly panted and puffed their way into bone-breathed docility. Posse was clearly a hunter for hire; he came decked with a bountiful sombrero, a bullet-stocked bandolier, handcuffs, two rifles, a pistol, a whip, and knives. Some called him "bandito."

FEETS

Feets knew he preferred Posse; he said so whenever he needed to have his horses shod.

Free blacks in Memphis, prior to the Civil War, were few and far between. Any process perceived to aid and abet communications among blacks was outlawed. Few blacks knew of the 1860 Crittenden Compromise, and fewer still possessed the skill to read it. Reading and writing were severely prohibited by law. In fact, the argument persisted, much like the appetite of mosquitoes for human flesh, that the ultimate recognition of personhood, in the form of the African slave, was the varied and sundry prohibitions against nourishing their literacy "to legally prevent communication and learning by a people is the ultimate recognition of humanity!"

But slaves knew the reason for war, drums or not, reading or not. Professionals among the race were, for all practicality, unheard of. Slave uprisings, revolts, rebellions were feared in the young Confederacy. Fugitive slave laws allowed bounty hunters to pursue, snare, and return runaway slaves to their owners irrespective of the jurisdiction, north or south. Bounty hunters were judged on their success to track and find – to fetch for reward.

MEMPHIS

Their ranks included whites, Creoles, Cherokees, Apaches – anyone with a record of success in search and find. "I part Creole, part Cajun, part French, part Cherokee. I search for refugee from sea to shining sea," chanted Posse's calling card. He framed a picture of "bandito" brave, foxy, intrepid marksman, and scavenger, part everything, mostly Cajun. He sat quietly examining the midday auction as it unfolded, his bay tied to the hitching post, his feet crossed lazily on the rail of the general store.

"Gather round folks if you plan to bid today," trumpeted the auctioneer. "Gather around and get out your notepads and pocketbooks!"

The fellow seemed gay enough and positioned himself on a wooden platform, more back than centered on the large, open, square-shaped park and a bit to the left of the colossal, rectangular block of granite standing at its center. He blew his nose several times in an unsuccessful attempt to free it from congestion. Feets, positioned as he was next to him, wondered why; most passersby couldn't breathe either. In fact, no one downtown after this brief shower, with the sun pounding every creature relentlessly, could breathe easily. The combination of heat, steam, and humidity made oxygen a banished commodity. The red polka-dotted tie the auctioneer wore stood in stark contrast to the loose white suit that seemed a little large. The polka dots stuttered in singsong under his chin, much as his words stuttered up Front Street. In fact, the man seemed clown-like; the face, the voice, the garb all appeared to Feets out of joint and context. "This is more of a circus than a sale or auction. I thought auctions were serious matters," he thought. "Mom should have let us come to these. This guy is funny!"

In his mind's eye, he pictured the man with painted lips and oversized shoes, just as if he were under that main tent he witnessed a few years ago. "Posse, this fella is a clown!" he voiced out loud. "Does he have a band with him?" The man next to him shifted his posture a bit and responded, "Is funny on top, but more serious it becomes." The crowd around them grew and chattered in comic disbelief. A small boy in the vicinity pointed to the man saying, "Daddy is the circus coming?" Feets kept his eyes glued to the brass megaphone the man used to shop upcoming events. Although the red nose never appeared, he thought it would come into view any moment. "Magic, it will come like magic," he thought.

The gaiety of Front Street was infectious. Men and women making grocery purchases coupled with tourists of every size and description staring wide-eyed at red polka dots, a brass megaphone, and the great expanse of the Mississippi. Golden rays of sunlight had pierced the clouds right after the storm and seemed brighter than ever. The Union flag which had draped the post office since 1862 spangled in the breeze, its furls untangled by the combination of a slight breeze and glowing sunlight. Buckboards rolled by, somewhat less dusty in their passing because of the quick shower. Traffic became diverted because of the gathering crowd still moving north and south down the narrow avenue. Parasols and umbrellas stayed open, first to protect from rain, and now to shadow from the glare of the sun. Two or three bent black men collected the droppings of horses so as to prevent pedestrians from being "splattered with horseshit," as one of the passersby aptly stated.

FEETS

In the distance, Feets Roche spotted the dark outline of a vessel, a good-sized ship, moving with regular motion, past the sun-spiked bluffs of Memphis and approaching the town from the south. The vessel seemed to crawl, revealing more of its true speed as it rounded the bend where Fort Pickering blistered the bluff. It crested and drew into full view. An eerie silence accompanied the boat. With the imposition of martial law in Memphis, the gathering crowd of bystanders knew that slave auctions in Memphis were now illegal. Most law-abiding Memphians had taken an oath of allegiance to the Union. Those in resistance had been run out of town. Just north of Memphis, the town of Randolph, itself a burgeoning crossroad of commerce, had been burned "beyond blackness!" That was one of Feets sister's favorite phrases, and as she stated it, she always remained absolutely flat-faced and watched those within earshot erupt with laughter at the sheer wonder of its meaning. He wondered too, spinning the phrase on its axis of *into, out of, and beyond blackness!*

"Crews for Hire" was painted along the sides of the vessel. Feets erupted, "Look Posse, here comes the band and maybe some more clowns!"

MEMPHIS

The ensuing minutes were occupied with regular blasts of a foghorn coupled with the panting of a large bell located on its starboard side. Eventually, a gangplank emerged from deep in the hull and lengthened accordion-style to the cobblestones at the lowest portion of the docking area. The ship threw anchor next to the landing bay like a roach in copulation. The resultant snuggle with the cobblestoned embankment delivered a load of hirelings in the color of brown and black who, according to the auctioneer, were chained for their own protection. The chime of chains mingled with the soft slosh of waves slapping against the ship's hull. In order to improve their perceptions of events, the crowd, which had grown even larger and sported parasols of every hue to shield bland complexion, lengthened monoculars and peered into binoculars.

"Get your worker here! Keep your notebooks special with entries about the finest, able-bodied help and sharecroppers you would ever expect to see!"

A hush crawled across the crowd as a line of bedraggled slaves, African in appearance, inched its way down the gangplank nearing the bottom of a hill yet to be negotiated, for arrival at Auction

FEETS

Square. Their mindless march mimicked marionettes minus a will to live. Mosquitoes, flies, and grasshoppers, the cannibalized detritus of once teeming insects lay strewn about the pathway up to the square. The swallows had feasted. Soldiers garrisoned at the fort and stationed throughout the city stood quietly by, unsure of how to handle the event. Indeed, it looked more like a slave auction than an employment festival or a circus. At the sight of the gloomy parade, a drunk dancer, festooned in rags almost identical to those of the dismal marchers, broke into a chorus of "Mine Eyes Have Seen the Glory" and circled the auctioneer in a curious series of weaves before shouting vulgarities and shuffling farther up Front Street. He never spilled a drop of liquor in his jaunty and syncope-loaded foray. Yankees, Yankee-haters, assorted couples, rouged whores, Saturday afternoon picnickers, and merchants all jockeyed for prime watching spots. Feets Roche decided he would stay one more minute before returning to his chores at the blacksmith shop, his spirits sunken by the gang of despondents who favored him in color.

"Feets," drawled Posse in his clear articulated Cajun

accent, "Be *tres interessant*, watch the johnnies un-load this cargo." He adjusted his bullet bandolier and climbed to a slightly higher position on the higher porch of a nearby furniture store. The line of hirelings crept closer, winding their way to Front Street and towards the middle of Auction Square. Although the home guard was not clearly visible, a band of ruffians hooted at the show. To the trained eye of Posse, they ostensibly maintained a defen-sive positioning alert to movements of the Union soldiers. Yankees posted as checkpoints, clenched their weapons while remaining invisible to the av-erage eye. Feets momentarily wondered if any extra rifles or pistols were stashed in wagons or closeted nearby. A stone's throw from Posse, he watched the sad gang climb the Mississippi's torrid banks. Through the eyepiece of a Whitworth rifle Posse had allowed him to watch the procession through the magnifying eyepiece. He refined the image as he altered the position on his face. The makeshift eyepiece, black in color, contrasted markedly from the golden barrel of the rifle.

"Not the original eyepiece," mumbled Posse, "but almost magnify same." Feets studied the monocu-lar briefly, and returned it to his eye for a closer study of the grave lineup. Rumor had it that Posse worked for the council, actually called a syndicate, which included among its benefactors none other than Nathan Bedford, slave-holding millionaire of the Memphis slave trade, himself.

Posse tapped Feets quickly on the shoulder saying, "Feets, what sign say? Read to me out loud."

"Faudree Auctioneers, Twelve, Noon, Saturday!" spoke Feets quietly. Posse took a deep drag off his cigar, inhaling its rich aroma. He blew thick, bluish rings of smoke from half-puffed cheeks, positioned his sombrero backwards from the crown of his head, and stood on the railing of the building. He appeared relaxed and in thought. Feets marveled at how close the marchers seemed and felt heart struck at the sad, hopeless gravity with which they proceeded. The gay mood of the gathering crowd modulated into increased emotion now. Even so, the crowd grew, drawn in by the drama that was about to unfold. The throng massed into a hushed herd of expectant flies. It seemed as if it imbibed a mean-spirited hunger to suck what little remained of life from those within the bonds of chains. Just as the flies and pigeons had pecked at cakes of shit left by pass-ing horses and oxen; just as the birds had sucked the life from the mass of cannibalized carcasses that littered the grounds; just as the detritus of hungry spiders hung in the silky webs of a thou-sand corners. Feets unconsciously finger-flicked the black half-mooned medallion that graced his neck.

"This operation is sloppy," added Posse, "Usually, more armed shipmates on hand to insure no trouble. They ask for trouble, this crew." A dark-skinned, almost purplish-black male buck, close to the end of the procession and ominously mus-cular in appearance, wore leg irons though his arms and torso were free. Posse excused himself, gently relieved the boy of the golden Whitworth, and studied the scene himself through the single lens, itself mismatched, from the Davidson scope, which usually found itself in the company of the famed Whitworth rifle.

"Buck could cause big trouble; should be restrained in arms, aussi!" he commented. The auctioneers chatted vividly in preparation for the twelve o'clock event, lifting to their faces brown bags of liquid,

and joking in murmurs that, even from a short distance, revealed the barrenness of their hearts and
souls. A bright reflection bounced off the window
behind the produce stand farther down the street.
Feets eyes clockwised the street northward, barely
catching Posse's movement towards the auction
block, his chestnut in tow, his Whit casting rays of
sunlight much larger than those twinkling off the
rippled sheen of the Mississippi.

He tongue tossed words back at Feets, "Mare is *tres
bonne*, a healthy heifer!" Beautiful skin and teeth ain't
been matched up in this line. Where I come from,"
and he cupped his large hands around his mouth
to hide his words from the comprehension of the
crowd, "Palomino pussy art in motion." Dropping
his hands now, he continued, "Two younguns. Bet
her and the kids go for the highest prices here today. You a bettin' man, I mean boy?"

Feets thought he detected a snicker from behind
the sombrero and his thoughts registered the comments, much as an accountant registers double
entry in an accounting book; a rational item to be
added and mulled over later to help more clearly
define the person behind the words. He winked his

right eye in understanding while thinking, "This Cajun bounty hunter playing both sides of the scene; spews words of hatred about the event, but ready to control it no matter what happens. The money must be real good!" His thoughts stammered. Falling short of understanding, his instincts slanted towards mistrust and his emotions stayed poised so as not to reveal a decision. Stoic.

II

Memphis

*Slaves obey your earthly masters with fear and trembling,
with sincere heart, as you would Christ, not by way of eye-
service, as people pleasers, but as slaves of Christ, doing the
will of God from the heart.*

Ephesians 6:5-6

The voice of the bishop, rich and well intoned,
floated across the dank, humidity-laden air and
into the congregation. Unforced, it glided as if
airborne by the strong wings of a hawk. In fact,
if Feets' mental focus were not outside on the
crows periodically darkening the bright sky, he
might have thought of the personae of Bishop
Hightower as hawkish, a hooked nose cloaked

over a baritone-rich mouth in the mighty power of the mysterious. Bishop had danced on the final words of the verse, "sits at the right hand of God, doing the will of God FROM THE HEART!" The sermon had never considered the undercurrent feelings of its black parishioners, most of who stood in the upper balcony, separated from the white members of Calvary Church. It never even broached the subject of yesterday's murder. Questions murdered Feets' concentration. Was it natural for the black buck (he never had learned his name), to allow himself to be put up for auction? Wasn't it natural for him to try to escape this embarrassment? Wasn't he free to choose his means of employment? If he was a criminal, was this a forum for defining his guilt or innocence? What would happen to him now? Could he charge the captain with kidnapping (or buck-napping) and who, indeed, was the criminal? Feets' thoughts confused his heart for many moments as he eye-chased black crows across their arcs of flight outside the windows of Calvary. Reluctantly, he smiled at Penny.

Dara Roche was proud to be considered one of the black pillars of Calvary. She had been the Bishop's maid and domestic live-in since leaving Mississippi for work almost as the lips of Abraham Lincoln pronounced the Emancipation Proclamation. The seams of her broken heart had mended as she became more involved in her half-day job at the hospital and her responsibilities as a domestic.

"Why shouldn't I strive for respectability? My children can read and are clean, and Hawk will come to Memphis when he can," she thought. She was lucky to have landed the work and felt obligated to attend services here at the church, even though it lacked the political focus that captured her imagination, her desire to be free in the north. Even though she had come to yesterday's tragedy late, she could not help but notice the brokers as they examined their ledgers at the start of the auction; notice the gleam in their eyes as they surveyed the human chattel: the procession of black and brown contraband, of the dispossessed presented as helpers for work on the farm and in the kitchens of white folk in Memphis. "Yes, I am lucky," she repeated to herself.

Penny Roche wasn't about to think of respectability or big men falling into the river. She knew that the river had a huge appetite, just look at the thick lips of its riverbanks and the speed with which logs floated down its massive gullet. No, better to skip rope, help mom polish the beautiful glasses held in the cabinets of the Bishop's house. She drew four lines, two vertical and two horizontal, on the back of the Sunday program. "Feets," she whispered, "look." She pointed to the page so as to minimize speech. His reluctant smile grew warmer, "So!" he whispered. "You still are a loser and I can still beat you." Penny's legs, just shy of reaching the floor, swung back and forth scissor-like in glee and from her mouth escaped a mild shriek; "Ou-wei." She loved tic-tac-toe.

"Sh, shh," ordered Millicent Dara Roche, whose patients were already beginning to call her Mother Roche. She had worked to banish poor deportment from the garment of her carriage and also from the undergarments of the deportment of her children. Her unerring glance had caught the o placed on the tic-tac-toe template drawn by Penny and the hefty nudge Penny's elbow had planted in Feets' gut. Feets had drawn his x, once again trapping Penny in a variation of the flanking attack that she almost always fell into. He surprised her by the trap, and surprised himself by the use of the word "flanked."

Had he been following the war too closely? Was the jargon of war starting to populate his thinking? Flanked: to address the side of a military formation, putting the largest numbers of the enemy at risk. The definition had stuck and he prided himself on the ability to accurately memorize his homemade flashcards. *Education is emancipation,* he conjured, rapping his knee with his knuckle. Maddened by the inevitable loss that would follow, Penny stomped one patent leather shoe and crashed the other into the second of two pews that the Roches were lucky enough to capture for seats. The bang clapped loudly, magnified by the ceiling, which acted as if a baffle for an organ or woodwind instrument. Interestingly, the arched eyebrows and recriminatory stares were not turned on Penny, but on her mother. Feets smiled at the attempt by the black womenfolk to keep his mother in her place. Even though she was hardnosed on keeping her kids on the straight and narrow, she herself was fiercely independent. "Lord give me strength," she had whispered as she rolled her eyes upwards toward heaven. For good measure, she gave Feets her behave-yourself-in-church glance, sometimes called her "killer stare."

Penny thought quietly to herself, gently pulling her long pigtail that she and her mother concocted to draw attention to the spring-like mahogany beauty of her face. Feets thought she might try to slap him with it, so he pulled away from her ever so slightly, and her eyes traveled up his chest in search of a target at which to shoot.

"Your plait ain't no whip lil' goil," he said teasingly. "Goil" met the icy stare of Dara Roche and the rhythm of her first finger movement was an ancient reminder of the pace of weeping willow switches, stripped of leaves and pulsating across his wiry six-year-old legs. She leaned across Penny, still seated as the recessional hymn began, and whispered, "Feets Roche, you ain't no baby. You may be ten plus six, but you ain't grown yet. Mind your manners."

For his part, Bishop Hightower was proud that his sermon was apolitical, antiseptic, indeed respectably liturgical and non-inflammatory. He had focused on the abstract to the pleasure of the vestry. The business stalwarts of the town were pleased that his sermons did not agitate the colored folk of Memphis to wish beyond their means. They were not bookish but simple people. "We want our niggers simple, too!" A century later, humorists and scholars would emphasize "service-oriented" as an euphemism for its great disparities in income and education.

Posse was not interested in church. For him, it was a foolish pastime for those expressing superstitious natures about what might happen in the future. He knew what needed to be done in the future and that was to make money. He studied the sketches in the paper and pondered on the words that engulfed each page, not that they meant anything to him; he could not make hide or hair out of any of the sentences. He couldn't read. But he had an appointment with the kid he had met named Feets. He knew Feets could read and he also needed to have new shoes put on his chestnut.

III

Memphis

Headlines in the morning's *Memphis Daily* made prominent mention of Saturday's events. The Sunday and daily papers rested in a neat stack outside the small shop known as Fauks' Blacksmithing. They were enclosed by an iron bin that also housed a waist-high enclosure reserved for mail. Feets had asked blacksmith Fauks why he hadn't built a sturdier receptacle for receiving mail, checks, orders, and such. His response came quickly, "No time!" Now that the man had left him momentarily in charge before his Confederate enlistment, Feets was starting to understand exactly what the man meant. Feets felt as though most of his waking hours were spent working in the shop.

FEETS

The newspaper read:

Captain Henry O'Malley, skipper of the boat Shrine Chaser *was brutally murdered at the hands of a lunatic sharecropper at midday on Saturday close to Mud Island. The captain was busily unloading contraband when brutally accosted by an African male buck of muscular stature. As the African savage choked him lifeless, Posse Raiford fired a spectacular shot unleashed from the heights of Front Street to wound said buck in the shoulder. Unfortunately, the captain suffered a broken neck and fell into the murky undercurrents of the Mississippi River. All that could be recovered of his former presence was his uniform cap, conspicuously decorated on the bill with bright yellow scrambled eggs. Local residents are angered over the incident, which further demonstrates the savagery of the Africans in our midst. Given the lack of all civilized grace among these strangers to American shores, we find it unimaginable that the Union seeks to arm the African buck to further insult and disgrace the Southern way of life.*

The day was almost saved by a gentleman called Posse. In full possession of his faculties and equipped with a trusty Whitworth of the kind used by General Nathan Forrest, Posse severely wounded the buck as Captain O'Malley, broken neck and all, fell to his death. He was pronounced dead

MEMPHIS

at the Army Hospital on Union Avenue. Funeral plans are unknown.

Feets glanced around the shop quickly before starting the routine Fauks had given him. He then fetched a large pail of water from the water pump, swept loose hay from the entrance, and made sure than his tools, hammer, nails, prying forks, bellows, anvils, and files were in their places on the wall. He then lightly oiled the vice and hand-powered jigsaw, fetched some additional coal for the brick hearth, and emptied the wooden baskets underneath wooden tables. Many of the tools had penciled drawings to outline their correct wall position. With broom in hand, he whisked away old filings from the plane sander and on top of the wooden tables. There was method to the routine: water first for emergency fire extinguishing, oil next for tool protection, and hearth fire last. He used the bellows to initiate this last step and had solid flames and heat rolling as Posse strolled in.

"Hey, Feets, morning to ya!" The hand-cranked drill on the wall next to the window caught his attention. "That's an interesting equipment piece! Use you to drill holes, *n'est pas?*" Posse fumbled with the deck of playing cards he had in his shirt pocket adding, "You still auction think of as carnival?"

Feets thought, "Once you get past the order and arrangement of the words, he's not hard to understand," and said, "Yeah, I use it to drill holes." Feets turned to grab the bellows, pointed them at the lower portion of the mound of coals supporting the robust flames and up-cranked the volume of his voice, continuing, "You still need those shoes for your horses?" The silence that answered caused him to glance over his shoulder at Posse, who stared at the newspaper clippings Feets had installed on the wall of the shop; he often read the paper as he worked. Posse caught Feets' stare and proffered, "Sorry, wasn't paying attention. I missed what you said! The paper you can read!"

"Oh yeah, and no. I know that was no carnival! I asked if you still needed those shoes for your horse?"

"Uh-huh, *oui*, I four way need. Just replace them all. Since you know how to read, you think you can me some pointers give on reading?"

MEMPHIS

"Well I got some tricks that the schoolmarm taught me; actually, my mom taught me mainly." Increasingly aware of the man's infirmity, and not wishing to call attention to it he gracefully added, "We must start first with the alphabet. Start very slowly if you are out of practice, and then add words. A man as smart as you will have no difficulty in learning how to read." Without waiting for an answer he added, "Have you had reading lessons before?"

Posse nodded in the affirmative without making eye contact. After he quick-glanced Posse and rummaged his imagination, Feets picked up a bucket of whitewash standing in a far off corner thinking, "Make flashcards using that card deck in his pocket and use the words from the newspaper."

"I will need that deck of cards, Posse. You can use this old bench behind the door to paint them and then we'll start right now; business is a little slow now, so the more we can get done, the further along we'll be when things pick up. In the meantime, bring your horse around to the side alley and I can get started on him."

FEETS

Before walking the horse to the shop's side, Posse grabbed the broom standing behind the bench, brushed off the bench quickly, and laid all the cards out, face up. The ads of the paper had been tossed in the trash bin; he salvaged that two-page section. Neatly smoothing these pages out, he moved each card to a separate place atop the newspaper pages.

"You have brush, *n'est pas?*" he quizzed. "Oh yes, that *n'est pas*. It means 'do you not,' right?"

"Uh-huh, *mais oui*. I mean yes!" was Posse's response.

Feets gave him the brush, added water to the white-wash, and delivered both to Posse, demonstrating on one card how the cards should be painted. It didn't take long for the man to finish. While the man was earnestly attuned to the task, Feets gathered four bars of iron and fired them in the hearth. He rounded them on the anvil using a hammer slightly lighter than the one used by Mister Fauks until they came close to the traces he had made of the chestnut's hooves. Posse took some hand-bills from his saddlebags and studied them as Feets went about his task. From his position at the anvil,

MEMPHIS

Feets couldn't see the pictures clearly but noted that they were daguerreotypes of black men and women. Before giving the words a second thought, he asked, "You said you hunt runaways for bounty. That means money, right? Are you chasing those men you have in those handbills?"

Posse quick-swept the establishment and lowered his voice somewhat before landing his eyes on Feets, answering, "*Oui*, many of them are not valuable, except two or three. They run up north usually. But trip is difficult and is very long way. Syndicate many dollars pay Posse, even though black is now free, to bring back more expensive slave to plantation. I chase and bring back one or two; many dollars of money keep in my pocket. My puppies need de exercise and Posse can do nothing else. Not as good a job as being a blacksmith, but we all must work. This is what Posse do best!"

The answer was plaintive in its tone and seemed to grow out of embarrassment rather than pride. A sudden smile appeared on the face of the man and he added, "The slave often has not the use, even of a horseshoe, to make his escape easier; no shoe for the feets. You not have been out of Tennessee, but is very, very long way for slave to walk to escape clutches of Tennessee—for the old, *c'est* impossible." He cast a glance at the dried cards adding, "What we do next to the cards?"

The subject change quick-registered with Feets. "Okay, next we take your bowie knife and neatly cut out the alphabet and words; we put definitions on the back. So first the alphabet, then the syllables, and then the word. I will show you and write those three steps. I write that out for you. Put word on one side and definition on the other side. Definition is the same as meaning. So we put the meaning or definition of the word on one side and the alphabet, the syllables, and the word itself on the other. He continued, "When you practice, you shuffle cards up many, many time, just like in poker, and practice. It's good to practice many, many times each day. But first, before we start, you also have to whitewash the other side."

While the cards dried after Posse attended to the other sides, Feets finished rounding off the shoes and applied files to the hooves of the Chestnut after removing the old shoes from the horses' hooves.

"Yeah," he spoke, adding enough energy to his words to draw Posse's attention away from the handbills to which he had returned. "You can memorize these cards just as if you were studying those handbills and determining the character of those men you are after. Words have just as much character as people and do not allow yourself the luxury of becoming frustrated."

"Aye, frustration is a dilemma to study very interesting. Often Posse think of ways to measure the level of frustration slave can stand, the level of determination in the mind of slave. It is true, when I study these pictures I try to see how much determination, joyfulness, smartness, is in the eyes of the runaway. Syndicate may not understand the mind behind the eyes, the quality of judgment and creativeness of slave. Posse has to know these things—try to outguess where refugee go, east or west, cross stream, down stream, or up mountain, use nose and eyes. Sometimes Posse even have eyes in the air to chase slave.

He said slave at first and then said refugee. Which does he think is true, slave runaway or African refugee? Which of

FEETS

the two is a person, a thinking, feeling, and fearful person? Eyes in the air—in the air?

"Oh, you mean a map! So, do you think of slave or refugee as a human being, as someone who desires to be free, have family, learn to read, and have an interesting job?"

"Posse no think about such things. If Posse ponder about this question, Posse can no longer do job; no longer do whatever necessary bring back slave to plantation. The master, he sometimes very, very angry at slave; just want back property for which he spend money. Master no care always about the feeling of slave; that I see very rare. Anyway, now you show Posse what is next with the cards."

Eyes in the air—what does this mean? Use map, perhaps a bird? "Alright! Now we have to cut out the words. I sharpened your knife and now it's quite sharp. Cut out these words I have circles around—captain, close, arm, trusty, neck—and I will put definitions on the backs of these cards. I will pick out some additional words. Start slowly, adding more cards each week."

Feets wrote out some definitions, finished with the re-shodding and was about to close some flutes over the hearth when Belle, the manager of the restaurant across the street, peeked in, slid her wide-brim back to unshield her eyes, and spoke, "You boys look like you could use some of my biscuits! Whaddaya think? Posse, almost every other person is talking about that shot you made yesterday. Course I am one of the few who understand that it's those carrots that you get at my place that helps that happen. Oooohhhh, now you got Feets trying to learn you some readin'. Told you already, get out your Bible. Surest way anybody could ever have of learning reading."

Feets smiled as Belle sashayed into the shop, a modest basket loaded with buttered biscuits swung from her elbow, and retorted playfully, "We ain't even begun to talk about my fee, but I been thinkin' 'bout getting some shooting lessons, once I get him set up for learning."

"My, my Miss Belle." Posse had already moved in on the biscuits and spoke simultaneously with Feets' "fee," making the rest of the boy's comments unintelligible, at least to Cajun ears adding,

FEETS

"been practicing that shot ever since I was in the crib, Miss Belle. We boys down in Louisiana learn to protect ourselves real early; guess that just cause we learn to do most things on the early side. Me and Feets gone strike upon a deal."

The moccasins he wore gave not the slightest hint that his feet had touched the ground. It was almost as if he floated across the room, his nose leading him toward the aroma of hot bread.

"Focus, flex, fire. You inhale across all three. Inhale real slowly, and you almost can't miss. Now we know that. You shoot Miss Belle, don't cha?"

"Where did you EVAH get a thought in your head like that, Posse? You know that I couldn't possibly hurt a li'l old fly!" She slid off her straw hat, the brim seeming to grow ever larger, and hadn't noticed Posse slipping the handbills of runaways into his pocket. Belle had owned the restaurant for many years and was known for her personal warmth and her shrewdness with a dollar.

"Took some biscuits out to some those contraband camps last week. Some of those folks are in terrible condition and those camps are nowheres near as well organized as that one down in Corinth. I guess they be trying though! Here is some coffee to go along with those biscuits. Wash 'em down, don't cha know! Brought some hot chocolate for you Feets."

"Thanks, Miss Belle. Smells delicious and tastes even better! I did some work over at Camp Dixie last week myself—never seen Camps Chelsea or Fiske!"

"Feets, you know how I enjoy cooking and how wonderful it is to have your family here in Memphis. We can be friends here, go for occasional walks and have tea together. Hell, in Mississippi, we might get shot at just on sight. Your mom is such a sweetheart. There is so much going on these days with the war and all. They said Vicksburg couldn't hold out much longer under the pounding of all those Union canons last summer. Grant gave them all the hell they could stand up under! The Cotton Syndicate, that group of plantation owners, is still around trying to do things the old way—got some kind of power psychosis. They over there going back and forth about that recent battle. Seems they can't make heads nor tails out of who won that battle outside of Chattanooga—place called Chickamauga. That Union general, General George Thomas, doesn't say a whole lot in the newspapers, but he sure carries a fierce punch. Being from Virginny and all, they can't stand to hear the name mentioned! One of my helpers says he was Provost Marshall down in Corinth. Anyway, Rosecrans left the field. Thomas almost single-handedly saved the Union's right wing from a complete rout. Forrest was supremely pissed! Imagine that, Bragg had Rosecrans on the run, ran him all the way back to Chattanooga. Apparently Longstreet punched through a breech. They got the map right on the wall, so as to follow the movements and such."

Posse: "*C'est vraie.* I seen some of them in the market the yesterday and they speak of Thomas, say he do good job as general. Strange though, that he be from Virginia and still with Union."

Belle: "Speaking of jobs, Posse, you 'bout ready to make steady money and come work for me over at the restaurant? We still get some of those ruffians in the place and we must have better security, especially on the weekends. You'd be much better off than chasing refugees all over yonder, specially since its illegal anyway."

Posse said nothing right away. He collected the cards, which had dried and took another swig of coffee from his tin cup. "I think real hard about it Ms. Belle. I stop by this evening so we chat, *tête-à-tête*, about it. Feets, I leave the Whitworth up against the wall over there if you want to take closer look; it is unloaded." He looked at Ms. Belle adding, "Feets never seen hexagonal bore before in rifle—wonder how the accuracy of Posse is possible. I tell him simple: focus, flex, fire and inhale over all three!"

It was rare for Posse to feel appreciated. Standing in the middle of Belle's Biscuits restaurant, being invited to sit with the Cotton Syndicate, being recognized as the center of attention, held no particular fascination for him. "What is the job they want now?" passed through his facile mind quickly as he sauntered towards the group. The poster they had discussed was placed in an envelope. Boss Noland started the discussion as Posse beckoned to Belle, pointing to a coffee cup.

FEETS

"Posse, we have a wager going and most of the fellas believe that you are the man for the job!"

Posse merely nodded his skeptical approval, knowing that he was never invited to discussions other than slave catching,so as not to be drawn into the lowest price too early in their negotiations. To his credit, he was a student of human beings. As an accomplished tracker, he always tried to understand what choices a refugee might make, what direction he or she would take. He did often call "runaways" refugees; he knew of the squalor, deprivation, and hopelessness under which these people lived their lives. Put in their place, he would have done the same. Perhaps he would have been even more desperately revengeful. To test the magic of assuming the "refugee" mindset in order to confirm his strategic tracking decisions, he often shadowed the refugee for days, even when he could have crippled or hobbled the target before making a final assault. He responded to the offer, "I see."

Belle brought over some freshly brewed coffee. "Thanks," proffered Posse throwing a glance in Belle's direction. "More than welcome," added Belle.

MEMPHIS

Boss Noland continued, 'Stands about six feet two and missing one foot and colored coconut brown. Our offer starts at $1,000." After making the offer, Noland, eyes uplifted, counterclockwised a smile to the group.

Posse sniffed the air like a bloodhound and smiled. W*hat kinda bullshit do these jacks take me for?* If outside, he would have held up his finger to test the wind. Since he was inside, he alternated closing and inhaling through first left and then right nostrils, and then spoke, "*Mon ami je*. I am interested in this chase, this search for the single-footed one. You give me poster, I study face for a while. Posse tell you what I think is at stake in the chase of this runaway."

There were two daguerreotypes. One, taken from the shoulders up, exhibited pride in the large and intense eyes, focus of purpose in the somewhat angular, yet broad, base of the nose and the heft of muscle throughout the upper body showed significant strength. The other, taken at full length of the "single-footed one," showed a concentrated athleticism, taunt lower limbs (even with the foot missing), and a distinct nimbleness than was still

within purchase of the body. Posse posed a question, *"Tres dangereuse,* you say is blacksmith? This
one is quick-witted and could be dangerous; the
price will be higher. I assistance maybe for handcuffs, shackles, horseshoes, and ammunition. Oh,
yes, and food! My rifle, she require bullets very
special. Bullets not always available. See if I can
duplicate model bullet made like this!" Posse
showed them one of the bullets specially made for
the Whitworth. Its convex, angular grooves glinted
in the minimal indoor sunlight. If you wish, I can
suggest some names to you that—"

"No," interrupted Boss Noland who had seen
Whitworths before, "We want you; name your
price!"

Old Jack pitched in, "Yeah, with the caveat that
the expenses vary according to state boundaries.
We do expect higher fees if you have to cross state
boundaries and—"

"Contract with you or Old Jack," interrupted Posse
looking at Boss Noland who nodded affirmatively,
"Me!"

"Two thousand dollars up front, the balance—

$3.000—when I return with the contraband. I will need one other person for this job. Will let you know when I decide to leave and set schedule for trapping refugee. Offer like Grant, unconditional!"

If Posse had been able to read, he might have signed the contract as "Posse Raiford." As it was, he signed with an X. For now he applied skill at visual memory beyond the mere tracking of this one-footed African buck, this black American male slave to be captured on this trip. He memorized: *six feet, two inches, chocolate bronze in color and sharp of feature, muscular torso and missing one foot—maybe headed for Fort Pillow or Memphis, last seen in Oakland.* Later, he would cut out the words and use them for reading lessons with Feets. He added muttering, "I memorize the face! You say called Hawksmith?"

Memphis forlornly flew the Union flag on June 6, 1862. African American slaves, known also as "thinking property," streamed out of Union-occupied towns and villages towards Federal lines. Spies, home-guardsmen and guerrillas crawled throughout the western theater, including New Orleans and Memphis, plying their trade and seeking new opportunities for turning a dollar. Already

FEETS

before 1864, the war for the Union begat two confiscation acts, which nullified owners' claims to fugitive slaves and freeing slaves of owners' disloyalties to the Union as an article of war that refused the return of fugitive slaves to former owners, and the Emancipation Proclamation.

At Fort Pickering, located on the banks of the Mississippi at Memphis and a block from Beale Street, contraband were employed as laborers, commissary workers, teamsters, and for garrison duty. One day a week, or more when she could manage, Mother Roche volunteered for duty at the Veterans Army Hospital cheering patients, scrubbing floors, ironing, and doing laundry to assist the Union effort. She had the blessing of her employer, Bishop Hightower, and remained loyal to him, just in case the divine deemed the Confederate cause just and victorious. Her ultimate superior was Mother Byckersdyke appointed to Memphis by General Sherman and held in esteem by hospitalized war veterans, both federal and rebel, black and white. Mother Roche became known as the "Angel of Front Street." Because of her position with the Bishop, she was treated with a dignity and respect unknown to most black and tan ladies of Memphis.

Before the Vicksburg campaign, Grant had designated Memphis as the center-post of his medical and convalescent operations for the Western theater. The hospital center would receive sick soldiers from Arkansas, West Tennessee, and northern Mississippi. Mother Byckersdyke had been monumental in helping to organize volunteers for the hospitals.

"Morning, Mother Roche," chirped the bishop as he joined her in the kitchen for biscuits, scrambled eggs, grapefruit, and coffee, what he called his "preacher breakfast." Things are changing fast in this war zone—topsy-turvy, chaos really. Every hospital in Memphis jammed-packed, black refugees all over the place. Being an interim bishop is real tough work. Memphis might need a full-time clergy. I get caught in this amazing straddle of politics inflected, countered even with abstract interpretations of the gospel. I feel such horror at the tragic suffering of our black brothers and sisters. The city fathers are most inflexible about how we should deal with this. Your people are the pivot on which all this tumult seems to rest. It is a very perplexing situation," mused Bishop Hightower almost talking to himself.

Millicent Dara parried, "Can you take a man, beat and work him to death, revoke his access to education and self-development with black codes, hang him at whim, rape his women, sell his sons and daughters, mock the golden rule at every turn, breed the crime through generations, and expect him NOT to fight for his liberty? Bishop," continued Millicent Dara, "I ain't no religious scholar, but I know that the black spirit ain't broken. Tell the truth, maybe your pivot is under the wrong place, or I should say race. 'Long as I hear the music, see the dancing and industry for a dollar, I know—" and she broke into the melody of "My Eye Is on the Sparrow" and singing put forth, "And I know he's watching me! And thee! That's the truth Rev. Bishop, even those slaves cooped up General Forrest's den right there behind Calvary 'Piscopal. Oh no, they ain't let their spirit die. You can hear 'em singing and humming right along with 'Amazing Grace!'"

"How far would you go Dara? Would you, would

Mother Roche, as many call you, kill to protect her children even though killing—taking what you cannot give back—is a sin according to the good book?"

"Well, I ain't never been put in that position to make that choice. I imagine that it would be a mighty tough one, mighty tough. What about you?" she answered as her soul veered away from her lips sneering back. *Damn it, Millicent, you know full-fucking well you been put in that position time and time again, when your daddy was shot, when your mother was shipped, and when you was sold right here in Memphis; but you best be keeping that to yourself, lest you and yours be split up if you can't earn a dollar.*

"Well the journey through 'ifs' doesn't always crack the hulls of tough, menacing questions," voiced the bishop as he washed down a fork full of scrambled eggs and a quarter bite of biscuit with coffee.

Millicent thought of her Hawk later that day as she made her rounds at the hospital for the colored. She new that the unsanitary conditions under which black soldiers were housed combined with sloven-ly-provided medical care caused many deaths and severe sickness among the Negro troops. Many of the newly minted black soldiers were here already; a sizable majority of them had embossed on their backs keloided reminders of disobedience or mis-obedience to white masters. Labyrinthine scars crisscrossed keloids were crudely etched at cotton farms where 'white gold' was king. Amputations were performed to limit mobility , though nothing staunched the exodus, nothing froze the desired metamorphosis from slave to refugee!

She had consciously raised both her children with the attention that she knew would be denied them in adult life. She spoiled them with kisses, she fed them generously, she taught them to read. *Oh Jesus, what a wonderful library*; nothing could have reined in her joy at seeing the library of Bishop Hightower. It was all she could do to maintain her gravity as she watched her spirit bump around the ceiling like a balloon gone wild, farting with glee as it bounced around the English chandelier and the wooden staircase, landing, air poor, on the Bible, Keats, and Shakespeare. She didn't know what the names meant, but her children would, just read one page after the other. "I think I would like it here," was all she had said when interviewed.

MEMPHIS

Now her children's intellects festered with a bubbly curiosity. Both asked many questions: Ma, what will we do if you get sick? Ma, when will we see our daddy? Ma, what do you do at the hospital?

"Feets, Penny, I told you—everything! I change bandages, apply iodine. I read out loud to the men from the newspapers, stories about the battles. About Bull Run, about Manassas, about President Lincoln." Because she could read, she was one of the first to know about the Emancipation Proclamation

"But Ma," Penny had said, "If you get sick from the men at the hospital, would me and Feets go stay with Daddy? Would Bishop Hightower help us find him? Is he still working on that plantation in Mississippi?"

She answered, "Maybe yes, maybe no, but rest assured that Mr. Lincoln will help you find him. Abe Lincoln will help you find your daddy!" She put her arm around both her children adding, "Things are changing all across the land, even here in Memphis. The wounded from Shiloh speak of great determination of Northern soldiers. My supervisor, Mother Byckersdyke, asks me to read and sing to the patients. It keeps up their spirits. I make pretty necklaces and tie them around their necks, especially for the colored soldiers. Many of them are very superstitious and like to have trinkets around their necks just like that half-mooned medallion you have, the one with the hawk on it."

Her brisk walk had taken her to the hospital. She remembered that she was preparing a special dinner that night. Bishop Hightower had invited a guest to the parsonage and she had to buy some chickens and other groceries. The money in her pocket would buy an ample supply of groceries and, being the careful domestic that she was, she would spend it wisely.

She was proud of her Feets, newly apprenticed to Mr. Fauks, a local blacksmith. At the behest of the bishop, Fauks had consented to take on the boy because of his "brights" and general industriousness. *He shows the same bent for mechanics and smattering of artistry in his drawings that characterized his dad,* thought Millicent. Also, the boy's quick grasp of words and numbers had not gone wanting to the Bishop's quick eye.

"Feets, you got the same talent for metal work and design that was your daddy's. It was rumored that Hawk could turn a slab of iron ore into the prettiest butterfly you ever did see—birds and horses, too. Fact of the matter is if he made a hawk, you could bet that it could fly, or at least make you think it could." She laughed to herself. The smile that crossed that boy's face, quick-flashed over his lips and rested, gleaming in his eyes, gave her the blush of pleasure that she had reserved for his father. She had not lain with him out of duty or order; no, she considered the work of his hands miraculous and was immediately attracted to his wit and personal, imaginative industry. It had been years now since she had seen Hawk; she often wondered how he was and when, if ever, she would see him again.

"Where is Daddy now?" the boy had asked when younger, at one stage over and over.

"Everywhere," she'd answered, "wherever you are, he is!" and that seemed to satisfy him. "You can see him hiding in the sky. That's why they call him Hawk, cause he is up there in the sky cruisin' and floatin' 'round. Anytime you see a hawk, you might

FEETS

as well be looking at your daddy; he be strong and powerful jus' like that hawk floating free in the clear blue sky." She remembered Hawk by the deep rasp in his singing voice and the strong muscular grip of his arms around her as he sang, holding her body to his chest.

IV

Memphis

The blackness of Memphis nights within the now newly refurbished gas-lit north district was pitched at a level far beyond that seen in darkest Africa. Superstition prevailed that the squeals of the blues emanated from such a darkness. Tales persisted that this darkness emanated from the cries of a pig when clutched by the hug of a huge bear— the sad music of the engulfed and surrounded. As a refuge hostel, Fort Pickering was far and away, one of the most active, mainly due to its proximity to the Mississippi Delta. As a military compound, it emitted an aura of safety that was unknown in the eastern-most extremes of Memphis. Most notably, given the summer 1864 presence of General

FEETS

Forrest, the contraband camp at Grand Junction was moved to Memphis exactly for reasons of safety.

A single lantern lit the home of Bishop Hightower located as it was in a residential corner situated close to Calvary Episcopal Church. Its flickering flames gently pierced the night, causing dancing shadows to taunt trees and passersby. On this quiet evening, one could almost feel the gentle lapping of waves against the banks of the Mississippi. Farther south, past Tennessee Street and west on Beale, a figure had limped along on its uptown journey. Union soldiers, disheveled and loud of voice, ambled and stumbled their way back to Fort Pickering. In the shadowy corners of the street, black laborers and teamsters sat talking, comparing notes of the day, negotiating with prostitutes, and listening to the wails of music floating out from the bars and restaurants. Union soldiers anxious for entertainment caroused the various establishments, enchanted by the skits, fellowship, and follies designed to separate them from their dollars. The stench of alcohol and cigar smoke blended with the aromas of women's undergarments. The composite rendered a special musk peculiar to that part of town. Two soldiers, dressed in union blues, stumbled down the boardwalk, stopping at an alley.

"Gotta take a piss!"

"Well hold it, damn it. We almost at the barracks. You can piss to your heart's content once we get to the river. Fact of the matter is you can piss a stream right into the Mississippi long as you can keep the levee rats from pock marking your pecker. Put some starch in your spine if you plan to get by the duty officer."

"Can't make it. Where's my damn revolver?"

"Right there in your belt loop. What the hell do you need that for?"

"Its New Year's and we toast to the new year. Hey, you over there, you in that long-ass officer's coat! Get your black ass over here! Know you niggahs is grateful to us Yankees for helping Johnny down to his knees! Keeping these Rebs in their place is cause for celebration. We been drinkin' a blue streak. Minnesota peeeee! Niggah, hold this lamp while we piss. Whoopeee." the soldier muttered to

FEETS

himself and lateral-waved the gun in the direction of Marcus Roche.

Marcus Roche stepped towards the white officers, took the lamp, and held it high. He had already seen two posters with his faces on them, so he obliqued his face under the lantern, grabbed it, and hand-covered the half-mooned medallion draped around his neck, finger rimming the brass buttons on the oversized, long navy coat as if he were twisting his thoughts into focus. He fish-eyed both bluecoats, "No problem, for a damn dollar, and the deal is off if you don't holster that revolver."

"Damned contraband be smart-mouthed soon as they get off these damned plantations—here's your dollar and the lamp!" The flame of the lamp frolicked and threw bizarre silhouettes against the dark pith of evening. The shorter man of the two replied, "Damn good idea," and took the revolver from the other as steam rose from the arch of urine careening off the walls of the alleyway. Marcus held the lantern and backed out of the alleyway as the two finished their water business. He readjusted the peg on his leg, straightened himself with one crutch, pulled up his collar, and swung into a gait that muted his limp. The stops that he made along the way only minimally betrayed his furtive search for the house numbers that recently installed gaslights still rendered dim.

Fog of increasing density augmented the luminescence of the nearby Fort and threw a glassy glow over the whole of downtown Memphis. A drunk, holding high his liquor bottle, gestured wildly in his direction, wretched vomit in the yard of a close by establishment, sidestepped Marcus, and danced a series of jagged bounds, spirited head jerks, and backwards sidesteps. Marcus was stunned that the bottle never broke or spilled liquid! The only verbal part he could clearly understand was, "Damn!"

Occasionally, a small glimmer of light whisked by his head, but any witness could recall no clear form of face. In this gas-lit gloaming, even the most astute student of movement could not readily identify Marcus Roche. The eyes of both Union sentries and hell bent home guerrillas had missed him. For one dark, gray, misty night, luck was on his side and had hidden the measured hobble of Hawksmith.

FEETS

It was in this dimly lit darkness that Bishop Hightower's outdoor lantern, often refueled to define the entryway revealed the identical number written on the crumpled sheet of paper in his shirt pocket. In the flickering light, the figure appeared too lean to be the owner of the house, too self-conscious even to be in the neighborhood, but yet aware that the modest abode was exactly the correct domicile that bore the distinct ingredients he identified as correct: the correct address, correct colors, the correct street positioning, and the correct street numbers. Self aware of his movements in the dappled light, Marcus Hawksmith moved efficiently, hobbled manner to the side, then to the back, and bear hugged the shadows in the backyard. Crouched, caged-monkey-like, he alternately glanced over both shoulders then rapped on the windowpane of the servants' quarters of Bishop Hightower's modest dwelling. The hollow sound drew numb silence. If someone had seen him, even at a close distance, the figure might have suggested the experience of watching a dancer through wax-papered windows of a blues club on Beale Street. A gentle triplet of raps was magically followed by darting glances followed by the quiet raising of the single window through which the unusually bent male figure, clothed in a full length officer's blue navy coat, balanced itself on the tall crutch. He mounted the sill precariously equipoised against gravity, hoisted and rebalanced himself perilously on the self-same sill, flutters, balances and then rolls over the ledge onto the tall stick, posted militantly in the middle of a small. Squared on the wooden floor, he landed safely.

"Whew!"

Muted candlelight flickered around the window's rim, aggravated by a ripple of breeze shunted by the crutch. The astonished, over-opened eyes of the "Front Street Angle" met him and his shoulders melted in her arms.

"Marcus, you made it! Oh you taste—look so good, baby." Millicent Dara clutched her arms around the sweaty neck of Marcus Roche. Tears of joy, armpit sweat, and the smell of oven-baked rolls that she had left on the table to cool co-mingled. True to his nature, Marcus, mitigating his need for her, stood smelling the smell of her hair and bathing in the warmth of her touch, the glorious silk of her skin. For several minutes they stood mute in the joy that flowed from months turned to years of separation.

"Cheeks just the same. Those pretty brown eyes still dancing in their sockets. You smell luscious, too, like honey." They kissed tenderly at first, and then the memory of their lips took hold, making their kisses harder as if to immortalize a tactile joy that both knew might not last or be oft repeated. He put her face between his hands and held it there, mind-traced her face for a future sculpture, then rubbed her back and toyed with the sway that flanked into her buns, "These golden buns! Always did fancy those riverbank buns!" They hugged, tickled, and tussled, skylarking in the small room's darkness.

"Sh-sh Hawk," for she almost always called him by his nickname, unless she was angry, "You gone wake up the house."

"Where are the kids? Are they asleep?" he whispered.

"Right next door. Where you think they'd be, out foraging in the night? They been missing their daddy something awful, too. Feets is blacksmithing and I'm teaching Penny to sew. She's not very patient but she has real good hands!"

"Lemme see, I promise not to wake 'em up," and he hobbled past the doorway, spying Feets and Penny on pallets in the larger of the two rooms. Slicing the room in two with his crutch, he swings around to the boy and caresses the chain and coin around his neck. "I love this boy and his beautiful sister." He threw an uncaptured wink to Millicent, leaned to kiss Penny, and studied the ever-lengthening feet of his son.

"This boy's feet are almost wings; he done growed since the last time I saw him!" And he narrowed his gaze to see if the half-mooned token, the medallion as he called it, was still in place. He could hardly believe his eyes as he watched, listening to their breaths, and saw himself in their sleep.

"Yes," said Millicent taking his arm "He gone be tall and handsome, jus' like his daddy! I love you Hawk," and she moved his hand to her waist, grazing a taunt nipple. She had known his ways early and profoundly understood his love for his children. He had made up in his mind that he would wait for her to initiate their lovemaking, if there was to be any lovemaking. He always regarded their time together as a great gift. One that he perhaps had not deserved, but one that made him feel special, even preordained in some far away place. In his own mind, she was pure luck for him. Pure unadulterated luck, and he pinched himself each time he found himself engulfed, bathed in a rendezvous of their love. He knew by the taste, the smell, touch, and feel of her in his arms. Strangely enough, her cinnamon smell was what first attracted him to her, magnetized his affection, drew him to her thoughts and mental agility. Then, he began to see her more and more as a woman and in that crucible of smell and thought, his appreciation fired into lust, love, and then devotion. He was transported by their love and felt refreshed emotionally, psychologically, and physically from the time he spent with her. He was prepared to continue his journey north if her desires had changed, if her needs were new, and if she felt committed to her life in Memphis. He had prepared himself for rejection. But he did want, desperately, to see both his children.

"They be growin, that boys feet!"

"Yeah, he gone be tall and handsome, jus' like his daddy."

"Those your daddy's feet, my daddy had medium-sized feet!"

Under a normal circumstance, she would have parried insult with him, blow for blow, played the dozens with him far into the late hours, but time was short. She took his forefinger and placed it in her mouth, sucking it gently and asking, "Have you eaten? I have some leftover chicken and rolls. Wash yourself in that water over there and I will fix you a plate." She took his overcoat and stretched it out over the pallet. He washed, ate, and they talked.

"I hope and pray for you Hawk, ever since we left. We all fine now, kids healthy. Might be better chance for us to be a family all together up north. Even so, I seen handbills describing you and offering a right big bounty! I can't bring myself to mention them to the children."

Marcus smiled, "Just means I got to be invisible on occasion."

FEETS

She carried the washbasin over to his feet, removed his shoes and began to wash his feet. As she washed them, she massaged the foot, still healthy but strangely deformed from the slice of its Achilles tendon, delivered to keep him rooted on the plantation from which he had run. She massaged it with olive oil. "Where you be headed now?"

"Well I went to Pickering and signed up! Joined the Union Army, right there at Fort Pickering. They need all the blacksmiths they can find. My unit is assigned to garrison Fort Pillow. We leave tomorrow. I am a free man at the end of the war and I will send for you and the children. I'll send my medallion when it's time. I've money for you."

"Be careful, Hawk. Please be careful," she whispered, pleading for his dedication to his own safety.

"I plan to," he replied as he finger-grabbed a sandwich and checked the window and foot-checks the door. "They gave me a post at Fort Pillow; say they need all the help they can get up there. At first, they didn't want to let me join, because of my foot and all. But I helped in the shop for a day and they were impressed by my work. Heading up there in the morning if a train comes through. If'n don' none show, then I wait for the next supply train."

Dara pinched the flame that had grown brighter and reduced it to its previous minute flicker. Placing her finger against a small spoon, she convexes, then concaves the spoon to extinguish the flame.

"Hawk, did you miss me? I have missed you and the good times we had. You're always on my mind. Bishop here's been good to us. He's a fair and honest enough man," she spoke as she caressed his chest and thighs then toweled dry his arms and neck. "I want you to make yourself a man for me Hawk, want to feel you inside me, baby," whispers Millicent in his ear. The music of her words enchanted him and he ran his fingers up her neck, around and through her hair.

"My time is short, baby. Make sure Feets keeps up with his medallion and Penny keeps her anklet on, too. You got yours on?" He examined her ankle and seeing the small iron casted bracelet around her ankle, smiled, kissing her from the length of her leg up to her belly button. "Tell them everyday I love them."

She knew he was leaving soon—could sense it in his voice—and placed her forefinger on his lips. He sensed her excitement, smelled the musk of her rise and intertwine itself with the cinnamon of her skin. He teased her smallest of nipples between his thumb and index finger and bathed in touch of as her fingers reached inside his pants to massage his thighs. His manhood was made even stiffer by the soft flecks of her fingernails. Millicent, back arched bridge-like, inhaled deeply and pulled him inside her, polishing his erection with the satin juices flowing from her labia. Her thighs glistened in the candlelight as they sought, then found the wheel of rhythm familiar to their union. Candlelight spidered then splintered around her neck.

"Ooouuuhhh," "That feels sooo good. Made yourself a real big man for me, didn't you, baby?" He slipped into quarter consciousness and pumped slowly, panting as she spoke, "Hawk, you feel better than ever; do me baby, do me real good!"

MEMPHIS

Been a man for you since I was born, sounded in the back of his mind, *ever since I seen you in the flesh.* Dara juked left, then right, and he trapped her, pulling her down closer to the heat of his scrotum. "Soon gone be one for you year round," he slurred.

The completion of their circle rolled into deeper thrusts. As their thrust grew stronger, they showered one another with kisses of increased delight. At the peak of their frenzy, they quaked simultaneously, their mutual exhalation clapped out in staccato-like flickers of candlelight that warmed their journey into joy.

"Now you smell just like me," she laughed softly. "Let me wash you." She rinsed and dried him in the dark as they kissed in relief. He strummed his crutch like a guitar softly humming, "Under the willow tree, made love to by a smoked Yankee."

"You still smell like me," and they both laughed.

"When I get to Ohio, after this whole thing is over, I'll send you a full medallion in a perfect circle and get word to you of my location. I will send travel money too; it will look just like this one." The red-tailed hawks that he loved watching were a natural source of inspiration to him, even as he slipped on his pants and kissed her in preparation to return to the fort. He showed her the black hawk coin he had fashioned and cut in "S" like halves, one half held by a chain around his neck, just like half he fixed for Feets. Marcus had similarly fashioned two smaller medallions for Millicent and for Penny to wear around their ankles.

"My 'smoked Yankee,'" she teased, handing him a sandwich and thankful that their romp went undetected. "I made up these envelopes. Each one has my name, our address, and some stamps on it. Be sure to send us something in it that tells us where you are and how you're doing." She looked at his foot and thought to say, *Even with your one foot, you act like you gone perform the feats sometimes accorded to two*, but thought better of it and said nothing. They hugged and Marcus "Hawk" Roche left the small hut and disappeared into the darkness of the late February 1864 night.

V

Memphis

The American Episcopal Church could take one hundred years, maybe more, to escape the stink of its ambivalence to slavery in the American South. The golden rule, "Do unto others as you would have them do unto you," is central to every great world theology; I grieve for the church profoundly.

-Anonymous

"Par Excellence!" That was the phrase Bishop Hightower had used to describe the table he approached that she had prepared for his dinner guest. It was also the phrase he had used to describe her cooking on occasion.

"Looks magnificent—and the food! The chicken

smells just awesome. Can I do anything?" he asked. She loved preparing meals for dining in the library. *All these wonderful books,* she thought in private. And the music on the spinet made those evenings perfect; she thirsted for those times when the church organist would play Chopin and Bach. She hungered for time to read Hume, Schopenhuer, and Hegel. In short, she adored the access her position as mistress of the house gave her to the intellectual jewels of the West. What she could not reconcile was its wanton exclusion of works about the black experience in the country in general, and about blacks in Memphis in particular.

Her purr-pitched response bristled with friendly sarcasm, "Bishop, after all those inspired speeches on Sunday mornings, you just take a seat. Feets will get the door when Mr. Noland arrives. I been quizzing and schooling Feets and Penny on that Golden Rule—especially when Mr. Noland starts to retort, hold forth on slavery and all!" She flashed on the long talk she had managed with them adding, "Boss Noland be coming through that door any second now and, of course, we want you to be rested and calm when you bring up that anti-lynching campaign!" She knew she had stoked the coals a bit on that issue, quickly dousing it with, "Just ring this bell if you need something quickly. Me and the kids will be eating right here in the kitchen. We'll bring in each course on the menu. Do you want the order to be soup, salad, main course, desert, and coffee?"

"That sounds marvelous," replied the Bishop, straining to keep his eyes off the bowl of fried chicken he saw in the kitchen.

"You say my sermons are good, eh? That's a good thing with politics in such an uproar, loyalty oaths and our faithful sheep being banished from their own houses. I would never have imagined that these good people, our very way of living and breathing could be threatened so. We must try to be appreciative of one another—and of our property!" she interrupted, finishing his sentence in midstream and thinking of property as contraband. Of course there was no doubt in Millicent Dara's mind: *The golden rules applies to thinking property.*

The loud knuckle-rap on the door severed their chat. The misty aroma of a cigar announced the arrival of Boss Noland. He was immediately preceded by a small could of billowing blue smoke, which evaporated, blurring the image of the carriage in which he had arrived.

"Millicent, that boy of yours sure is shootin' right up in the air—fine looking boy, too! Evening, Bishop!" and he quick-flashed a smile in the preacher's direction. "Heard he be right handy with those tools in the blacksmith shop—hammer, anvil, wheel cone. That's a great thing 'cause we need all the extra help we can get, muscle, sweat, and energy to keep Memphis rolling during these hard, hard times! Especially with Fauks' gone to the war and all! Yes sirree, he be a welcome addition to the Bluff City."

Penny circled the table with a pitcher of sweetened tea. *Darn tooting*, she thought to herself, *my brother ain't no fossil*. She then disappeared behind the swinging door after checking the tea levels all around the table. Millicent followed with a bowl of ice, making sure that the two men had enough tea and soup to start the meal off.

Bishop Hightower broke into his traditional prayer before he began a meal as she laid the bowl at the corner of the table, disappearing through the swinging door. Feets waited for the prayer's end. In the space of very few seconds, he stepped and reached backwards to purloin a crispy wing from the bowl of chicken behind him. He stuffed two-thirds of it into it his pocket and slow-chewed the tip. He knew that his initial success would not be repeated and enjoyed nibbles of the tempting flappers as dinner progressed. Millicent made plates of the meal for her children, offering them a prayer dedicated to "freedom for our folk." They proceeded with their meal in the kitchen. As was her custom, she had briefly added words of hope for the success of the "Marcus mission," thanked the Lord for the Emancipation Proclamation, blessed the food, and each little medallion and bracelet in the family. When the bell rung, she quickly traipsed past the door, into the library, forked out the salad, and ladled more soup. She calmed her body so as not to detect the interruption she had caused in their conversation.

"Bishop," Noland continued, "we got Yankees—smoked, closeted, and homegrown— brandishing firearms right here in Memphis. That damned Sherman started that mean-spirited shit with this

FEETS

'loyalty oath' crap! My daddy would flip in his grave and spit if this shit had ever graced his eyesight. Citizens, good Memphis landowners, burned right the hell out of their own houses for refusing to kneel to the Yankee rod! We got niggers streaming out of the Delta like an open artery. Who in the fuck is gone pick the cotton and bale the hay?"

I knew that was coming, thought Millicent. She tossed a quick smile in the direction of the bishop, who unobtrusively snatched it midair, responding to Noland, "I understand your concern Noland, but damn it—forgive me blessed father—" and he crossed himself, "We will never be appreciated as a civilized, God-fearing society if we are always sparking these lynching and damned quasi-slave auctions. Those squatters and sharecropping fees are a farce."

Noland's teeth clacked and stuttered before he could emit a sound. He splattered chicken as he tried to speak through stammers. Half-chewed pieces of chicken flew airborne from his mouth. Embarrassed, he napkined his lips adding, "You Bible-toting clowns! You mi-mi-missed," and with the words he gaveled his fist on the table, "the goddamned point! I have lost money, lost crops on every one of these Saturdays. In *your* damn parish, folk have had their houses burned, niggers taken, cotton confiscated. Niggers are roamin', runnin' like loose deer to these damned contraband camps at Dixie, Fisk, Chelsea, Corinth, and Nashville. The home guard guerrillas are doing all they can to recapture and restrain some of the pests and keep law and order intact, but you can bet your bottom dollar that the economic losses will be staggering. Bishop, they are contraband, our fucking property. Thinking property got no truck with the golden rule—do unto others—all that crap! If they got feet, no matter if they are bunioned, hammer-toed, blistered, burnt, or broke, those feet be pointed north when they should be planted south!"

Krrhiggghe-pow! A loud crash erupted from the swinging door and Penny suddenly lay sprawled across the floor. Her dress ripped and several glasses atop her tray broke upon impact, splattering shattered glass dancing across the floor along the walkway to the kitchen. Millicent Roche, Feets, and Penny had been eating at the kitchen's small table when the girl had, absorbed as she was in the loud argument transpiring, lifted the tray to refill the tea glasses and mistakenly hauled a full glass pitcher of ice, instead of empty glasses. She had slipped, as the heavier weight of the pitcher unexpectedly shifted her weight, skidded and slid across the ice-diced wooden floor. Her focus on the conversation resulted in a loss of concentration. She had leaned against the door to overhear the conversation and unwittingly lost her balance against the doorjamb. Millicent shoveled her out of the library room, sweeping the ice to one side, adding, "We got the coffee made! Oh, yes, and dessert, Bishop and Boss Noland! That Penny never learns how to carry a simple tray and her ears are those of elephants! Anyway, you men are going to love this cheesecake!"

After tossing down his coffee, stoking his throat and locking his jaws around several pieces of cheesecake, and assuring Feets that he was going to come by the blacksmith shop to refit some yokes for his oxen, Noland bade goodnight to the bishop, Millicent Dara, and the children. He added, "The syndicate is meeting over the next few days at Belle's Biscuit House. I will let you know how the sessions go and what they decide. I can tell you that, for sure, their mood is not a hospitable one to your point of view!"

VI

Memphis

The earlier metallic blue sky had morphed into a blooming, mist-filled darkness; it closed in around the figure of Boss Noland as he departed. Feets felt a strange mixture of relief and anxiety as he looked out the window to track Noland's pathway to the carriage, but saw no motion that resembled the broad piston-like plunges of the man's step. He started washing the dishes and made sure that the dining room table was completely cleared. Bishop sat still at the table, wringing his hands at his inability to reach a thoughtful exchange about the comparative differences in his and Noland's thinking. Mother Roche cleared the plates of bones, leftovers, and residue as she pondered when, and if, she should congratulate the bishop for pushing the lynching point or play petulant because he didn't push hard enough. She flip-flopped through the balance of the evening, gratefully petulant.

"Thanks for helping your mother out with the dishes, Feets," Bishop mumbled. "Like Noland said, you—"

"I'm so sorry, Bishop!" Millicent offered. "That Penny of mine is kinda nosey. She didn't mean no harm by leaning on that door, She is just—"

"She is just a child, Millicent, and children have accidents! I think I will read just a bit before I retire for the evening. In the morning, I will walk with Feets to Fauks' place. I want to check on the syndicate. I think they might be watching his movements. I am sure Ms. Fauks appreciates his holding things down while her husband is away. Might as well check on her, too."

Feets flashed backwards on the lessons that Fauks had given him before his departure, and forward on the comment that they might be watching, but him? He had done nothing to them, so why watch him? He filed that question away until it might be answered by events. The lessons on the use of the bellows and hearth, the slap-dash lesson on gun-cleaning, and the precision steel balls that he mentioned in customizing the bore, the sight-setting process he used to coordinate the optical metal or monocular sight with the barrel for better marksmanship—was he supposed to remember the details of that one?

Mother Roche gave the stove a quick onceover with her dishcloth adding, "Okay, Penny and Feets, off to bed. Penny, anyone can have an accident, so rest your face and put some iodine on those scratches you have on your elbow. I have to re-check the library floor for any more glass pieces that could be lurking to cut someone." *If the sun exposes truth, then our folks are refugees from sunlight, unengaged by the ice of daylight!*

Feets looked forward to tomorrow, to his work in the shop. It had sharpened his sense of industry and strengthened him physically. He flashed on his interview with Mrs. Fauks, "Good morning, Mrs. Fauks. I appreciate this opportunity." He had practiced his greeting and his handshake, and the casual bow of the head, to show an understanding of his place and commitment to do good work. As he walked to the shop the next morning with the Bishop, he felt an onrush of pride and a lightness of gait caused by feeling creative and necessary.

"Have a great day, Feets," Bishop had said as he strode towards Belle's Biscuits.

"Yessir," Feets responded.

Feets made himself familiar with the tools of the shop. He struggled to banish the fear of firearms from his mind and focused on the hammer to be used for horseshoeing and the tall cone that Mr. Fauks had used for repairing wheels that had come out of round or had broken spokes. The manuals that Fauks had shown him were in a drawer, next to the vise. Bowls of potash bedecked the floor underneath the long wooden workbench. The imposing anvil stood on a wide log, almost at the very center of the shop, so as to be approached from any shop angle with equal efficiency. He knew he could make extra dollars by learning about gunsmithing as well as horseshoeing. He stuffed the gun manual in his shoulder pouch for later reading. He stole a quick glance in the direction of the shop keys that had been given him and repeated, "The keys are on the northwest table," to himself out loud. Then he proceeded to take every tool down, redraw the outlines of each tool on the wall, test the nails which held them in place, and reflect on where to arrange a place, somewhat more free from grime, where he could house gun-cleaning equipment. He resolved to diversify, hauled in some water, took floor measurements for a far corner, and moved one small desk from the doorway to the corner. *I need a long piece of canvas to separate this area, keep it somewhat cleaner, than the rest of the shop.*

"Bonjour, mon ami," barked Posse as he strode past the entryway. "How have you been? Me—I been just fine," and he started walking around looking at the varied implements Feets had placed in a pile on the table. I got some work for you and—I want to thank you for helping me to start on my reading." He took the pencil marker Feets had used to trace the outlines of tools and drew, P-O-S-S-E on the wall. "Spell my name, *n'est pas*? I also make cards to flash quickly, help me see letters of alphabet, too." He went outside, gathered his saddlebag, and stepped to Feets, showing him the cards.

FEETS

"Very good Posse, " responded Feets, fish eye-ing Posse and catching a glimpse of the Whit, still outside in the rifle holster. Posse had forgotten to leave it earlier. Feets pinched himself to banish the thought that Posse might have left it on purpose.

"Look Feets, I got a job for a little hustling entre-preneur like you. Something that would make you some extra money, perhaps enough to buy your freedom, for you, your mom, and your sister."

"How do you know all this about me?"

"I track people for a living, Feets. I track informa-tion, too!"

Maybe Posse would need that Whitworth cleaned and trued. *What a fascinating instrument, a hexagonal bore and the small tattoo on the stock, NBF.* He wondered about the emotions of a person who tracked black refugees for bounty. If the game was a fair one, where did the slaves have access to firearms? He had always loved the experience of being outside, breathing the fresh air, and the changes in seasons. He thought of the immense freedom that came with wandering around in the dense trees and the open farmlands of the south, free and unfettered, liberated from the double-think, the complex rummage through emotions and experience, thinking in two worlds, the habit of seeing the commonplace in the world, analyzing it from two different perspectives at once, the art of zeroing in on, balancing out experience with possibility, sifting through events for elements, nuggets of truth and trust. Is it possible for thinking property to act of free will? *When could property ever think? A conundrum of stupidity!* Mainly trust! "Gosh," he thought flashing again, "I sure wish I could shoot like that. One awesome shot at long range!" *The mighty Whitworth as my implement of protection!* He banished his jumble of thoughts from his mind and prepared himself for bed.

On the following day they arrived at the shop early. Bishop headed straight to Belle's and Feets pulled the canvas off the days' papers, setting them in the bin just beside the door, with the collection can next to it. Fauks had sold newspapers at the shop, a tradition Feets continued. Feets took one paper and posted it on the wall to keep up with news of the war himself. Fact of the matter was, as he became more established, he often tacked it to the wall on top of another out-of-town paper, essentially to get another perspective on how the war was progressing. The outdoor sign read: "Get your newspaper HERE," and he placed a heavy rock on top of the stack covered by rain canvas. The iron bin kept them from blowing. He started to work on his unfinished horseshoe pile.

"Feets!" Posse called, scratching his hair as he walked through the shop door, wearing a leather vest, and appearing somewhat more agitated and rumpled than usual. "You give to Posse a minute for speak."

"You always speaking, but you ain't saying a real whole lot. If you promise to leave that Whit today, I'll give you a minute. My business is picking up and you say you know my motivation. In two weeks, customers will be standing in line. Speak, speak, you gone say something. Otherwise you jus' taking up precious time!"

"Good you inspect Whit. Look at real good, but take with you always. Never leave in shop. I give you leather case. Citizen think it be trombone, think you be musician! I speak about time and you use time with Posse to make money, to buy freedom, of course. Posse has difficult detective work, tracking runaway to do. You help—*n'est pas*! Got poster of runaway name Hawksmith. I you show now, you maybe see face, claim bounty for self! Posse memorize face, make flashcards of words, get scent for puppies, get good bounty for to make chase! You join Posse, keep mother happy with stay out of war, buy freedom, and leave hell! Deal?"

"Posse throw in deal, aha, what's the catch! What's the deal?"

"Posse show Feets how to regulate and clean Whitworth. How to make weapon true friend and improve life and accuracy of weapon. Slaves headed north, not sure which side of river he take. We track this side of Mississippi as far as Fort Donelson. Try to pick up scent on this side or come down other. Let me know if you need I speak with Mother Roche."

VII

Memphis

A Butcher, A Baker, and
A Candlestick Maker?

Among the preeminent energy sources of 1864 Memphis was steam. Steam was central to hygienic efforts of the Memphis medical base of the Union army, established by Ulysses S. Grant in 1863. Steam was essential to the laundry organized by Mary Byckersdyke to clean and sterilize linens enjoyed by the Memphis Army Hospital Complex. Steam locomotives, boats, and steam fire engines provided propulsion to put out the fires, which torched the homes of banished citizens.

Bishop Hightower was a man trapped between the

old cotton syndicate and Deuteronomy: *Thou shalt not deliver unto his master the servant, which is escaped from his master unto thee.* His own conscience was horrified by slavery; his presence in slave society compromised him daily by his silent acceptance. He had to pray for Confederate families, counsel grieving widows and orphans, visit the infirm in hospitals, render homilies, and appear hostile to the Union, to the likes of both Boss Noland and Abolitionist Mother Byckersdyke. It was enough that John Brown's Raid on Harper's Ferry had robbed the South of its moral foundation and snatched away its sacred scaffolds. When the carriages pulled up to the parsonage, he was rooted, frozen to the plank, some would say astonished. He knew she had come to recruit nurses among the colored and his Millicent Roche wanted to serve.

"Good morning, Bishop," she smiled matter-of-factly.

"Greetings, Mother Byckersdyke."

"I'll get straight to the point, Bishop."

MEMPHIS

"Fine! Coffee?"

"Thank you," the terse words of the woman seemed well fitted to her austere manner of dress. "As you know, our situation here is one of great challenges. Not only must we contend with small pox, malaria, and dysentery, we are nearly overwhelmed with battle injuries of the most bizarre and grotesque proportions. It is absolutely necessary for me, therefore, to recruit nurses amongst both colored and white ladies of Memphis. Given this situation, I am requesting the opportunity to speak to your congregation about our needs and request volunteers for our Samaritan League. It would be a civilian adjunct to the Nurse Corps."

While Mother Byckersdyke spoke, Millicent Dara eavesdropped from the same door that sparked Penny's precipitous ice flight. She was riveted by the straightforward no-nonsense manner in which the woman spoke. Effortlessly, she floated a tray of tea and cookies, nodding to the Bishop and stooping to offer both to the guest. A flash of understanding conveyed in mutual smiles, cashiered all doubt of character as Millicent took the offensive. "The colored ladies of Memphis would be most proud to assist in any way, assuming, of course, that our superiors, our masters give their consent. I would be more than grateful to collect and present a group of such ladies, colored ladies, for your approval. Cookies, madam, tea? Master Hightower?"

"Ahem," answered the bishop, clearing his throat in the wake of Millicent's somewhat forward beneficence. "Of course, you can count on this household to support your efforts. However, it is rumored that your entourage includes significant numbers of contraband. We would require that your efforts are sensitive to the Ladies of Calvary to the extent that the coloreds and whites attend strictly to their own races. Otherwise, I see no difficulty in Millicent's involvement on the days when her duties here are not protracted or necessary."

Mother Byckersdyke smiled enjoying the oatmeal cookies and took a second cup of tea. "Thank you, Millicent. These cookies are delicious."

The bishop's offensive masqueraded as pontifications. "Afternoons on Mondays and Fridays might be a good start. In fact," he added as he surmised a firm bond of rapport existing instinctively between the two, "Mondays and Fridays it is," and excused himself with a backwards nod. Millicent passed an auxiliary tray of milk and sugar to Mother Byckersdyke offering flatware for stirring.

Before he could escape entirely, Mother Byckersdyke further trapped him. "Well, let us agree on a date, say Sunday evening next, for us to gather a group of local ladies at your church for the purpose of revealing our mission and seeking medical assistance that would benefit soldiers of both armies in recovering from their wounds and maintaining an environment of health that does not threaten the civilian population."

She continued, "We are concerned not only with the quality of care received by the soldiers, but also with the general hygienic state of the contraband camps. The Union has Federal jurisdiction over Camps Fiske, Dixie, Shiloh, Chelsea, and Grand Junction. I want Millicent to help us to minister Camps Fiske and Dixie. Keep out a sharp eye for general cleanliness and garbage disposal, monitor the health of the women and children, basically establish rolls and keep a journal of loose notes. Not anything final, just loose notes, if you agree to accept the appointment."

Millicent looked firmly at the mesmerized Bishop and spoke to Mother Byckersdyke saying, "I am most honored to accept your offer!"

Mother Byckersdyke rose to leave, adding, "Fine, you will start Friday; come as early as you can and for heaven's sake, please make the coffee!"

Millicent went on to effectively organize her work schedule to prevent conflict between her duties with Bishop Hightower and her volunteer work with Byckersdyke. She posted her schedule in the bishop's kitchen so that he, in no way, would feel impinged upon by the new arrangement. Her new assignment with the corps afforded her additional barters with which to purchase clothing and sewing paraphernalia.

"I am so happy that you have decided to work with us. It's important that you keep this letter of identification with you at all times if you are challenged by the guards posted throughout the city." Mother B, as she asked to be called, continued, "General Hurlbut was most impressed by your interview and delighted that you are so impressively literate." Their discussions had concluded with an assignment of rounds at the colored hospital on Monday and at the Gayoso laundry on the other, supervising washing, ironing, and starching of hospital linens, the preparation of bandages, and cleaning of surgical tools and instruments on Fridays.

"Mother Roche," as many of her clients now called her, learned much of the atrocities visited upon soldiers and slave refugees in the western theater. Much of her future advice, to both Penny and Feets, regarding health practices would be grounded in her nurse corps experiences.

Busy as she was, Mother Byckersdyke made sure-footed plans to maintain good contact with Millicent Roche. They evaluated the health status of the camps in biweekly evaluation sessions. They also conversed together shortly after making rounds at the hospitals, both black and white. Mother Byckersdyke offered in compliment, "Millicent, you're doing a wonderful job both at the laundry and with your inspection notes. You have a gift for nursing and your patients adore you. Some of the officers note that your writing is clear and concise. I agree! I have been asked to include the camps at Fiske and Grand Junction under my purview. I want you to continue as you're doing. Your instinct for health matters show initiative, common sense, and imagination. Oh yes, please include any military information you glean from contraband camps, about confederate issues, and troop movements in your reports. Of course, any information you gather will be treated confidentially."

"I see Mother B. Gladly!"

"Here is your office key and this is the dialog ledger we will use. It will always be in the top drawer of my desk. We should keep the office locked. Feel free to share any questions, observances, suggestions, and conclusions with me. Basically, it will give us opportunity to trap and refine emergency issues. I want to be sure that we are in good contact; think of it as written conversation." The diagram Mother Byckersdyke drew reminded Millicent Dara of the tic-tac-toe boxes her children drew in church. She smiled as she flashed on the "x's" and "o's" Penny and Feets elbowed one another over at the eleven o'clock hour.

February 1864

Mother Byckersdyke	Millicent Dara
Dear Millicent,	*Greetings!*
I hope your day has been good. Are you satisfied with the hygiene at Chelsea? I have asked them to identify three additional workers at Camp Fiske that can assist you in carrying food and lifting tubs.	*The new workers are a big help to me Mother B. Some of the contrabands report raids by General Bedford Forrest in northern Mississippi. He has kidnapped males for manual labor. Forrest uses them to help with the Calvary, build more entrenchments, and push artillery, or at least that's what my military friends tell me. Am using much new hygienic information at home!*
	Millicent Roche

FEETS

Do keep a map of Memphis and northern Mississippi with you, especially when visiting camps—and hospitals, too. Any trails and unmarked roads would help the cause. Let me know how the organization is coming along; of course, if you see something I have missed, be sure to make a note of it. *Mother Byckersdyke*	*Mother B -* *Will do! The keloids I have seen in some of the camps defied description, like a labyrinth of serpents choking a soul. Camp Fiske has a young talented drummer and the evenings are joyful and beautiful. I hope my son never has to endure the pain and hardship I see in the recovery world.* *Millicent Roche*
Be sure that your stores are counted and that nothing is stolen that belongs to the Union. We want to have plenty of iodine, soap, hot water kettles and irons on hand to do the work which God requests of us. *Mother B*	

African American refugees and runaways streamed

to Fort Pickering from all parts of the Mississippi Delta in the wake of Lincoln's Emancipation Proclamation of January 1, 1863. To say that they defied description is a compliment; certainly their description created a visual anachronism to the stories pictured in contemporary magazines of "happy darkies." The town was on its way to shantytown status. Added to this was the audio element ignited in music—drumming, banging, singing, tooting, and tonguing—all manner of every conceivable musical expression. Whatever could be struck to create pulse and rhythm—scraping, hammering, "back-beats," and syncope—accompanied their majestic wails in distinct cross rhythms. Whatever could inspire movement and courage was employed in moving the emotions, ferrying them to "the promised land." Millicent occasionally stopped to see the "dancing drunk," as folk were prone to call him, punctuating the pulses of Beale Street with toe, elbow, head shuffles, and mis-directs, all calculated to irrigate the atmosphere with joy. Folks far and wide lay bets on when, if ever, that fifth of rum would break on cobblestones or even spill a drop! Even the jailhouse was rocked by the drumming, as was the brig. And it was there that cries of "*Bertie, libertie pour l'homme noire!*" persisted, fueled

FEETS

by the drumming far into the dark late February nights. Mother Roche was glad to see the wounded spirits raised, glad to visit each hospital, especially the camps. They sported a strange potpourri of male runaways, refugees, and federal misfits seeking respite from the elements of weather and war. Who knew, perhaps one of them would have information about her Marcus?

VIII

Memphis

Male refugees of every height, weight, and color sought refuge at Fort Pickering of Memphis, ditto for Nashville and Corinth. As the cities of the South fell, the vacuum was redefined in chocolate. Feets and Posse watched as they walked from his Memphis shop, they saw the same sights, but listened for very different information.

"Feets, you thought any more about that offer I made you? Gone be hittin' trail soon and you would make helpful companion! Here are the bullets that Whit is designed to use."

Feets studied the metal gray-colored bullets, which

seemed shaved in clean, oblique lines to accommodate the hexagonal shape of the Whitfield bore. "I got to speak to my mom again about it. Don't think she is real keen about the idea. I told her it would be better than me volunteering for the Union like some of my friends. That seemed to rattle her a little. I bet I could make a die for this bullet, cast it in almost this same kinda metal. They might be able to give me some clues down at the fort about it!"

In this phase of the Civil War, the watchword had become recruitment. Slaves were recruited for the Union army; northern males were recruited for the army, spies were recruited for both armies, women were recruited for the nursing corps, and Feets was recruited to capture contraband. Anticipating raids by Nathan Forrest, now thought to be in West Tennessee and northern Mississippi, Washburn posted extra guards at hospitals, camps, and jails, lest prisoners, key personnel or vital troop movement information be compromised.

"Feets, this barrel is made of extraordinary hard material. See, I can hardly scratch it. The workmanship is extra special. I show you how to clean with rod, zero the scope, and check bore with gauge. Fauks did it once for me. I think he has steel balls in that drawer. You can you test and calibrate it with that stuff! I pay!"

"I can try to calibrate it. I can't shoot it here, but they may let me in at the Fort to shoot it. One of those generals, Hurlbut or Washburn, comes to the church on occasion; maybe they would let me talk to the ordnances folks at Pickering. They can help me to know how to work on your piece, maybe show me how to make the bullets also. That may take a few more days, okay? Tell you what, let's go to the fort now, see what we can find out."

"You go, I better not," Posse responded curtly. "Vibe me get from Fort Pickering is not good!"

"The ordnance division is located next to the firing range inside the fort," stated the guard posted at the entry. Wide-eyed, due to this first time inside the Fort's walls, Feets stared glued to warrior building in the personages of black soldiers drilling with firearms, marching, alternating ranks for firing, drilling for loading artillery. Contraband laborers engaged in a myriad of activities ranging from hauling crates, cleaning barracks, refreshing paint, and effecting stone masonry.

Feets saluted the duty officer, "I hope to find out information about a rifle I brought with me. Can you point me to the gunsmith?" After locating the division and explaining what he wished to accomplish, Sergeant O'Reilley commented, "Let's see what you got." Eyeing the military implement carefully, the man put on glasses, of the vintage Bishop Hightower used while reading, and reported, "Hmmph, looks like you got yourself a bona fide Whitworth .45 caliber rifle son, Same sort used by sharpshooting success with Forrest. We tested these. Most thought they were by far the better rifles. The tests were absolutely conclusive in my estimation, but politics being what they are, the secretary chose the Enfield instead. Whits do foul easily, but for me it's by far the better weapon. It is consistently more accurate at greater distances and made with much better precision and a higher grade of steel. The rifling, the number of twists in the bore, is quicker. It does have to be carefully cleaned. Is that what you are up to? Is it loaded?" Without waiting for a response and actively engrossed in the mechanics of the rile, he went on, drawing on a nearby piece of paper, "The bore is hexagonal like this, with rounded edges," and he quick checked to see if it indeed was loaded, which it wasn't.

"Good!" he exclaimed, "That would be a quick way of losing life and limb." Using a magnifying glass and a micrometer, he studied the markings and abruptly retreated to retrieve a long brush instrument. After inserting it into the bore, he said, "Hmm, fascinating instrument."

"Do you have a pass for the fort?" the man spoke smiling. "We haven't seen many of these here. Understand that top brass nixed them cause of the fouling problem. Are you the kid running the blacksmith shop up yonder?"

"Uh-huh." Feets spoke, sensing that the man communicated with him straightforwardly and without prejudice.

"Well, I have seen some of your work, the horse-shoeing part. You're getting pretty good. We could use some help from a fine lad like you at our shop, so think about coming aboard when Fauks gets back. Here's a pass with my name on it and a cleaning rod. If you come early, you can even test it on the firing range to adjust the scope. Your scope is not a Davidson, but it's pretty good. If you come late, I'm not around, but at dinner time, the range is all yours!"

Feets registered, weighing the importance of "if you come late" and "if you come early," but made no choice—yet. "Show me how to clean it!"

The burly man smiled," Okay."

Mother Millicent Dara Roche felt like an onion lately; each time she had toughened herself to the extreme horror of injury to the wounded, a new experience peeled back another layer to teach her numbness anew.

"Where you going so early?" Mother Roche tapped Feets on the shoulder while he sandwiched in another horseshoe and wrapped it in his burlap bag, placing the Whitworth, wrapped in a trombone case, over his shoulder.

"Oh, I want to get to the shop early; I need to swing by the fort after work, so I may be late tonight. I got permission to run some tests on this rifle," and avoided her glance.

Rifle, there is a rifle in that case. She almost said, "You have a rifle, a rifle in that case," but didn't, thinking that she would not start an argument so early in the day, but surely would after thinking on an approach, said merely, "I see."

Posse hailed him as he turned southward towards the Fort. "*Ami*, Feets, morning!" Joining in long unison steps, Posse continued, "What do you think of Posse's deal? You like *n'est pas?* I follow, track runaway; we not kill. You join *moi*, share profit, share bounty. I need a helper to smithiron, cover back, teach Posse reading! Might take a few days, maybe week."

The poster Posse carried had no picture, and was smaller with bold lettering. It read, "WANTED— Buck Slave named *HAWKSMITH. Dark brown to mahogany in color and stands about 6 feet 2 inches. Talented blacksmith and missing one foot. $1,000 reward if found in Memphis. $2,000 if found in Tennessee and $3,500*

FEETS

dollars if found outside the Tennessee State boundaries. Contact the Bolton and Crisp in Memphis, 101 Front Street."

For Posse's purposes, this smaller version was perfect. He had formed a mental picture of the face and the larger letters would help to promote his reading project.

"You read to Posse several times and he get words memorized. I cut up into cards of flash in next few days." The man grew positively giddy thinking about reading lessons.

Feets knew he was leaning towards the adventure and yet he also feared making a decision. Business at the shop was good; Sergeant O' Reilly himself recognized the quality of his work.

IX

Memphis

If Posse had been able to read, he might also have
been drawn to the larger handbill that had been
circulated about the town late yesterday. The one
he had cut into pieces had no picture and was
now flashcards for a grown man. Needless to
say, he waxed excited about the prospect of having teaching company in the grisly business of
bounty hunting. Under normal circumstances, he
would have had the poster read by someone else.
Hawksmith was a name he would not easily forget;
he could feel his excitement starting to gather in
his puppies.

Feets headed for the ordnance station. Officer

FEETS

O'Reilly, a muscular man, broad of shoulders, and thickly mustached; his intense, clear tan-brown eyes greeted the young man, "Top o' the morning, Feets. Good to see ya! Here is the old rifle manual I found. The procedures are pretty much the same for your Whitworth. I found some technical stuff, too. Take a gander, see for yourself!"

The manual read as follows: "The Whit has one turn in twenty inches, the Enfield, one turn in seventy-eight. Most importantly, the Whitworth bore is polygonal, hexagonal to be precise, with rounded edges! You can see that the differences in their accuracy are manifest even at 800 yards, with the Whitworth being twice as accurate as the Enfield at that distance. The tests that were run made the penetration and precision of the Whitworth exceptional, even at 1,700 yards, which was out of the range of the Enfield!"

"Let's test it ourselves. Here's how you clean it; a swaging die, brass jag on cleaning rod, toothbrush, soap, and hot water."

Feets read the passage aloud slowly, pointing his finger at each word for emphasis. At 500 yards, the "Figure of Merit" between the Whitworth and Enfield, Whit: 10.194, the Enfield: 25.535; at 800 yards, the Whit: 18.264, the Enfield: 45.750; at 1,700 yards, the Whit was 129.762; at 1,700 yards, gosh, that's out of the range of the Enfield. NO HITS.

"Note the faster twists of the Whitworth, that aids its precision also," added O'Reilly slowly. "That's why the edges of many battlefields were dominated by the rebels early in the war. This is an extremely accurate, lethal weapon."

"'Figure of Merit,' what does that mean, really?" inquired Feets.

"Well, that measures the rifle's ability to maintain its trajectory, the arch of the bullet, from point A to point B," explained O'Reilly.

"Trajectory," Feets underlined that word in his mind.

"Its ability to maintain its course and cut through air resistance. Let me show you on the rifle range. But before we do that, just a few words on cleaning.

FEETS

Take a sponge and wrap it around a jag of brass. Fit it on the end of the ramrod and swab the bore of the rifle with it. Then rinse the bore with hot water and dry the barrel with a dry swab. The main thing is to be sure that the barrel is absolutely dry, okay? When you load the cartridge, put the lubricating wand *between* the powder and bullet."

Feets thoughts scampered to the sign "CLOSED" on his shop, but he did not want to miss the testing. Lips pursed, he watched Officer O'Reilly fire-test both guns at 100 yards.

"Golly, the Whit is *much* more accurate and penetrating than the Enfield. It shattered the oak planks, passing through twice as many as the Enfield, with the planks stacked behind the bull's-eye located next to a dirt embankment." After this lesson, which he wrote and saved in the desk drawer with the gauges, he decided to practice at the range during dinnertime at the Fort.

"Sergeant O'Reilly, thanks for the cleaning lessons and running the tests for me, too. I will keep you posted on how I come along with the rifle. I'd better get to the shop!"

"Come down whenever you can and test them at greater distances. Happy to show you how to zero the sight; this particular sight magnifies your target four times," O'Reilly handed him a recruitment packet adding, "Feets, read this when you can. I hail from up-state New York and grew up not far from the stomping grounds of the Brown boys and their daddy. This is a book called *Hardee's Tactics*. Most of the African soldiers cannot read this manual. This one is an extra—one that I found digging around in the commissary. Take it and think about coming down and reading to some of the black recruits when you have time. Oh, I included some thoughtful words of Frederick Douglass and the Honorable John Brown."

A smiling Posse greeted him at the shop door. "Did you find the Enfield in your shop? Belle was going to get it to you."

"Oh yeah," he said sounding nonchalant. "It was there this morning. I'll clean it this afternoon."

"Thought about my offer?" asked Posse, noting that the Whitworth gun smelled freshly fired. Feets flinted sparks for a fire, flexed the bellows; the

FEETS

flame he needed for work started and re-channeled the conversation.

"I'll get started on the shoes for your horse. Tell me about how you track runaways. Do you shoot them? Are they hurt? How far will we go?"

Posse responded carefully, "Posse work hard not hurt runaway. Posse bring cards made by you. Too many handbills and posters to read, but sometimes I handcuff buck to keep safe. Main thing is Posse keep word on payment. Your cut may be dollars 250, maybe 500, for trip."

Feets smiled inwardly, his outward expression seemed bland and nondescript though the words danced inside his mouth and floated against his teeth, festooning his eyeballs with a flickering bonfire of dollar fairies. One thing he had not thought about was what amount of funds was necessary to leave Memphis and set up homesteading in an area north of the Mason-Dixon line?

Posse took out a card with "P-O-S-S-E" and pronounced it smiling, "We be Posse."

MEMPHIS

Mother Roche had her back up. Every vertebrae that existed in her back had a question, and they were good questions. If she voiced them in the tone in which they arose in her mind, she knew she would alienate the child that reminded her of his father and whom she found pure delight in raising. She didn't know this Posse fella and she didn't trust him. She hated the thought of her boy being out there somewhere where she could not put her hands on him. She had two jobs and he had an apprenticeship; that was enough money. After all, money ain't everything! Where would they go, even if they were millionaires; race and draft riots in major northern cities dominated the news when battles didn't!

First off, she translated that into questions, attacking every angle of the bounty adventure that she could imagine. "What if Forrest were in the area? What if you got sick? What if you got wounded? How would you get help? How will I know that you are safe? What if Posse sells you down river? How will you protect yourself if you cannot shoot? When will you get back? What if those guerrillas stop you, kill Posse, enslave you, and sell you down river? I don't like that man." Once she had reached

FEETS

180 degrees of questions, she started on the 360. Her questioning was nothing short of relentless. But the boy was not convinced, not once saying, "I won't do it, Ma!"

Then she attacked the result of the plan. "Freedom to do what? Starve up North? Buy a house in the North? Travel to Canada?" Her mental agility fermented as she thought, "He is at the age where he could volunteer and enlist alongside a growing majority of his friends. She sensed that he knew this and was trying to keep from challenging her decision-making authority. She also sensed that eventually he would follow his own heart and mind. Concluding that she would take a step that allowed them both to vent their thoughts without spouting venom, she developed a plan closely akin to that of Mother Byckersdyke.

"We need the money, Maybe we can buy our freedom beyond any shadow of doubt?"

Millicent Roche countered, "Who knows how this war will spin out! Could be that the South will win and your efforts—"

"Will be appreciated and treasured by the South," as he blushed, knowing his pugnacity annoyed her.

"—And we right back into slavery."

"I don't feel there's a choice. Either way, I earn money to secure our way out of here or I join the Union. I see those as my only options."

Millicent Dara did not dare tell him about his father's visit, about his plan to escape to free soil, about her plan to join him. That would have broken the backbone of her argument. But she went on, "Black folk, they're moving up there. Most Yanks don't care a whit 'bout damn darkies. You doing fine in the shop! 'Thou shalt not deliver unto his master that which is escaped unto thee.' Deuteronomy 23:15.' Read that to your friend, Posse."

"Mama! Down at Camp Dixie, they say Forrest is roaming round West Tennessee. They trying to train the colored soldiers for orders, but mostly they can't read." He didn't tell her that O'Reilly had recruited him for the Union with the words, "This army needs good blacksmiths. We could end this thing with a decent cavalry. With Forrest back in West Tennessee, speed, marksmanship, and horsemanship are the talents we need most. With that goes horseshoeing, gunsmithing! Think about it."

Feets did love his apprenticeship along with the smell of iron with its malleability to curve, bend, and contour to his patterns. He had a new plan to make a die for bullets. The money was decent since he brought home seven dollars a week to help his mom. That word "dollars" still danced inside his pursed lips.

"We'll talk about this later. I promised these linens for the Block hospital around the corner from you," added Millicent. "Leave this bottle of alcohol on top of them and drop them off on your way to the shop. I'll leave the basket right here by the door." She embraced and kissed him as he mowed down his sandwich. Soon he was on the street. Wooden-wheeled carts, drawn by majestic oxen, drawn by combinations of mules and horses, drawn by donkeys, and sometimes yoked to men, were pointed northward hauling the complete earthly goods of every color of brown and black in the worldwide spectrum of color. Sociologists of a later age would claim it as a great migration. Slaves of the era laughed when birds migrated south and chuckled, "We know better!" Daily could be seen at least one ox, behemoths of wheeled locomotion, a tired horse or mule yoked to carts with oxen with worldly possessions. Basket atop his head, he outlined his afternoon workload: Twenty horseshoes, three pairs of handcuffs, the rifle cleaning, and added *zero that toughie!* He would drop off the basket after he quickly checked the shop to see if any customers were waiting. Rounding the corner, he approached then sidestepped three men who eyed him carefully appraising his awkward posture and extra luggage.

X

Memphis

"Mornin," spoke Feets, "What can I do for you?" since they seemed to be waiting for his shop to open. Imitating the music of his words, one rosy-necked, blond bearded, buckskin-clad customer skited tobacco juice over his shoulder crooning "Do for you boys, we got us a smoked-Yankee b-b-bblacksmith, a money-making darky-smith, sliding right past us on Front Street in Memphis fixing to turn down Union to his Yankee-ass blacksmith shop!"

"Mornin'—and wha—what was the rest of that?"

Feets felt his heart quicken, felt his brain slow

down as he quick-scanned the immediate environment for a weapon. Every spine-tingling floor creak on the boardwalk, every necklace of words, every movement became a symphony of seconds. He studied the score vertically and horizontally. *Nigger or man—your choice. H*is own word tackled him! He arrowed his voice in their direction, flattened it to a telegraph monotone, "If you need shoes, perhaps I can fit you in."

"Fit us in!" was followed by laconic, raucous laughter. "Oh, my lord, is that a bottle of gin? Vodka? Boys we got us a vodka-gin drinkin' darky-smith! You dance like that rummy that prances around town?"

The more reserved of the trio spoke, "Fellas, that's hospital alcohol, best not to drink it."

"Somebody say you can read, too, Sonny. I betcha you kin read—selling them newspapers and all. Kin you read dis' here paper?"

"I do have several—" the words assumed a flat dryness while his brain thundered along a divergent path: *The gun is inside, unloaded, behind the door.*

"—extra horseshoes if that is what you need. You boys have a good day. I'm in the shop today 'til three!" He back-stepped and swung out towards the street, almost evading an outstretched foot, which tipped his gait just enough to throw him off balance. The tumbled sprawl which followed was inevitable. The silence which followed it was shattered with, "You be aiding the enemy boy. Niggahs that aids the enemy come to a breezy ending!"

He knew he should have brought the Whit, but it sat at the house and the Enfield, behind the door. Neither was of help to him now. Sweat pasted his shirt against his torso as his pulse clicked faster; a breeze splattered through the trees exposing the wild glitter of sunlight on a rounded mirror. He caught sight of Posse stepping from Belle's, and jerked sideways as the blast from Posse's pistol spun the tobacco bin on the floor dancing off the boardwalk into the grimy street.

"You boys need to be movin' on! The next one might be closer." The blond eyed him suspiciously, then the three made for their horses, mumbling in the distance. "Homeguard fellas gets a little excited, *n'est pas*! Takin' care of the citizens and all."

Sweat became the rain of his purpose. The juices and minerals that made it grow. Sweat flowed from his arms and chest, cooled him in the face of the fiery furnace. Sweat insulated him from inflamed belches when he opened its front gate. Sweat rimmed the rich black color of the iron, the malleable, bent, curved modes it assumed under his prongs, and sweat cooled its redesign to fit his purpose. After he had delivered the slightly mussed mess of linen his mom had bundled, his swipes at the shoes were slightly harder, his brow a bit more furrowed, his timing and lashes at the iron bars somewhat more staccato. *Caught without a goddamned weapon, dead in a macadamized Memphis street.* He allowed the sweat to fuel his imagination and put on gloves to aid his grip. He hammered for hours. Feets Roche hammered horseshoes until his arms were numb, and even then he did not stop. It was ten when he started and four when he stopped. For a brief moment, he paused to stuff the rifle manual in his bag, and returned to the anvil, focused on developing the technical skill that takes craftsmanship to artistry. He had asked Posse to come back by the shop at three o'clock. He wanted to exploit his knowledge for now, embellish upon it later, perhaps on the hunt.

Caught without a weapon; trapped without a defensive maneuver. His eyes came to rest on a yellowed news article, the paper rumpled and the print mildly blurred.

"Armchair generals following the battle movements during the battle of Chickamauga, continue to debate the full meaning and impact of that battle and its implications for the Confederate war effort. The gap in the Union line, so perfectly exploited by the irrepressible Longstreet, forced Rosecrans off the field, thus corrupting his military career. With Confederate Crittenden on his right and Forrest on his left, Thomas saved the Union army with his application of the defensive perimeter." If you stay in a circle and fight, no one can defeat you. "The 'Indomitable Warrior' of Chickamauga had his soldiers practice that philosophy in small reconnaissance groups ordered to scout enemy positions during non-engagement hours; they went on duty with a day's rations, ammunition, iodine, and detailed maps of Snodgrass Hill—meticulous preparation."

Feets skimmed to a later sentence. "When Bragg refused to attack the retreated Federals in Chattanooga, Gen'r'l N. B. Forrest, hero of the threatened Confederacy, threatened to quit the Army vowing never again to serve under Bragg. It is rumored in some quarters that he slapped and cursed the man."

"*N'est pas*," thought Feets to himself. What the devil does that mean? Got to ask that question. A papa bird? That's it! The daddy. "N'est paw," he said to himself. "No paw? No father?" He wiped his brow—sweat! Mom hadn't mentioned his father lately. He decided to call it a day. Posse came through the door as he turned, and Feets grinned, saying, "*N'est pas*, what does it mean?"

Posse had spoken with Mother Roche on her way from Camp Dixie to the hospital. He knew she was adverse to the boy accompanying him on this mission, knew that she was very, very proud to have Feets for a son. He also knew that she would want to keep him from enlisting for duty with the Union. To her he said, "If he is with me, he will not be volunteering for service with the Federals. I promise you that I will protect him, with my life if necessary!" She decided not to allow that then she thought about it, thought about the thirst the boy had for male guidance, the vacuum created by his father, who loved him but was absent, and about the rifle, the golden bright rifle the boy had brought home just a few nights ago. I *cannot leave it in the shop, Ma. Somebody might steal her!* Her, indeed. She had relented, "I will hold you personally responsible, Posse."

Posse added, "By the way, explain Feets, *n'est pas* means 'is it not'!"

As Feets reminisced, squirrels scurried frantically to escape the speedy shadows crisscrossing his path like a mad opponent trying to beat him at tic-tac-toe. There was no logic to *buteo jamaicensis*, also known as a chicken hawk, which drew occasional attention for target practice. Its Latin name gave no indication of its powerful lethality, engineered by its ability to see clearly at very great distances. Once before, Feets, without knowing the species, espied the majestic bird in full speed, talons and wingtips literally walking on a lake surface. "That's freedom," he had murmured.

In order to head off the showdown she knew was coming with Feets, primarily regarding bringing a rifle in the house, Mother Roche and Penny made one of his favorite meals. Penny whipped up a cake to take some sting out of the street altercation that she and her mom had heard about. Millicent resolved to try Mother Byckersdyke's strategy of "written conversation" to reach a compromise, a non-destructive compromise, to discuss what Bishop Hightower called an "unfortunate decision" he felt had compromised his stature as a peaceful man.

They joked at first. "We all laughed," Millicent had said, "when your daddy saw those feet!"

At first the boy balked at the suggestion of writing.

"We can talk!"

But Millicent knew the treachery of discussing

emotionally explosive issues and how quickly they could become stalemates, or worse, islands of ego posturing frozen in right or wrong.

"Let's just try it." The boy relented out of love and the desire to develop a creative and new response to his mother's thinking.

Millicent	Feets
My responsibility to you is to honor the love I have for your father and the ancestral spirits that look over my shoulders: your grandfathers and mothers, our African ancestors, and the community of descendants that bid me do excellence in your rearing, even in spite of the white sin that persists with regard to your color.	Mom, I know that you do and have done that! And father too, even though he be absent many years in raising us. The rebuke of the whites, in addition to the sin of the Confederates, defies understanding. They mock the Rule of Golden-ness. But my heart is troubled and my mind disturbed by the sacrifices I see around me of my fellow Africans.

FEETS

I know troubles of
the heart and they are
not easily put to rest.
But before acting out
of rage, or anger, or
rebelliousness—be sure
that your knowledge
brims with the history
and understanding, that it
learns all it is able of the
struggle of good people
of all colors to eliminate
slavery.

I hear the discussions,
read what books I can,
listen to and learn of the
theological hypocrisy of
slavers. Newspapers have
daily plumed the varied
strands of the customs
and policies, the differ-
ences of views that fuel
the war. We know not
when our father can join
us as a family; my friends
volunteer for war and I
feel the need to act, lest I
be labeled cowardly

I sense this urge of yours
to act and I see your
friends respond to the
call of Fred Douglass.
He has issued a call to
arms, much as Lincoln
issued a call for nurses; I
know you must act and
I fear for your life. I also
fear that my example has
been a poor one.

Ma, my first responsibil-
ity is to you and Penny,
to stand by you and see
that you are safe and en-
joy good welfare. Should
the war end tomorrow,
then I have learned a
good trade and I can
earn a good living by my
sweat. My apprentice-
ship serves this end.

MEMPHIS

Yes. That decision would be a smart and honorable one; you are lucky for its presence. I shudder to think that your father may be in harms way at this instant. The disease and battle wounds take many lives; the numbers are augmented for black soldiers. I do not like Posse; what he stands for disgusts me, but his survival skills are undisputed and that is important to your survival.

I enjoy the steady salary I receive from the wife of Fauks to keep the shop open. Posse has offered me the chance to make three times that, for one week of work. The officer of the Fort has already recruited me as a blacksmith. They teach me how to gunsmith and value my learning. They say I can teach the black recruits how to read; read aloud to them the manual and the rules of military conduct and tactics. African regiments are active after Chickamauga. If the Confederacy wins, I can still buy our freedom.

XI

Memphis

Dara Roche did not like to be called by her first name, Millicent. She thought it compromised her fierceness and she fought racial stereotypes with every breath she took. "Call me Dara," she would say to those with whom she formed solid friendships. When pissed off by those who had the effrontery to call her Millicent or, even worse, "girl," she would simply reply, "You have my permission to call me Ms. Roche." That usually ended the matter. She'd been lucky in Memphis. She could sew and allotted a certain portion of her day to enterprise as a seamstress. She could read and had dreamed of being a nurse as a young child watching doctors examine and ply their trade, rarely on persons of color. She had received an unusual number of compliments on her black wide-brimmed straw hat at Sundays' service, however, the ones she received on how beautifully her children had grown pleased her most.

"Oh, Dara, your Penny is so beautiful," or "Ms Roche, that Feets of yours is such a responsible young man!" The comments took her back to the first time she had seen their father, Hawk. He had been sweating over an anvil, tears of perspiration rinsing his taunt muscles, soaking his shirt and the front of his pants. There was a problem with the weathervane he was making. He could see its shape in his minds' eye, but to him the outcome was out of balance, crude, and misshaped. Something was wrong with the mold and now he had to redo it, start over again. She could see his features in the children, the way he held his shoulders back, the smooth dark skin of her daughter, the sharp angular features of her son—their son and their daughter. *I miss you, Hawk!* She remembered the wheelbarrows, wagon wheels, and rifle bores he had repaired; saw his artistry reborn, especially in the drawings and handiwork of Feets. Penny was learning to sew and she reveled in the young girl's love of color; her pattern making artistry sprouted from her daddy.

"How do you like this pattern, Mama?" she'd commented when making a tie for the bishop.

She recalled the play wheel that Hawk had made for the children on the plantation and how the two of them, she and Hawk, had tried it out before he set it up in the field behind the big house. It rotated clock and counterclockwise, and he pushed the wheel fast, making her so dizzy she couldn't possibly walk afterwards.

"This is the stallions part," he had said of a huge replica of a stallion's phallus. "You can rub it for good luck!" he teased. He had made a slingshot of metal, and together they used it for target practice; they gathered stones and made shooting dates to compare notes on who the better marksman—or markswoman," as she called herself. *It has been such a long time since I have seen you, held you in my arms.* She had helped him to learn to write and, occasionally, if a refugee could find where she lived, she would find an iron casting at her doorstep or receive a casting in the mail with the initial "H" on it.

FEETS

Those moments made her heart leap, something that did not happen as she left the plantation, which would not unfasten the invisible irons of "the money massa pays me to stay will support you until I can join you." She knew, though, that Master Partridge would kill him, rather than see him escape to freedom. "He is my most valuable slave. I cannot part with him," the man had said in a drunken stupor. "The whole place goes to hell without Hawk!"

"Ma," Feets had said later that Sunday after the service, "Ma, Posse fired only one shot when he broke that chain from around the Captain's neck, one shot! It ricocheted and split that buck's shoulder!"

"Feets," she responded, "don't tell me about those damned guns. Don't tell me 'bout no shootins'. They should put that Cajun on trial for shooting an unarmed man, chokehold or no, ricochet! I respect his skill and know that we all got to make a dollar somehow, but his actions keep our people in bondage, chasing folks down with dogs. They might just put his bandolier-ass on trial!"

MEMPHIS

It distressed her to see the long lines of young
black men lined up and down Union Avenue to
volunteer for action with the Federal forces. Many
looked the same age as her Feets. She had overheard
their discussions. "Gone send my gal a picture of
me wid my Union brogans and rifle." Even the
songs that they sang at those honkytonks on Beale
Street spoke of "answering Old Frederick's call"
to the tune of "My Blues Done Chased the Grays
Away!" Cute euphemisms for volunteering for
Union duty.

Millicent Dara had seen the damage that military service could do firsthand. As an assistant
to Mother Byckersdyke, she had started as a
washerwoman, volunteering when her duties at
the Hightower household would allow, and then
moving up through the informal ranks to include
additional chores: washing, ironing, and sewing for
the Army Hospital on Union Avenue. The men
that this building housed suffered mightily from
all kinds of gunshot wounds: head, arm, thighs,
feet, even eyes and private parts. She knew that
many would die and witnessed the deaths that
were caused from malnutrition and disease. The
thought of Feets' fascination with that Whitworth

rifle, even if its color was stunning, deeply disturbed her. Lately, his reading had become much more technical in its character. He had even written to a Chicago gun manufacturer for cleaning and repair manuals. No, she would forbid Feets from ever becoming a victim of the carnage that she witnessed in Memphis, especially those poor fools they had wagoned in from Shiloh. He must not join the Union.

Better to be bounty hunting with me in Kentucky than volunteering right here in Memphis for death. The words of Posse started to leave a rut in her thinking.

The proud owner of Belle's Biscuits, Belle Fortune, enjoyed watching the Roche kids grow up. She thought of Ms. Dara as her friend and used adjectives like smart, mannerable, and well cultivated to describe her. She also liked Posse, though not as much as many thought. Belle had a nose for a dollar. It would flow much more easily if the serene atmosphere she imagined could be maintained. She surely would not tolerate the brawls and free-for alls that sometimes decorated Beale Street. Belle had seen Posse use minimum force, a special finger punch, a chokehold, and knife or stiletto, a gun abutment as necessary, to quietly subdue the unruly. She needed the swift and deadly if her vision of a restaurant and entertainment salon was to be realized. *I will sprinkle in the management skills personally,* she thought.

She had tested the entertainment salon idea out during Thanksgiving. The idea had worked well except the crowd control element had been less than acceptable. In today's crowd, top hats and homburgs bobbed like little birds atop a cragged lake. Below their hat bills, tongues and fingers wagged belligerently making points and berating perspectives on Chickamauga and Vicksburg.

"Cut right in two, from Gettysburg to Vicksburg and Grant perched right at Chattanooga," bellowed one voice. "Some shitty Christmas present for our johnnies. I suspect Grant will be heading towards Atlanta before too long, make another 'Chimney-ville' outa that place, jus' like Jackson. Niggers streamin' through Memphis like a night train outa hell. Forrest done turn't his back on Bragg, and Hood trying to smoke the Yankees outa Kentucky … my, my!"

Belle's restaurant was the town-gathering place for

war news. It was a simple place, a floor of brick and several pine-top tables, along with a huge map of the Confederate states, garnished with pins of various regimental battle markers. A large rectangular table stood square in the floor's middle. Common topics included who got whipped when, who died where, what implications flowed from factual outcomes, and who was headed where next. Sometimes bets were laid on an array of strategic choices. Arguments always ensued. For many, it was also a place of business, and posters of runaway slaves sometimes made it to "the wall." For sure, the quietest conversations that took place in this room focused on how to get important runaways back behind the curtain of cotton. For those conversations, Posse was often the outcast attendee along with the membership of the Cotton Planters' Association also known as "The Cotton Syndicate."

Few of the patrons knew the end point of the spiral staircase that stood behind the door, closeted inside her office. There was for sure an upstairs, which served as a meeting space for gatherings: poker, religious, small recitals, and such. It had a piano. There were no public stairs for the larger rooms downstairs. Subsequent to his commission by the syndicate, a meeting that was conducted very privately, he was summarily shown down the spiral staircase by a wordless butler.

"Madame Belle will be down in a moment," pitched a lithesome Negress, her features obviously luxurious at every point and her manner conducted so as to make him experience only a feeling of complete and utter ease. "May I fix you a drink? Of course, you know that Ms. Belle has requested your company. Monsieur likes the hideaway?"

Posse was not remotely aware that this caliber of luxury existed in the basement of the restaurant. A large bed stood in the far corner, separated from the fire only by a Japanese divider made of rice paper. In the opposite corner was constructed a fireplace, made of Arkansas fieldstone, and shielded from the room by an ember catcher built of wrought iron. Positioned next to the fireplace was a tub large enough for two, already smelling of attractive vapors and emitting enough steam to show that the water was hot, and whose surface brimmed with soapy bubbles.

FEETS

"*Cest tres bonne. 'Est magnifique.* Bourbon, have you bourbon?" He studied the room carefully, almost not believing his eyes.

"You may rest your shoes and bandolier on the coat rack. Ms. Belle likes champagne. I will leave her glass on the tray in front of the sofa. If you wish to take a bath and relax, she will be down as soon as she attends to a trifle or two. Please be comfortable."

Belle had not explained any of this to him earlier, when he had finally decided to take her up on her offer of dinner. He had thoroughly enjoyed the conversation, mainly about her need for heightened security and her desire to see him ensconced in the job. He felt a tremendous surge of excitement and expectation when she wandered into the flat, somewhat aimlessly, dressed in a flowing black kimono, her tresses of blond backswept under her usual straw wide brim. His wide-eyed stare brought a throaty chuckle from her. Belle lowered her eyes slowly as she spoke.

"I have invited you here to strike a deal. Of course, I cannot consummate a bargain with which you have not agreed to. However, we can sit, talk, and share our appreciation for one another's views, perhaps discuss how best to proceed. Are you interested?"

Posse had been aboard a few floating vessels in his time, had developed the kind of sense of balance some called sea legs, had tracked many presences, wild and tame, across a wide variety of terrain. As he sipped the glass of bourbon earlier offered, he thought, "If this is quicksand, I am in it." The bulge in his pants gave away his desire and put him at a visible disadvantage. He thought it best to buy time. "Belle, I have nothing but admiration for your great beauty, both of intellect and of the body. Before, when I have come to your restaurant, I never expected this kind of extravagance. Now I see it with my own eyes and can hardly believe it."

Belle waved to the Negress to come over to Posse saying, "Please help Mr. Raiford with his moccasins and pants." The girl appeared from nowhere and affixed a towel to his waist after removing the very last stitch of clothing he ever thought about attaching to his waist, neck, or ankles.

FEETS

Posse leaned back in the long, deep recess of the hot tub of soapy water, took a long drag on his cigar, relished the blanket of soapy bubbles that defied gravity as he blew blue smoke into the rainbowed bubbles, and relaxed. *Shit, I'm so relaxed my dick seems to have gone limp forever,* he thought. Magically a mirage appeared. Belle clad in a terrycloth robe, the blond tassels of her hair swinging freely. A splash followed her feline entry into the tub.

Posse's hands and arms once tense, now relaxed into forgotten appendages and the thoughts of the day faded. Though he occasionally blinked to dredge up the day's events, they refused to rise to the surface. Faced with this unexpected turn of events, he couldn't will his mind into a state of alertness. The parts that defined his manliness spoke back to him *Sorry, buddy.* He was beginning to feel inept, incompetent, a languishing fool.

For her part, Belle was almost embarrassed by her connivances. "Here Posse, Posse," she meowed in successive diminuendos, casually exploding her consonances, his ears ever so slightly masked by the bubbles of soap.

MEMPHIS

The sounds that reached Posse's ears registered "here pussy, pussy," and he turned ever so slowly to see—was a cat in the house?

Belle spoke again, as if summoning a pet. "Some pussy for Posse," she purred, smiling at the comedy she had mounted, and rinsed her torso in the water's warmth and the intimacy created by two flickering candles simmering in the muted, underground darkness. "Here Posse, the hound of the rich," and cackled, allowing her nipples to pout at him just above the surface of the water. Belle reached over, lifting her glass of champagne to her lips. She drank, rubbing his thighs, chest, and submissive dick with the tips of her toes. She eyed him inconspicuously for his reaction. "And to think, I had the mistaken impression that you were a lover; shoulda known bet-tah!" The "tah" was spoken as her lips articulated a brusque, percussive "T" across the top of the soapy bubbles causing them to accent the air at just the right angle to become airborne. He moved closer to her feeling the temperature rise. The lights seemed lower—*was it dark*?

The Negress had approached Posse from the rear

now and gently sponged his chest and neck with layers of soap, refreshed his drink, and hummed as she rubbed. In the warmth of the tub, her hands cupped the now rigid post of the man she knew only as Posse. She covered his eyes with a warm, heated towel and massaged his temples and neck. *Now, for sure,* he thought, *ah, now, it is really dark.* In the darkness, his pleasure increased and he felt the weight of his body released from any hint of gravity. "Am I asleep?" A coy laugh followed his thought and he wondered if he had spoken out loud. As he thought, the water quivered and became much warmer, almost as if the tip of his most rigid member has been guided into the treasures of the goddess Venus. The calm, yet undulating movement of broad thighs cresting his thick phallus towed him into recognition of felicitous experience in the sublime. *Ah, the sublime. "C'est tres magifique!"* His hands clasped the silk waist that rode him past the present into a future of pleasure that yoked his inner being into territory often classified as transcendental; he felt expired. The Negress lit one candle then dried a smiling Belle before she dried herself.

Belle took the towel, continuing to dry her shoulders, breasts, and thighs, commenting to herself, "Perhaps one day you will possess the real thing, Posse."

"Perhaps you will consider more diligently the offer I have made to you, Posse. I have always thought that it is better, and much more fun, to pursue beauty than bounty. Of course many of the soldiers who are new to the South pursue booty. But booty can be such a crude term, for this joy we," and she cast a sly grin to the accomplice, "have just experienced, as you would say, '*n'est pas*!' You needn't answer now, but think about it."

XII

Memphis

The sign on Belle's Biscuits was in touchup mode. Belle had the background of the sign refurbished in more of a creamy, than bland straightforward shade of white. Before the Christmas holidays would set in, she wanted the lettering to be gay and multicolored, just like Memphis' Camp Dixie. She had never seen so many black folks, of every shade of brown imaginable, speak in high comedy, even though the conditions of life there were abominable. Even if the war was going badly for latitudes south of the Mason-Dixon line, her shop would be a centrifuge of joy and happiness, a place full of the Christmas spirit.

FEETS

Still the "massa" types congregated as the new year, 1864, approached. They shared stories, quarter-backed the war effort, discussed commodity prices, "nigger codes," and the South's ongoing answer to January 1863's Emancipation Proclamation.

"I don't give a shit 'bout none of that. All I care about is that my mules keep pullin' and my niggers keep pickin." As the man became more excited, the red clay around his shoes dried and flaked on the pine floor. Close by, another "Southern gentle-man" lamented, "wouldn't been so bad if'n I hadn't lost my entire buck crew!"

"Buck crew or buck shit, either way looked like your crew done bucked out to Yankee land, free-dom, and all that North star crap they been singing about."

"Well, my niggers is almost family, 'cepting of course that they can't come inside!" said Boss Noland. "We been good to our niggers down in Oakland—real good to 'em. They talk loyal, but when action time come 'round, they mostly still jus' as determined to bolt outa these parts as ever. Least-ways, they ain't rising up!"

MEMPHIS

"So," thought Belle, as she headed towards the kitchen for more sausage, "The death of the Shrine Chasers' Captain had heightened fears of the white majority. Here were their representatives, the Dixie Council, The Cotton Syndicate, for heaven's sake, chatting away first thing. If the slave buck alleged to have broken the man's neck had not been housed at Fort Pickering, there is no doubt he would have been strung up." Belle had seen the attitude before and had seen, felt, and witnessed lynching first-hand. A chill creased her spine.

When she returned, she heard, "You ain't gone get him outta the fort. I got a different idea. One of the owners down Tupelo way will put up money for a little wager. He got a 'limp-a-way' that he wants back! Wants back real bad! This coon is as close to a nigger genius as you 'll ever see with iron. Says this boy can make a Monarch out of iron that he guarantees, will damn near fly! He'll spend two to three thousand to have him back!"

"He can forget that'un, heard about that slave named Hawksmith! They tried to tether him to the plantation by severing his Achilles tendon. He probably sprouted wings outa some of that iron.

FEETS

If he's as good as they say he is, to wing his way to the damn North Star! Thataway, he can fly right over those Nigger Codes y'all done whipped up to keep 'em in their place!"

"Shit, them codes ain't about nothing. Designed to keep them in place, my foot! You can jus' look outside, anytime, day or night. They be all over the place, even sportin' guns down at the fort."

"Fuck a code," said another. "If any of those damn niggers get outa line on my property, I just string 'em up. Course I jus can't imagine that a slave on my property would ever want to read a book or carry a gun. Hell we give every one of these niggers a pass, jus' so they knows which nigger they is when the constable is around. Far as I can tell, they can't much remember their own name, lessen it's printed on their forehead."

"Mebbe they don't like the name!"

"Well, forehead or not, I seen a few here and there that could handle a gun, and don't you just know that I was down by the riverbank the other day, caught a few of those clownish niggers singing and hovering like they are prone to do, jus around the corner, few of those bucks gathered 'round a rifle! Old blacksmith Fauks upped and went off to help Hood after that terrible debacle at Atlanta and his apprentice, that nigger kid of the Roche woman, he was in the shop the other day, reading a manual bout rifles."

"Didn't know none of them niggers could read. How do you think the kid learnt? Had to kill one t'other day for callin' out letters of the alphabet! Head broke open like a watermelon when I pulled the trigger on that piece of musket. Wife was madder that shit, but that ole coon wasn't good for nothin' but a hard dick. Got to keep 'em in place."

"Don't matter none, 'cepting that we do need to keep our eye on that shop. Seen lot of blue uniforms going in and outa there, getting everything fixed—from buckboard and wheel refittings to horseshoes. Fauks is a good Christian man. He ain't gone jus' let out the place to any ole body! The kid's smart and he's trying to make hisself some money. Don't fret none about him. Spoke to Jack 'bout him just the other day. Ain't gone be no problem there!" He fired a wad of tobacco towards the spittoon and smiled as his lips quivered like a bowstring just relieved of an arrow.

"Jus' the same, that boy bears watching. Might be mite too smart for his britches!"

Belle, busy in the kitchen for the most part, overheard part of the conversation as she hefted plates across the table. Business was good when the propertied and ordained came together for breakfast. Being the good businesswoman she was, the electricity of their presence enlivened her.

She pitched, "Boys, y'all mighty energetic this mornin' but you worry too much. Y'all pretty much got these black folk caged up. It against the law for them to read, be taught reading, or even writing. By law they cannot carry guns and they gotta carry some sort of identification, a pass or loaner coin, and they gotta sign contracts in writing, even if they ain't had one lick of school. You can't tell me they would ever get out from under wid those rules in place! They got hell to pay if they get out of line with these codes or those sharecropping rules in place! Seems to me like the clamps are on pretty tight."

"C'mon Belle, right over at the fort they training 'em to fire guns. They think these niggahs have the right to raise up agin their masters and fight to give the Federals an edge! Used to be a time when a nigger best not breathe on a gun lessen he got strung up!"

"Aw, Miss Belle, you know what me mean, lookit! Bragg done got his comeuppance at Atlanta. Now, he's back peddling through the Carolinas. Jeff done given the troops over to Hood. Now thems that's close to him say he's jacked-up on Clementine cordial. Anybody with half a mind and two quarters worth of good sense knows that Cordial fries thinking. That jackass is headed back to Nashville. Shit, Washington is the other way. I guess he's trying to reclaim Tennessee! Just pisses me off. Damn it, they shoulda put Forrest in charge helluva long time ago!"

"Jeff Davis too damn aristocratic for that. Got to have those military blue bloods outta West Point! Forrest done showed that West Pointers can be whipped!" Boss Noland took out a cigar after that lecture, the spirit of which was continued by another syndicate member.

"All the Union got to do is send a boatload of ordnance to these here contraband camps and you'll see slaughter of the first order. Niggers wid guns is bad news, friends. It's hard to order around somebody that's looking at cha through a gun site! Look at the Daily, just look it. Fugitives lace its leaves through and through. Runaways peppered all through every page practically! I tell you, they are leaving us with crops unattended and cotton withering right in the fields. Shit, the other day I saw a nigger hopping through the field jus like a kangaroo!"

Boss Noland spoke with solemn gravity, "I need somebody to give me some leads, some names. Who can I get to act on this little wager, boys? Who can track this limp-a-way?"

"Well serves him right for breeding rabbits and niggers on the same farm!" A trickle of heavy laughter followed and Jack O'Day added, "Trackers, bounty hunters—all of 'em a dime a dozen if the money is right. Tell you what though, I'd put my money on Posse Raiford. Man can smell a grasshopper in a field of oats every time. My money's on him!"

"They tell me they are flooding Fort Pillow and enlisting right there on the spot. Can you imagine that? Gideon used 'em to help build the god-damned place, and the Union's got them enlisting there left and right. I hear tell that some make a pilgrimage to Pillow so's they can enlist without any whites seeing em do it, then you can't go after the relatives or whatever.

XIII

Memphis

Posse had fallen asleep after the former evening's frolic and as the water became colder during the night, he dried himself, and retired across the bed that stood in the corner of the basement. He awoke several times, always somewhat drowsy and, never completely alert, rolled over and went back to sleep.

Over his head in the restaurant, the syndicate discussed runaways, the price of cotton, how to best get it to the market. The word *refugee* was never heard. He woke up to the smell of a breakfast tray. Scrambled eggs, coffee, buttered toast, bacon, and ham sent arresting aromas to his bedside. He shook himself awake and smiled thinking, "It feels good to sleep in a soft bed, wake up to a warm breakfast, and be able to shave and bathe first thing in the morning. Life on the trail chasing these runaways, being a trail boss, or farm hand is nowhere as user-friendly as these scrambled eggs. Maybe it's time to think about this job offer Miss Belle has on the table."

Down by the fort, the day's cast of runaways filled the outside duty board and rim of slack boards that corralled the place. Posse half-blew his nose and repeated the operation on the other side. He washed down some coffee and pulled up his pants; he shaved with maddening slowness, savoring every stroke of the sharpened steel, and he thought about swinging by the fort to chat with the teamsters, laborers, and commissary workers. He traded cigars for information.

Buy some cigars. You can trade cigars for good up-to-date information on any slave still alive. Everybody loves to smoke a good cigar, he told himself, —*everybody! Some folks would sell their mother for a good cigar, especially folk with time on their hands.* His thoughts ambled past the brig where he knew the buck would be housed. *Stories and gossip about that buck had grown to mammoth proportions. Sure as hell won't go inside of the fort. Don't want no truck with those Union types.* Tres dangereuse, passed slowly over his lips. *Had the man been in a civilian jail, his neck by now, would have been long broke.*

Posse Raiford climbed up the stairs into the restaurant taking three steps at a time. He tipped his hat to Belle and smiled as he passed through the hall back of the kitchen and slipped into the main room of the restaurant. "Mornin' gents," he sang as he entered.

"Posse!" they cried in unison. "We was just talking about you!"

Mother Roche had seasoned the crispy fried chicken with her tears. The telling blow in the written conversation, the equitable discourse she so loved was, "We are free since January 1, 1863. We need money to exercise our opportunity."

Her registered apprehension for his safety was not a logical encounter. Bishop Hightower had read

FEETS

them both a poem Feets thought he would read to
Posse. Posse brought two rifles, his Whitworth and
an Enfield he affectionately called *les deuxieme*, and
two sets of handcuffs.

XIV

Memphis XIII

The owner's syndicate had sponsored travel paraphernalia, blankets, bullets, spare cash, rope, and saddlebags. Posse rode a horse, and Feets rode a mule. "Posse, you had better watch out for my boy," blurted out Mother Roche in the predawn hours of their departure. "Your son is my brother. We are seven days before return," said Posse.

Sparrows danced a fluttering frolic and sputtered over their banquet of mosquitoes near the riverbanks. Faithless to the undercurrents of the Mississippi, eddies chiseled the river's surface frequently lapping the edges in soft impulses of delight. South on the compass, smoke rose from the contraband Camp Dixie.

A dank, fetid stench hung over the Mississippi inhibiting the intake of deep breaths, embellished by clumps of horse manure lining the byway of Front Street. The hounds were reintroduced to scented rags that, according to Feets' best guess, had at one time belonged to the runaways they now chased. Impervious to the noxious atmosphere, the hounds barked and moaned in delight at the prospect of new olfactory adventure.

"Good, *c'est bon*!" commented Posse, stroking their heads and necks as their tails wagged furiously. After Feets kissed and hugged his mother and Penny, the tiny caravan moved northward on Front Street, beginning its trek in search of escapees from the cotton curtains of the Delta. Feets sat forward in wide-eyed alertness, calmly aware of the adventure that was at its very beginning. Posse slumped, bent backwards under his sombrero, as if he could fall asleep at any moment.

"Do you know what they call Camp Dixie?" murmured Feets.

MEMPHIS

"No. What?" questioned Posse.

"Little Africa," replied Feets.

"Oh yes, *comment on dite*, *petite l'Afrique!* " said Posse chuckling.

The grey haze, smoky stirrings, and daylight smells of late March and early April Memphis mornings, along with the granular shuffle of teamsters and laborers hoofing through the gates of Fort Pickering, bugled the start of daybreak."

While Feets thumbed through his mental checklist, glassy-eyed Posse yawned, adding,

"Keep your rifle and pistol loaded. Between here and Munford be roving bands of *rouge- necks*." Grimacing he added, "We want no surprises." The putrid funk of flotsam bore down on them as they skirted the Wolf River and headed due north.

"Rouge-necks?" questioned Feets innocently. "What does that mean?"

"Rouge is red; so rednecks—is what you call them,

is not?" chuckled Posse, his eyes quite closed, his arms cradling the Whitworth and readjusting it around his torso. Capturing flecks of sunlight from rising sun, Posse's golden Whitworth glinted mildly, its dull refractions totally oblivious and unsynchronized with the hoof beats of the north bearing animals. With a mischievous smile, Feets floated a bet to the comment,

"So your rouge-necks—they are the same as the home guard? They s'pose to protect the families and property of the Rebs that have gone off to war, right? Are they paid by the Cotton Syndicate?"

"Probably, and no, your mule can outrun yonder turtle! Believe me, if you say giddyup, it might walk backwards! Jibberish." laughed Posse. "But if we be challenged by rouge- necks, then I do talking. You keep pistol poised under blanket like this. Understand?" showing him where and how to cover his guns from sight.

As the humid haze of dawn yielded to the almost intoxicating, exhilarating, clear morning, they passed on the macadamized roadway by buggies, oxen, fugitives, and union guards chancing their way to Camp Chelsea and out past Camp Fiske.

MEMPHIS

The pup-horse-mule caravan lumbered on, passing a nearing drunk, dancing to a self-motored melody *Marchons, marchons! Qu'un sang impur!* Though the greenish liquor bottle swung precipitously in the air, its contents never spilled. The bottle itself was never dropped.

"You test Posse. Hold up card, see if Posse know," requested Posse.

"Okay, I can do that! I got two words for today: SAINTS. S-A-I-N-T-S and MOURN, M-O-U-R-N. Glad to know that you are still serious about reading," beamed Feets. Posse studied the cards MOURN and SAINTS and mouthed first the letters, then a phonetic flow of the syllables, and finally an awkward, mechanical flow of the words, one after the other.

"Got 'em," Posse says while holding up the old card and he smiled, "POSSE." They both laughed.

"How did you get into the bounty hunting business?" questioned Feets.

"How Posse begin? Well, Posse track for a long

time. Scout too for government in Mexico. Scout for snipers, for deer, for army … money. *Si bon n'est pas?"*

"Of course, now bounty hunt more dangerous, but pay much better!" exclaimed Posse while rubbing his thumbs and index finger.

The animals settled into an easy gait seemingly aware of their need for sustained, long- term energy. The hot air occasionally punctuated a brisk, dusty breeze as tree shadows played hide-and-seek with leaves upturned and lusting for rain showers. Feets thought he saw the streaking dive of a hawk nearby; the angle of sunlight intercepted a clear view, and he dismissed the thought.

"C-U-R-S-E equals 'curse,' means a foul or demonic evocation," voiced Feets.

"Yes! Words that damn a person or a thing," voiced Posse. "I heard many a curse in Mexico!"

Dead leaves, caked together by rain and dust, stood in piles on the roadside. Here and there, old cardboard boxes and crates stood next to blackened piles of rubble. *The aftermath of attempts to destroy scents and leave an untraveled get-a-way trail,* thought Posse. As late afternoon commenced, the air became more chilled and Posse picked up the pace.

Tangled vines, thick-branched undergrowth, and trees drowned in the watery marshes of late winter mixed with the expectant onset of spring, as a budding scent of freshness carried by occasional breezes outlined exactly the lagoon they now passed. Beavers snare-drummed their signatures on selected timbers, erecting stick tepees of wood, mud, and cloves of lumber, arranged in every equivalent angle.

The hounds bayed loudly and relished the scent of clothing Posse periodically whisked under their noses. They appeared to almost consider the rags as food of some sort and inhaled with great delight. Posse named the horse Mary and the mule Maude. Both animals seemed pleased with the dew-hazed embankments; they snorted the air so as not to miss surprises and sent, from their hindquarters, sizzling approvals of the early morning breakfast they had consumed. The hounds zigzagged excitedly making stiff-tailed sallies into underbrush and blackjack. The lines, arcs, loops, and dashes left by their tracks was evidence of the desperate trail of human scent left by determined refugees. The image of the singing, dancing drunk captivated his mind's eye. *Marchon, marchon, Qu'un sang impur.*

"What does that part—the part 'the drunk up high'—what does it mean? Do you understand?"

"My friend Feets, so many, many question! Concentrate on the road. I understand a bit of it, think it be a French song of liberty. It is mere music that trails backwards, backwards and off in the distance. Our trail is forward, a money trail that helps you to liberty, not—"

"But is not liberty a birthright, not something that needs to be bought? Not something that you have to earn or seek in total desperation like these slaves we are tracking?"

"It is true that these we follow seek freedom and a chance for liberty. But my friend, it is their liberty, their freedom or yours, *n'est pas?*"

"Maude, whoaaa," Posse barked, keeping his voice husky at the hounds.

MEMPHIS

"Ruuugh, Gruuuruff," the dogs repeatedly yapped. Usually the dogs explored and returned, explored and returned. Now they concentrated and focused in their runs, almost as if they were fish hooked by the bait, and running straight towards their target, as opposed to away from capture. The dogs generally stayed close, orbiting home base. Whenever they roamed too far, a whistle brought them back from stiff-tailed, quick dashes, arcs, and loops in the underbrush.

"Grrrr, woof!" barked one to the other playfully.

"Stay on the road, stay on the road dogs! Don't wanna have you scratched and cut up by thorns, tangled up with underbrush, snakes, and shit. Better stay in close to us and not go too far down the road." Posse snarled again shouting, "Stay on the road!"

"Did you use the Whit for bounty hunting?" queried Feets.

"Oh no. Posse no hurt slave. Whit for snipers and thieves. Posse use shotgun to flush runaway from hiding place. Cut the muzzle, use eggbeater drill to dress muzzle and gauge pins to straighten bore. I show you when we get back! Dogs chase runaway. Slave smart, use rivers, lakes, creeks to kill scent. But snakes in water, rattlers, moccasins. Many slave *morte* of snakebite," explained Posse.

"*Morte?*" Feets asked.

"Die from snakebite," Posse translated. "*Morte* be dead."

"Oh," responded Feets in a spurt of understanding.

A short whinny from Mary provoked protruding ears from Maude as the dogs headed northward away from the more southeastward location of Camp Fiske.

"Aiiee, aiiieyaeii," yelped two bronzed, burlap-clad females suddenly appearing from the tangled underbrush. "We's headed north by the North Star," uttered the older woman. "You gentlemens headed north? Up Ohio?" and she nodded her headed, sputtering, "We needs 'tection from doggone Rebs." Juice from the wad of tobacco she chewed spurted past her lips leaving a reddish trail on one side of her dress.

"Whar's y'all headed?" asked the younger, peeking out from behind the older, then stepping forward with her arms behind her, obviously grasping a weapon of some sort, meant not to be seen at first glance.

Looking at each other, Posse hacked past the phlegm in his mouth from the cigar he nursed, stroked Mary to a standstill, halted the caravan, saying, "Headin' to Fort Donelson ma'am. Up the road a piece is Fort Pillow. These parts are infested with rebel deserters and home guard. We can't take you far with us, but you are welcome to join us 'til we get to the next camp or church. Reckon dat be the bes we can do, escort you to the next contraband camp."

The road past Millington showed signs of hasty movements: bits of clothing, evidence of reckless passage, carved walking sticks, dead animals, scraps of newspaper, charred wood, and the ashes of cooking fires, decked shoulders of the byways. The detritus also suggested the work of raiding parties. Occasional fires still burned in open fields and

smoldering embers from hastily doused encamp-
ments peppered the woods. An occasional wagon
marked "U.S. Government" laid in a trench, either
part of a raid on Federal troops or a charitable
donation from Union forces to serve as firewood.
They may have been left to help sustain those unable to spend time in a mode of protection.

Posse and Feets dismounted and allowed both
women to ride. Mary and Maude acknowledged
appreciation of the lightened weight of their new
riders and snorted their approval. Close by, a fire
burned in an open field. From the smell, it was
designed to burn old clothes and dead animals.
Even slaves knew that garbage spread disease and
death so matches were a premium item. Fires also
covered many scents, so not only were matches
premium items, to a runaway, they were a precious
commodity. Feets said little, using his eyes to examine, codify, and arrest the symphony of images
that, taken by themselves, made little or no sense.

For the most part, he tried to eliminate the timing
of the hierarchy in which events were perceived by
him, and attempted to let the forensic facts speak
for themselves. Despite his attempts to picture the

raid as the women described it, he found his attention drawn away from the vivid and sometimes
humorous descriptions of the raid. "Black folk
high-tailing it every which away, praying as they
be runnin', singing while they kicking at maraud-
ers, singing while they being shot at! Rebels gits
whacked off dat horse by a tree limb! Dat horse so
happy to be nigger driven, it flew from Tennessee,
right into Lincoln's office in Washington, D.C.!"

His brain sped in search of answers for these
events. The girl on the mule was wreathed in beauty. The long, purplish plait down her back shone
in the sunlight. Her brownish, tan complexion re-
minding Feets of the color of cashews that Bishop
preferred, and her scent surging of cinnamon.

"I be Eggplant. What's your name?" continuing
before he answered, she added, "What in de world
is dis man in front of us. He look white, sound lil'
black, and dress funny. He be your massa?"

"Not right now," countered Feets, "We out cher
looking for some folk he needs to talk to."

"Don't look like he about no talk! Look to me more

like he gone chasing slaves. Got those guns, ammo, a knife, a rope, iron cuffs. Look at 'im. Be putting his ear to the ground and such, just like an old Indian. He be trackin sumthin'! He be trackin' and catchin'. You be his helper? Him be looking for footprints, dogs be sniffing footprints! Ear cupped to the ground. Ma, Ma!"

"Girl, what in the hell you yelling for?" Feets sputtered as the hawk spun down from the trees, magically landing on Posse 's arm. The bird seemed to be spun right from the sun. It caused the girl to look on in astonished disbelief. Posse gave the bird some bits of corn and it flew off just as quickly as it came. Posse cast them both a smirk and smile, adding, "Takes more than a ear to the ground to track these runaways. They ain't no good to anyone *morte*!" He fetched some bits of corn from his pocket and sprayed them on the ground. "See, told ya."

Turning to Posse, she countered, "Yeah, but I betcha they might think it's better to be dead than a slave. Even more so if they got a half-breed like you chasing em. We been slaves and it ain't no glorious thing to think that your children be slaves, too, wid no way to climb outa it."

"Miss, you sound just like a philosopher. Monsieur Feets, he come along for the money! I didn't hear him complaining about that earlier. Anyway, there are lots of ways of locating most any kind of animal or person. If you track by sound, you can sometimes just put your ear to the ground, or you can use these dogs to track their scents. We have no plan to kill them, just return them to their masters. We didn't come to catch you or *votre bouche* large! Now stop yelling or you 'll bring the white Confederate army right to where we stand. How would you like that?"

Feets tried to strengthen Posse's argument, "I be trying to buy my way outa slavery, so I came here to make some money. Now we can help you ladies out or, if you prefer, leave you right here. It's up to you! See these here footprints, wheel tracks, and clothes? Could be wagon tracks, shoe and horse markings, could be Confederate or Union. Whatever came this way came recently."

Posse added, "Merely a business enterprise. Now we be trying to act as good Samaritans. Please help us by being quiet and we'll help you get to safety. For ze runaway, if they in the hands of guerrillas, then we could maybe make a bargain, maybe take away. It could be the difference in taking another breath for the slave. I knows I love to breathe. Seen every kind of possible runaway, quick, slow, runner, walker, except for swim-aways. Don' see too many swim-aways. That ol' Mississippi being a major deterrent. Now, those syndicate fellas think Nathan Bedford been round these parts. After Chickamauga, he been reassigned to Tennessee. He been hackin' away at the Federals, been burning these nigger camps. That's probably what hit these two!"

The trail they were now on showed signs of the dispossessed: bits of clothing, evidence of passages, curved walking sticks, wagon wheel tracks, burned wood and evidence of campfires. The bones of dead animals and the grim skeletons of the elderly, the infirmed, and useless littered the pathways, often unseen by these caravan of twos— two dogs, two men, two women, and two of four hooves. Even where the snows of late March and the rains of early April had come, the bare and browned grass left evidence of travelers on foot, a virtual army of refugees leaving plantations of the Mississippi Delta for territories unknown, places where their hopeful claim on the gifts and rewards of their humanness would be treasured.

Ammunition crates, marked US GOVERNMENT, stolen from wagon trucks once owned by the Federals were strewn about. Perhaps the boxes had been gifts from sympathetic Union regiments. Perhaps they were the results of raids by the Rebels. Almost for sure, they had been boxes used by contraband campers as protection from the deep and icy winter days that now faded into the distance with the onslaught of spring. The caravan plodded on. Swampy bayous, populated by tree stumps, illustrated previous visitors. Feets cast around about, glanced one hundred and eighty degrees. He reached into his pouch to pull out a string of tough beef jerky, offering it first to the rider who called herself Eggplant. She accepted quietly.

"If," wishing to take back the word as he spoke it, thinking it may have sounded like a blurt, he continued, "we find a camp or a Union wagon train headed to Memphis, it might be a good idea for y'all to put yourselves under Federal protection. They can keep you there for protection until this fever is all over!"

FEETS

"Fever!" spoke the girl in a half shout. Her mother looked back at her with eyes bulging out of their sockets, "This ain't no fever! This is a war! My mother done birthed children into slavery. What kinda of life is dat to be born into—no daddy, sometimes no ma, no money in one of dem banks. Slave by heredity. Folks ain't felt no guilt. No guilt for hangings, no guilt for poverty, no guilt for the ignorance, no guilt for living without doing the cotton picking, no guilt for de ghosts I sees dancing on their unmarked graves, no guilt for nuttin'! Thank you, no! Ain't no fever. Dis here is a battle to de death!"

The mother chimed in plaintively, "Sho' glad you take us on your mule's backside." She said with a beseeching glance towards Feets, "Me been walking and running for long time. My feets is all blistered up."

The young fugitive, deer-eyed and squaw-like in dress, chewed still on the jerky, tearing off a small piece with her teeth. The older woman swayed from side to side on Posse's mare, swaying weakly in the saddle.

MEMPHIS

"We sure has been walking for a long time," said the younger. "I wrapped ma's feet, wrapped mine, too. Don't make no difference, they almost numb just the same! We been dodging damn rednecks for day and a half. Lucky we's smoked out by your dogs and not theirs!"

"Girl, you sure are one angry heifer; calm yourself and we gone do our business and help you to live to do yours," spoke Posse in modulated tones adding, "Some would say you lucky, others might say you blessed. Either way, speak less to stay breathing longer! Feets, check out this map against the compass. We should probably get off the main road 'til we see the next church or camp. Crisscrossing gives us a lesser chance of being scouted by home guards, guerrillas, or rebels."

Feets nodded, "Okay!"

The younger fugitive possessed physical features that captivated Feets. Her silent intelligence was as vivid as when she spoke. Her keen awareness and obvious sense of disenfranchisement were enhanced by the understated simplicity of her garments. The lilt in her voice and her self-assuredness calmed him. He fell in to the unhurried but alert pace into which the group had fallen and turned occasionally to examine the rear, looking to tease danger from the majestic trees and songful birds, should it there be lurking. The long braid down her back dangled across her wide firm buttocks. He compared the map with the compass adding, "I think we are right on course."

"Me Eggplant," she said softly, "I like your mule, but mule needs water, water up ahead over there." Heeding her voice, Posse pointed Mary in the direction of her pointed finger. A creek emerged over a slanted ridge, its clearness unequaled even by the crisp visibility of the April day. Echelons of stair step pebbles lined the crooked creek floor; the travelers watered the horses, resting momentarily. Feets offered Eggplant a chicken wing. The elder refugee munched a proffered thigh. He ate a biscuit. Posse cupped his ear to the ground listening for movement.

"We'll have visitors soon, Feets," warned Posse. He used his fingers across his lips to indicate silence. He whispered, "Ladies, say nothing out loud and please remain very, very quiet. If you dismount, they will not see you if you hide behind yonder trees." He repeated himself, "Please, get off the horse and the mule and aussi, stay out of sight! We come back for you," and he put his hands over his lips for reinforcement.

"Feets, we leave the women here to stay out of sight and, later, clear area for camp! You and me ride to the road and meet riders, I think, maybe, guerillas."

Nearing the road at a trot, Posse barked orders, "Check pistol, rifle. You my body servant. Stay behind me, finger on trigger. *Compris?*"

Feets followed with a blank stare. "Yes, *compris*. That reminds me of those reading cards you wanted to learn. I had almost forgotten about those." nodded Feets and spun his revolver for bullets.

Posse put a handbill in his mouth, repeatedly checking over his shoulder as the dogs chased them. Stopping to strike a match, he lit a cigar and barked out, "I not forget the cards. Holster your rifle and cover your pistol under the blanket, but keep pointed at the one in front!" Suddenly, his chestnut reared and snorted. Posse fired several shots into the ground and backed the frantic horse away from the dust spiraling upwards from the ground they had covered. He calmly advised, "Boldness, Feets, Boldness!" Feets quick-scanned the now dead halves of a rattlesnake, its sections yet writhing from the shots, and made a wide circle around the reptile's remains.

Stunned by the apparent confusion of the scene, the three guerillas paused in the roadway unsure of the antics of this madman on horseback. Upon closer observation of their silence, Posse exclaimed, "Gentlemen, *mes amis,* good day. This damned snake startled my horse, a grave insult punishable by death and for him a most sobering experience. Your ride today has been a good one, *n'est pas*? You have a very good day for adventure."

"No problem," warily countered the lead rider. "Better you spend your bullets on that rattler then we spend ours. You fellas okay?

"But of course, *monsieur,* of course. Would you care to examine the result of this belly crawlers poisonous charge at my horse?" Posse quizzed. Feets backed away from the ruthless trio, recognizing the rouge neck who attacked him outside the shop. He kept his head downward, his rifle holstered, and his finger firm against the trigger of the pistol hidden under the blanket across his saddle.

"May I present belly zigzagger minus the kiss—I mean, the hiss?" pointing his revolver at the rattler.

"Pretty good shot Mister, uh mister..."

"Posse," mouthed Posse, quickly surveying the trio for which of the three would be the most trigger-happy. "Posse the name." He flashed his whip and unfurled it towards the remnants of the snake, wrist-flicked towards the reptile and breaking it into more individuated pieces. Almost on cue the hawk dived, swanlike towards the stalemated group. In doing so, it startled that member of the trio into drawing his gun. As he fingered the trigger, Posse lashed out at the gun hand with his rope, causing a wild misfire.

"The bird be mine and will not hurt you. She is hungry for snake meat. Accept my apologies please. I hope I did not hurt your hand!"

FEETS

"Goddamn Ca—"

Before the obvious invective could be finished, the more diplomatic of the three, the one farthest forward and in the middle, spoke, "That bird is no doubt trained and owned by our Cajun comrade. Be a real shame to kill that bird. No way a dead bird could roost on his arm like we saw through that spyglass. Looked like we saw some women folk riding long wid' y'all! From a distance, looked like one of those vaudeville caravans. Kinda funny, musta been mistaken!"

"Musta been," replied Posse, noting the slight rise in voice of the leader. The bird had risen to its full wingspan, a piece of snake dangling from its beak. It rose, banked, and flapped off powerfully to rest behind the same embankment, which hid the women. "Musta been."

"Well, there are many critters lurking hereabouts especially fugitive niggers. That's there your…"

"Body servant, *monsieur,*" as Posse filled in the questioning space left hanging by the lead rider.

"Well, we're home guard officers patrolling these here highways for runaways, fugitives, Union supplies, and such. Federals trying to keep this artery open for Pickering supplies and freeing niggers since that Proclamation. Ain't no such parchment ever been recognized in Dixie."

Posse nodded his acknowledgment. "Well to be sure, we plan to track down a darky or two."

The lead rider pitched his voice just a shade higher, "Darkies need to be aiding the cause, protecting their masters' plantations, and tending the crops. Your uh 'body servant' seems like he be a good nigger. A'int that right boy?"

Feets nodded the affirmative, saying nothing. He felt the eyes of all on him, noting the flash of recognition that crossed the face of the roughneck who had attacked him a month or two ago.

"*Mes amies!* We appreciate your checking on us." Feets kept his eyes shielded and his six-shooter under the blanket. His hand twitched slightly against the cocked trigger.

FEETS

Posse inhaled deeply on his cigar, noticing the bandage on the thin man's foot and commented, "Looks like your partner's hand was only nicked, just grazed by the rope. Now that foot! I would say that the foot needs attention before it gets gangrene. Might need attention real quick. Please accept my apologies for disturbing the aim. The hawk was raised by me for hunting and I cannot afford to lose it."

The quietest of the home guard now spoke up, "Yeah, we heading up the road now. Doc is in the next town over."

"Heard tell that Forrest is expected in these parts," added Posse.

"Oh, yeah. You could be seeing him any day now." The three tipped their hats to Posse and backed away, adding, "You fellas be real careful. You see any of them contraband niggers heading North, y' all just fire into the air. We be right over to check 'em out. That goes for any damned deserters you see, too!" A trail of dust marked their exit away from the road and southward towards Memphis.

MEMPHIS

"You notice their mounts? Just like those at the shop the other day," observed Posse.

"Yeah," replied Feets, "that was the same bunch that greeted me at the shop asking for horseshoe refits. His shooting hand was bandaged."

"Well, if you recognized him, he probably pegged you. We'll zigzag up this pike for the next four days. We'll have to ditch our lady friends when we spot a convoy heading to Memphis. Tie up the hooves with burlap in the morning."

When they reached creek side, their female fugitives had collected and piled stones to imitate a small fire pit. Pointing to herself first, the younger one spoke slowly at first, "Me, Eggplant," and then pointing to the elder, "Mother, mmm-oth-errr."

"Eggplant and Mother, *c'est bon*, Eggplant and Mother." Posse introduced himself and then Feets while making fine reed twigs and stocks for fire. "You make fire, we brush down horse and mule. We make camp here by creek, eat, sleep on west side." Posse commanded.

FEETS

"Uh-uh." nodded Eggplant walking towards the creek. "Eggplant and Mother catch fish for dinner. We fix for you."

A small team of fish was soon neatly tied to rawhide in the creek water. Feets tended to the horses. "I've got to scout this terrain," shouted Posse, heading northwest of the creek bed. "How did you do that? How did you catch them?" queried Feets. "I tell you tomorrow," answered Eggplant while she rapidly devoured the tasty dinner.

Upon returning, Posse reappeared simulating the professional and efficient topographer who was precise in his mental snapshots of the physical terrain. He gathered the small party together.
"Compadres, our visitors have positioned themselves between us and the military installation that exists to our north, not our south! They may observe us for the next few days or decide to attack us tonight. Among us, we have six guns, three rifles and three pistols. We'll do the following to prepare: keep the fire burning all night, gather wood for it, and load every gun with extra ammo."

"Eggplant, you and your mom will sleep behind

the horses. Feets, you are close to the crest of the ridge and I am close to the circle." He traced a wide circle around the fire with a radius of twenty yards. Then he quickly gathered twigs, and added, "Gather leaves, too." He added gunpowder to the levee of leaves, adding twigs and small logs to the centerpiece.

"We sleep outside the circle. They have to cross the creek and will probably fire at our blankets if they attack. Eggplant, can you shoot a rifle?" "Uh-huh," affirmed Eggplant.

"Okay, you will get the extra rifle and take this revolver. Make sure your weapons are loaded completely. Take extra cartridges. I will set fire to this perimeter once they are inside the circle. Do not discharge your weapons before then. From our positions, they should be visible targets from the fire. Aim well, *mes amis*, you might only get one shot."

Posse marked off appropriate places for each individual and then tied up the dogs a hundred yards to the north. Posse smiled, sopping up food with his biscuit on his tin plate. "We'll bed the horses here on the west side of the creek. Ladies, you will be on the perimeter behind the horses. Feets, you and me behind the tree by the boulder next to the trunk. We stand watch. I'm sure we will have visitors tonight."

As darkness descended, Posse rekindled the cooking fire, cleaned the cooking pan, and rechecked sight lines. Feets sighted the campfire from his position precisely at the tactical crest approaching the ridge.

"You help Eggplant with rifle?" asked Eggplant turning to Posse.

"Sure," replied Posse, knowing that her rifle had no telescope. He pulled up the sight and said to Eggplant, "Look down the barrel and through this metal aperture. Squeeze the trigger and don't yank it. Point this viewer up and look through this aperture." Posse knew that every gun, knife, handcuff, and iron in his possession could summon his own death. *Bolted in with a lock of a hundred keys*, he shuddered and rechecked their armaments as Eggplant stretched out sleepily next to her momma.

MEMPHIS

"Why do you think they will come back, Posse?"

"For you, me, the girls, dust fly only short distance and we no see at night, all of the reasons. I embarrassed them and now they know that they can sell you as a high priced slave, Eggplant for booty, and older woman for cook. Perhaps, they're just mean."

"Why do you think that they will come from the east?"

"'Cause the terrain shows the dust. The wind is from west and the bushes make noise. Before you sack out, sprinkle kerosene around this second circle I etched around the perimeter." Posse commented out loud, "We ain't bolted in, we not locked in. We make defensive perimeter! Lace the dogs' ropes to your feet."

XV

Memphis

"Bolted in," jogged Feets' memory as he back-flashed, fingering his medallion. Its shape was asymmetrical, the outer rim being round and the other rim shaped in an "S" fashion. Thinking of something he'd read: *All the powers of earth seem rapidly combining against him. Mammon is after him; ambition follows, and philosophy follows, and the theology of the day is fast joining the cry. They have him in his prison house; they have searched his person, and left no prying instrument with him. One after another they have closed the heavy iron doors upon him, and now they have him, as it were, **bolted in** with a lock of a hundred keys, which can never be unlocked without the concurrence of every key; the keys in the hands of a hundred different men, and they*

FEETS

scattered to a hundred different and distant places; and they stand musing as to what invention, in all the dominions of mind and matter, can be produced to make the impossibility of his escape more complete than it is.

"Have you ever killed a man?"

"No," replied Feets as he drove spikes into the ground, placed handcuffs around them to hold the tent taunt. He placed rolled blankets just inside the tent, gracing both blankets with hats: a sombrero and a soup tin turned upside down.

"Different from practice, from target shooting. Take steady finger like these that play banjos," smiled Posse, placing his banjo outside the perimeter, out past the horses, face up with tightened strings. The lariat, he strung out across the entryway to this cul-de-sac and it tied to the banjo strings. Feets completed the task, rechecked the rolled up tented blankets inside the perimeter; he placed new timbers on the fire and repositioned the hats. Posse stood first watch.

"Load your rifle before you sleep, Feets! I speak to ladies. Eggplant looks like she might really know a thing or two about guns. When they come, I take one, you take three, she take two. Understand!"

Feets nodded his approval. He visualized the defensive perimeter established by Posse and felt in his pocket for matches. *No matches*, he thought ransacking his saddlebags for small wooden sticks. *Not there*, he said to himself, and quietly studying the damp soil where Posse had poured kerosene, he walked towards Posse's position saying, "I have no matches!"

"Okay, here you go." The creek was ten yards east of the twenty-yard diameter. Posse's sleeping position was at six o'clock, Feets' at nine, and Eggplant's at ten feet west of the circle. Have to be quick in response, he thought to himself. Hopefully the banjo would sound with a loud bong if and when the rope attached to it was tripped.

Feets slept quietly at first and more deeply after midnight. Posse awoke him for the second shift and he cataloged items he would need. He had matches, bullets, shotgun, Whitworth, loaded pistol, and extra ammo. There was no sound from the quarter in which Eggplant and her mom slept, but he thought there was a trace of movement just east of the circle—the same direction which Posse thought would be the approach of the guardsmen. He shook Posse lightly, both straining to hear movement in the water. At the faint sloshing of footfalls, both men spread out away from each other, craning forward and extending their arms with pistols pointed and rifles at the ready. They laid down to minimize their bodies as targets.

"Squeeze, do not yank." whispered Posse, edging in closer to the perimeter. Just then the banjo sounded a comic arpeggio.

"Ba-jo-in—Bajoing—ing," went the fragile instrument, its unmistakable sound fractured into unstructured noises, a music indicative of footfalls in slow motion. The dogs growled.

"Damn," vented a strange male voice. The caravan awaited their breaking moment to meet their visitors. Posse smiled at the steps of the three silhouettes as they approached the dummy figures. Feets struck three successive matches at the kerosened perimeter. A "sa-whoosh" roared rapidly around the circle in spectacular tongues of yellowish and orange hue. The circle of fire trapped the trio inside the planned compound. The first and third were lifeless against the flaring perimeter, the blaze gaining strength as the wind lifted it skyward. The second stumbled and shouted a volley of epithets, "Damn it—shit" and moved, trotting and spinning, towards Feets as he attempted to reload.

"CRACK!" A burst of white steel burst forth, spinning the second around and into the jagged edge of Posse's saber. Before blinking, he pierced all three bodies repeatedly with his saber and kicked their weapons free before grasping them. Posse rolled backwards from the flame, firing at the first silhouette. Eggplant fired two pistol shots at the third, and Feets unloaded buckshot at the second. One and three when down quietly with voiceless immobility. Two struggled against the blaze, his jacket ablaze, his ten-gallon hat flipping sideways. He whirled quickly, unloading two shots towards the direction of Eggplant. They missed. Feets, sliding sideways, fired his revolver again at two, who still stood upright, both noting two rounds gone in his chamber. On one knee, he fired the Whit, missing a third time! The thought, *Perhaps I am already an angel, without existence, beyond the realm of affecting the physical,* rampaged his mind.

Posse groaned slightly as he returned with the trio's horses. "Feets, I got grazed across the shoulder rolling backwards."

"I'll look at it, let me see," spoke Eggplant while boldly examining the injury. Feets took the horses and tied them with the other horses to the tethered handcuffs. Momma and Feets then dragged the bodies to the creek, dumping them in a sand bar. Eggplant bandaged Posse's flesh wound and as dawned approached, they set their minuscule caravan off to the north.

"Ladies, if we run across a Union convoy, you should head back to Memphis. You'll be safer there at the fort," Posses suggested. Feets stood, embarrassed by his misses, and said nothing. He waited for chastisement from either Eggplant or Posse, but none occurred. Momma grunted but agreed.

"Ask for Mother Roche, either at Cavalry Church or Fort Pickering, she's my mother and please give her a hug for me." Feets wrote on a paper card:

MEMPHIS

"Hi, Mom!" on one side and the flip side he scribed MOTHER ROCHE/FORT PICKERING/ MEMPHIS. He handed the card to Eggplant. Posse then emphasized to the womenfolk, "We travel along the side roads. Listen carefully and keep your eyes peeled for horses and Union convoys! Keep your revolvers and rifles loaded."

Near daybreak they spotted a Union convoy traveling southward towards a small camp of contraband and explained their adventure of the previous evening. The commanding officer took notes of their description, asked for and received a crude map of where it took place, dropped off one box of supplies at the contraband camp at which it was parked.

"Be most careful, Feets and Posse!" warned Eggplant. "Yes, careful!" added her mother, and the convoy moved out, disappearing in the southward direction of Memphis. The women started southward, Memphis bound. They reached a small church just north of Millington on April 12.

Feets read aloud from an old *Daily Appeal* as he rode backwards in the saddle and in front of Posse.

FEETS

For his part, Posse plucked on the banjo he had bandaged after its fight with the guard of home. Amazingly, the bong of its strings was not absent without leave.

"The double envelopment combined with perfect timing encircled the enemy capturing or rupturing his supply lines." Posse's sombrero bounced with each horse trot, his shaded eyes glanced at Feets, "That is considered to be the most perfect accomplishment in battle."

"Yet to be pulled off perfectly," yawned Posse, "that girl Eggplant fired a good shot." He motioned his fingers across his head and chest as he crossed himself praying for their safety and mumbled, "*Mon Dieu*! May our crab caravan move to the delight of Thee!"

When contrabands were gained or captured during the midst of war, they were put to use as teamsters, laborers, and construction workers. Camps established outside of the Federal installations housed these individuals. "She be cute, too," he hollered back at Feets.

MEMPHIS

Feets kept reading the paper, ignoring both compliments, neither of which referred to him and read on: "Invaders of the North camped at Chattanooga after our victorious heroes ran them and their master, Rosecrans, from the field at Chickamauga Creek. In what was one of the bloodiest days of the war, General Longstreet arrived just in time to exploit a breech in the line extended from Snodgrass Hill to McLemore Cove. Bragg's intent was to crush the Federals, once they were hemmed in by the cove. Bragg slammed a double envelopment against the Union, using McLemore Cove as left side of a power intent. Forrest and his cavalry were positioned at the northwest, left of the Federal's approach from Chattanooga. General George A. Thomas, traitor to the southern homeland, allowed the Federals to escape imminent ruin through his defensive rally at Snodgrass Hill. Foiled in his desire to ardently pursue the Federal retreat into Chattanooga, Forrest repudiated Bragg and was repositioned in the northern Delta. Tennessee expects great things from her homegrown heir."

"So you think Forrest might be roaming around the countryside?" Feets pondered. Posse nodded, pursed his lips and casted a quick glance to either side of him. Following a quixotic smile, he added, "You ever met Forrest?" Answering his own question, he continued, "'Cording to rumor, he likes to put the skeer in folks and keep it on them. What you got to do, under those conditions, is be *skeerproof!* Prepare for the worst and all those petite increments betwixt and between. Make sure equipment works, triple check rifle, practice shootin'." The smile vanished. "Shootin' under ever conceivable circumstance!"

He added comically, "And be damn sure horses got rest and don't go lame. Fact is, we can water our horses right over there by that creek."

Offensive forces under Generals Grant and Thomas won Chattanooga for the Union later at Missionary Ridge. Frustrated with General Bragg's refusal to attack Chattanooga after Chickamauga, General Forrest personally chastised General Bragg and actively sought reassignment in West Tennessee. Newspaper accounts reported Chickamauga a win for the Rebels. After landing back in Tennessee, Forrest, also known as the Wizard of the Saddle, unleashed his magic unpredictably throughout Northern Mississippi and Western Tennessee.

MEMPHIS

The hawk and hounds had routed them westward from Henning towards Fort Pillow. "You'd be hard pressed to escape from these parts without wings or wheels," thought Feets looking at vast fields of such farmlands populated with nests of slaves plowing, planting, hammering, or waving at their party of twos. The air was crisp and he felt the air blowing cooler as they moved westward towards the Mississippi.

"The skirmish from the other night might have been some of Forrest's boys," Feets noted. Throwing Feets a second quixotic smile, Posse ruminated out loud, "That rumor that Forrest's motto is to throw the skeer on 'em and keep it on 'em: believe it! Looks like these puppies are leading us up to Fort Pillow way."

"So, have you met Forrest?" asked Feets naively.

"Those ladies be damned lucky to get back to Memphis in one piece and, no, not directly. The syndicate knows him well." Posse added.

"Would you head for Fort Pillow if you was a runaway?"

FEETS

"Not sure, would depend on what I'm up against. Might be a good stopover to be closer to the river, the water disguises tracks, cover scent, but patrollers, homeguard's cronies can hide there, aussie, sometimes rebel prostitutes."

"Scuttlebutt around the fort was that a Union garrison—your friend O'Reilly called 'em smoked Yankees—was sent to hold Fort Pillow. Seems like one runaway mighta followed 'em or even joined up!"

Feets dismounted his mule, noticing a limp in the animal's gait. Posse dismounted, too, and both men started walking.

"Tell me about the runaway. You got a picture? How would you recognize him?"

"Well, he's one legged, actually one-footed, no footed. 'Scaped from the Roberts' Plantation in Holly Springs. S'posed to be real good in iron works. They clubbed his left foot to keep him plantation bound. Other slaves called him Hawk. Seems like he always thirsted for freedom. Spent hours looking at hawks gliding in the sky, even made iron images of hawks. They say this Hawk could build anything: gates, doorstops, cuffs, chairs, door-knockers. Could draw anything whatever he saw and make very artistic like your father, real handy with iron works.

"Reckon that's why bounty is high," turning to Feets with an unfamiliarly ragged smile. "For sure, it would cost more than either one of us could afford!"

"Bounty is $1,200. Hawk looks like this, very golden in color and wears the Roberts' brand. S'posed to be a boat floating on clove of cotton." Feets fingered his medallion and felt his imagination scamper his brain, remembering old stories, but failing to find an unassailable connection to himself. The words, "very artistic like your father, real handy with iron works," spoken by the good Bishop never logically gained traction.

"Now Roberts and Forrest they do have business. Robert calls him General Ghost Rider now, since that business in Fort Donelson. Forrest escaped at night and all. Now, since January, 1863, fugitive, contraband, runaways, whatever you call' em, been striking north in droves just north of Fort Pillow, heading for Kentucky. Lots of 'em enlist up there!"

"See Forrest met Grant at Fort Donelson. Grant's idea was to use the infantry and Navy in attacking at Fort Henry. Henry is at the juncture of the Tennessee and Cumberland, right at Kentucky. Henry was low and flood prone and it fell first.

"I'll walk awhile; you can ride the mare for a bit 'til we get close to someplace where we can look at that hoof. Can you imagine trying to escape from Tennessee on barefoot? You have cuts—lacerations, bleeding, whelps—every kinda thorn imaginable raking your feet, not to mention the stones and hundreds of miles!"

Feets thought, "This mare rides much better than the mule." He recorded bits of Posse's conversation in mental shorthand: coordinated navy and infantry, marched infantry over land seventy miles, Grant stalled at first then captured Donelson.

"Both Forrest and Roberts have pretty good sized plantations. Called him The Ghost Rider mainly 'cause of his escape from Fort Donelson over Lick's Creek in the snow and ice storm."

Drawing close to water where the terrain became more hilly, a toothless white bearded slave appeared with reptilian suddenness. He was quite dark, almost purple in color, and short of stature. He approached them in a state of moderate hysteria, smiling while shooing them away. He pointed towards the east and swung his head eerily from side to side and going up and down, bobbing as if he had been hung. As they drew closer, he grabbed a shovel and tried to shoo them away; all his movements were voiceless. When he saw that they would not be deterred, he offered a candle and some matches. Then, he beckoned them to a hut and by a drum, pounding a steady, but intricate pulse and enunciating slowly. He appeared to be singing at the top of his lungs, but no tones were transmitted, only a kind of low-grade groan. When he stopped, his voiceless chanting and drumming, he stirred gruel over an open flame before the hut, secured their horses and tossed huge bones to the hounds. Posse asked the man, who stood no more than five feet, questions. The man nodded or wagged, depending on the question.

FEETS

"Do you have iodine?" Posse asked, concerned that his wound might get infected. The little man raced inside his hut, and brought out a small valve marked with a skull and bones to Posse. Posse thanked him, wondering about the date. *Was it the 13th or 14th of April?* The dwarf-like man motioned both Posse and Feets to open ground and drew stick men hanging from trees along a road stretching from "For Pill-OH" to "Brown Vile." After he finished the map, he drew one large eye and pointed to himself, gesticulating wildly.

"Thank you, old man," Posse said reflective. "He is telling us that a battle took place and he wants us to be careful. Brownsville is due east of Pillow, he thinks we might be in danger!"

Feets thanked the white-haired old man. Upon close inspection, he realized that, in addition to his missing teeth, the man's tongue was missing. It had either been burned out, cut out, or some combination of both. Feets shuddered. Feets thanked the old man and quietly dislodged a stone from the mule's hoof.

"We'll eat while it is still light and bivouac overnight in that cornfield beside the hut. The old man brought grain and straw for the animals. Feets brushed them down.

Posse spoke in cautionary tones, "We have a big day tomorrow. Should make Pillow fairly early."

XVI

Memphis

The old man's mono-groan with drum accompaniment reminded Feets of a prayer he heard in Memphis. As darkness lifted, Feets was momentarily dazed by the figure, which blocked the grayish light momentarily blurred by drowsiness. He blinked several times towards the direction of the tent's door. The beat of his heart jack-knifed until he heard the familiar voice of Posse.

"*Bon jour, mon ami.* Time to shine and rise." Posse led the bounty party into a thick misty haze.

Bogs, blackjack, thorny thistle, and barren bottoms covered with fallen leaves, hollowed logs, and flot-

FEETS

sam appeared, disappeared, and reappeared as if it were a school of fish teasing a hypnotized angler. Trunks of trees, branches, and lively bogs appeared suspended in a fog, as in a Japanese painting. A bloodied skull roped to an oak tree branch lynched Feet's pulse, chilled their advance, and froze discussion. The cackle of crows blended with the falls of their animals' hooves. Sunlight sparkled on the surface of the river, seen in the distance.

The ears of the bloodhounds pricked eagerly in expecting their instructions. Posse extracted a brown paper wrapped parcel from his saddlebag and untied the package. He knelt down to both dogs and presented them a piece of clothing to sniff. The tail-wagging detectives excitedly lunged forward, strained their leashes, and pulled the mounted figures down a lengthy slope, which curved gradually downward. The road sideswiped a low lagoon forested with dead tree stumps and flotsam.

"Would a fort be this low in the river?" The wobble in his voice barely masked the creeping disquietude, smoldering agitation, and flooding fearfulness in his emotions. "Easy now, easy, girl," he said, patting his mare's mane as both of them backed away from the slithering noise. Taunt, strained leashes, stretched by the muscular shoulders of the hounds pointed towards the west like needles. Posse led the bounty party through another thick misty haze. As they progressed, the fog peeled back, lifting as if to give them a better look. Raptors banked and weaved through keyholes of mist, claiming sovereignty amid the dense brush and brownish overgrowth.

Cool, damp air and the vibrant hum of flies clasped the attention of both. Posse quietly checked his revolvers. Feets followed suit. The putrid stench of death and blood rose above the humidity, guiding them to the defensive perimeter manned by pickets fringed with thick underbrush revealing blue uniformed bodies caked with flies. "Fort Pillow is up ahead. There's fighting here," Posse reported. "The coolness is from the river." Apprehensively, they continued forward slowly to take quick cover if confronted by snipers.

The golden sheen of morning sunlight peeled back and gleamed with haze as hoof falls plodded sullenly forward.

FEETS

"The pickets pushed in," explained Posse while continuing, "then—"

Posse fingered his gun but resisted the urge to shoot. He rose slightly in the saddle shifting for an upward view. A particular broken limb attached to the hefty grain of the oak tree still held the raptor-ravaged and bullet-riddled skull with a tightened noose as necktie.

"Ugh," cried Feets, "he's sizzling with flies!" Posse looked and had to close his nostrils with his left arm. A silent darkness scooted across the ground. "Scavengers," added Feets while loosening his bandanna.

Posse took out a flask of whiskey, poured whiskey on his handkerchief, and wrapped it around his face. "This is a hell hole, Feets!" mumbled Posse under his handkerchief. Occasional Confederate gray mingled in a sea of blackened Union blue. Broken sabers and bloodstained bayonets were strewn about the battlefield.

"Damn it," cursed Feets through clenched teeth. A swarm of flies rose swirling from their ghastly feast startling both he and frightening his chestnut. The bodies of Union soldiers, many of them black, lay strewn across the morning landscape, covered by blankets of leaves. Others swung like dried grapes from trees, ropes around their necks. Feets vomited as he passed masses of flies feasting on the bludgeoned and decapitated carcasses of bodies in blue. Blues, he thought, realizing that blues stretched the widest of emotional range, from the joy of freedom fighters, newly knighted in blue, to the horror of battlefield death purpled and marinated in blood.

Posse reined in the startled mount and continued, "The rest attacked with artillery from the look of wheel marks." He scanned and countered-scanned the scene, trying to rebuild the chain of events from the view of retro-analysis. Moving forward he spoke, "See that deep gully." As the scene gathered focus and the mist and fog dissolved, he resumed, "If they had cannons at the fort, they would be useless against soldiers in this ravine." Beneath their feet, a thick sheet of ash gradually solidified proportionally to dead bodies in accelerating numbers.

"*Grotesque est la morte!*"

FEETS

Many of the soldiers, grizzled from voracious carnivores and ravaged by cranial wounds, rested in unconventional stupors made concrete by *rigor mortis*. The silk screen of death seemed mirrored in every direction, three hundred and sixty degrees. Mounds of brown soldiers mimed the slaughter of a herd of blue-coated buffaloes.

Light from the morning sun crept past a dimly lit theater. Both men's minds ran in reverse logic. They silently attempted to fully fathom the contortions accomplished by the dead: arms twisted, feet mangled, agglutinated blood, mangled arms and legs, necks axed, and skin burnt. Feets tightened the neckerchief saturated with alcohol and camphor around his nose, but his stomach churned anyway. A hurricane inside his stomach bubbled forth, and volcanoes of vomit spewed from his mouth. Posse hung his head. These men were bolted in death— the keys had not concurred.

The snowy mist, rising more quickly now, hung more thickly over a distant patch of the smoky thicket, a floating battle scene. There a billowing cloud floated over the turrets. Bastions, loopholes, wooden archways, and tunneled entrenchments revealed still more among the dead. A blackened blanket of crows banded perched on tree branches, their squawks and caws peppered death with ricochets, scalding the bottoms of burnt trees with the lava of their vocal venom.

"Surrounded!" bleated Posse. The hawk cruised through the tunnels and loopholes, unlocking brutal secrets of death's wizardly enterprise. The hounds shrugged, countering their nasal instincts to seek.

"Finish on foot, we tie horses up here!" They walked a narrow crescent pathway to Fort Pillow's peak as a lifting haze uncovered ash littered by the dead, mostly blue uniforms, mainly black soldiers, intermittent swaths of whites, and an occasional woman or child. Ravenous raptors clawed and pecked, oblivious to the rustle of leaves under the foot of visitors. A ray of sunlit candescence glinted, pitched by metal from a man's chest, and slammed into Feets' eyeshot. With stunning immediacy, he fired two shots at the pecking crow, clearing it from its fiendish feast. The meal had been a feed on the hollowed eye sockets of a body chained and pinioned to a wagon wheel. Other scavengers scattered, uncovering the chained medallion on the cadaver's chest. The lifeless body was bent back against a wagon wheel, arms raised, hands nailed to the wheels, and head slumped to the side. Feets used his rifle barrel to unhook the medallion and raised it over the limp head. *No foot!* he noted inwardly. *No foot!*

The burnt bodies of two soldiers cuffed at the wrists, swung from railroad spikes driven into a chain wall of logs. The fires beneath their feet still smoldered. Feets scoured the medallion's chain in dirt to free it of maggots and stuffed it in his pocket.

The occasional hammer of woodpeckers startled the horde of crows, arthritic arrowheads chipping into mounds of maggots. Flash fires inflamed brutalized trophies of death, black carcasses made darker amidst random butternuts. The iron loins of dismounted cannons silently cursed bullet-riddled skulls.

Past the earthen breastworks, the fort stood still. *Mammon's Hymn.* Hell had flushed forth its fury and the keys had not concurred! Swoosh! To look death in the eye, their eyes became stone, carved of black granite, seared red in the heat of hate. Both were beyond tears, afar from words, and devoid of condemnation.

Cottonwood trees garnished by clumps of blackjack and rooted in black topsoil, sloped downward into a steep ravine. Leaves crunched as Posse, followed by Feets, stepped over bodies butternut and blue.

"Walk carefully, we may not be alone," cautioned Posse. At the physical crest of the fort, bullet-riddled severed skulls marked uncovered graves around its edges. Its tactical peak, which Confederate sharpshooters had ravaged, was compromised by the tall trees amidst the somber battlefield.

"Sharpshooters had a field day," added Posse. "From that vantage, this is a chicken coop." The majestic Mississippi murmured in the short distance. Feets slipped in blood from a child's body nearby. A lone woodpecker rapped a solemn rhythm hammering upon the door of death.

Dead, smoked Yankees festooned mounds of

earth, their hacked bodies bludgeoned, bayonet-ed, burned, and beheaded. The crack and sizzle of leaves underfoot stampeded flutters of black wings, a fleeting daguerreotype scribed against the morning sun.

Rays of sun sliced through the mist, as if through a cathedral window, punctuating the truth of power psychosis, momentarily capturing the terror-strick-en existence of African life under the absolute power and authority of American slavers.

A breeze, soft and long-winded, sang in a trembling soprano of pistols. The chorale whistled longer, harmonizing with alto intonations of carbines, baritone expressions of rifles, and a profoundly deep, growling bass of cannon. They listened to this hush in the chorale of *Mammon's Hymn,* a fer-mata in the battle chatter of Tennessee.

Posse suddenly uttered a precautionary note. "Load your pistol, Feets, put some of this whis-key on your handkerchief to stay alert and load it, check it, and reload rifle."

The ash grew thicker now among the deserted

levy where spent artillery, grapeshot bits, canisters, cartridges, and corpses were more abundant. Cannons turned inward stood with their back to the windows in breastworks. The sun, a melon of golden red and rebellious hues, painted a yawning synopsis of the brutal day. Feets rubbed the medallion affirming its location in his pocket. The band of crows cackled chaotically. As best as he could, Feets cleaned grit and grime off the medallion before slipping the half-mooned shape into his shoe bottom.

— XVII —

Memphis

"Halt! Raise your hands! Put your weapons on the ground slowly! Now!" boomed the clear voice.

They dropped their pieces, laying them on the ground between them in a neat pile. The footfalls of several men clattered through leaves behind them. A squad of bluecoats gradually appeared surrounding them.

"This is a Federal reserve! Until we determine exactly what happened here, you both are under arrest!" shouted the officer.

Feets stumbled backwards as he bent, securing his

own medallion against his chest. The band of crows cackled grim choruses of damnation. His cursory comparison of the two medallions renewed his curiosity at its oneness. The flock of crows perched silently in the trees now, tuxedoed deacons in a dark pious, lecherous ruse designed to facilitate their wild carnivorism waiting below. Blood besmirched the yellowed beaks of the elders.

They walked with their fingers locked, hands behind their heads. As they walked, Feets toyed with his fingers thinking, "Without the concurrence of every key!" A heaviness of heart snared his focus and as he walked, following in the steps of Posse, he felt the thunderous gongs of his heart announce an undefined meaning. Their Union guards had gathered the dogs, the horse and mule, and their guns.

"I'd like to help bury the dead," announced Feets hoping to at least study and cover the body of the corpse's which previously held the charred medallion.

"Damn it boy," shouted the sergeant, "You ain't gone bury shit. Shut your nigger mouth and be quiet!" He handcuffed Feets and Posse one to another and shackled them likewise. "Your partner there has been arrested before for purloining. I suspect he'll get some time." The burly sergeant stuffed papers into Feets' chest pocket continuing, "You fellas stink to high heaven. These are chits for your firearms, we are requisitioning the horse and mule."

Bloated, petrified bodies hugged the mud, frozen in their grasp for a casket of dirt and occasionally bumped against the boat's hull, scraping the bottom and rendering a bizarre chromatic scale.

"Damn it boy!" the sergeant's tone jarred Feets' spine, leaving him in the mood of a minor key. He knew any appeal would be hopeless, any question would be extinguished, and any reason rendered ridiculous. Questions came in colors: black ones were ignored or ridiculed based on genesis. Both men were brusquely taken aboard and barnacled to the small gunboat amid sounds of picks and shovels. As the boat turned towards Memphis, the cuffs and shackles were rechecked and doubly secured.

FEETS

"Ain't gone be no swimming tonight," he chuckled.

"What will you tell the syndicate?" asked Feets, turning to Posse.

Posse replied, "Probably nothing. I know too much. I know faces, bank accounts, meeting places, history! In Federal custody like this, my ass is almost dead already. Plus, I lost money they invested in this hunt. Horse gone, mule gone, supplies half gone. Posse say nothin'. In fact, if your fingers were free, I ask you to write it out for me. I put on my sombrero and point to it for anyone who ask question. Then Posse point and hide tongue," he chuckled with resignation.

"There's a price to be paid for bounty expeditions," tossed in one if the soldiers who overheard Posse's words. "You shouda left this boy, your horse, and your two asses at home!"

Another laughed adding, "Yeah, both asses—yours and that stinky mule's!" The guards stood directly behind and beside them, barrels gleaming. They rolled two cigarettes and mumbled out of earshot.

MEMPHIS

Feets' instincts stood in the midst of extreme confusion. In fact, confusion kicked down the door of his personal privacy, parked at the intersection of his heart and brain, and directed his survival skills to lose hope. He couldn't get straight answers from Union soldiers, death faced him from the Rebels, and no lanterns for truthful facts lit his way: hopeless! He felt doubly trapped; the jaws of the corrugated shoreline gradually diminished, littered as it was with odd scraps of clothing and besmirched with assorted body parts. The undulating, vicious undercurrents of the Mississippi sloshed as they back-paddled the small gunboat away from the shoreline filling the void. Nearby sandbars still dripped with fresh blood, crimson flecks of the once living.

"What about the dogs?" blurted Feets. The squad leader hollered, "Sonny, your damn lucky Johnny Reb didn't find your ass and sell y'all downstream for a can of molasses! Now shut up! Gave you and your Massa here requisition chits." He bellowed, "Go through their bags ag'in and rope both their legs together. Make 'em think twice about swimmin'!"

FEETS

A soft drizzle began as the small boat moved southward under a cloudy, grayish sky. "Can you ... would you read that out loud?" Feets politely asked the Union guard who had long yellowish white mustache whiskers that hung down like walrus tusks. The guard read, "Wizard of the Saddle strikes Fort Pillow" on the newspaper page. Rifle across his lap, he cast an oblique glance and pursed his thin, pink lips.

"Here are your requisition chits for the dogs! They will join you in Memphis," growled the unit leader. "Guard them carefully," he reiterated to his lieutenant.

Starlings skipped, dove, skylarked, and sprinted at the landing. Their play was a stark contrast to the limp lifeless bodies that littered the slope into the landing. The small boat seemed to glide through the waves as if it had wings, weightless. Feets wondered if this was what it felt like to levitate, to fly! In his heart, he glided like a bird.

"Rest on me, kid," said Posse. Bloated bodies, some still floating, limbs entangled around rotted tree roots, and flotsam peppered the landing.

MEMPHIS

Feets collapsed and Posse slowly smoked his last cigar.

Fear, hostility, anger, and rage commandeered the small prison of iron bars inside Fort Pickering known as the "Brig." News accounts of Forrest's "storming Fort Pillow" ranged from victorious reminders of black impotency against their masters to calls for revenge against mindless laughter of a surrendered fortress. The issue of arming brainwashed slaves against their masters received fatherly, paternalistic attention from news editors, North and South. By the time the gunboat docked, curious bystanders and a military squad stood with Mother Roche and Eggplant; reporters seeking news of the arrest posed questions about their journey, arrest, and arraignment.

President Lincoln had requested a congressional investigation. Rumors escalated around what to some was fact, to others, fiction. Some doubted that the lynched corpses of "smoked Yankees" lined the highway from Fort Pillow to Brownsville, Tennessee. Military minds wondered about the bewildering twists of fate that shaped the battle. Feets fought the shame and embarrassment that gripped his body, shook his spine, strangled his speech, and knit his face in a tight knot. Tears smoldered behind his eyeballs, frisking a great flowing sadness outward in miniature blinks; rage blossomed. If he was the son of a corpse, did he have a ghost on his back?

"*Bertie, libertie pour l'homme noir!*" screeched above the tattered voices mired in questions, greetings, orders, and the disorder of the landing. The cries of the "killer buck," rented the brisk April night in turbulent cries for answers. The next morning's headlines would read, "The Ill-fated Feats of Feets!"

"*Make feet your wings.*" The man re-laced his boots; the boy fought back his tears; the ghost glued both together. Inside the one sock lay his question and his instinct, his gift brought from the brink of hell to initiation into flight. Clutching the medallion around his neck, the spiritual link to a charred, burnt body nailed to the spokes of a collapsed wagon wheel, Feets trudged towards the jail that would protect his sleep.

XVIII

Memphis

"What does this note say?" inquired Posse comparably housed next door to Feets. "Says our bail has been posted by Belle. We'll be released after the morning hearing with General Hurlbut," Feets distilled from the note.

The next morning, Feets and Posse stood in front of General Hurlbut who spoke with a loud clear voice, "I am releasing you…" However, after that brief glint of relief flowered in the face of Feets, the words, "into your mother's custody. As for you, Posse, we must hold you in the military brig, both for your own protection and for further questioning. You have violated both the law regarding bounty expeditions in search of refugee slaves and you have trespassed on Federal property."

"Posse will stand trial as an enemy combatant. In your case, Feets, you have steadfastly supported our military efforts through your expertise as a blacksmith, and on occasion with your gunsmith skills. The Union Army is actively recruiting African soldiers. We invite you to consider joining our ranks. In the meantime, these expeditions, bounty or otherwise, will cease. Understood?"

Newspapers would recount stories of the Fort Pillow Massacre for several days. They were sidelined with notes about the "bounty expedition." Posse beckoned to Feets before leaving under armed guard. "Visit me soon, *n'est pas*? That killer buck, he speak in French. He say, 'Liberty for the black man!'"

Eggplant had rushed into the courtroom and froze abruptly upon contact with the deep solemnity of the moment. "Oh," General Hurlbut continued speaking to the general audience, "The Emancipation Proclamation overrides the Fugitive Slave Law in this military jurisdiction.

MEMPHIS

Anyone aiding or abetting bounty hunters will face trial and is subject to punishment in the fullest extent of the law."

"Let's get out of here, Feets, get out before he changes his mind. These, these clowns want to keep their little darkies boxed in, hemmed in, slaved in. They got to have their foots on the neck—what you call that—power psychosis? Their personal servants from wandering around the countryside, confused and hungry like little lost, illiterate sheep. They be the kinda folks hired Posse in the first instance. You seen that picture of the camp meeting at Corinth, the one with the 'scription underneath it, the one taken after Shiloh fell? *General George H. Thomas/Military Provost in Corinth, MS/Addresses troops regarding black contraband/JUNE 1862.* General Thomas grew up wid black peoples, listening to their stories and songs and such. 'Least, that what my paw told me. Pap said way back den wasn't but one Union General he knew could whup old Forrest. Say Forrest too magical and unconventional to mos' West Pointers. Somebody gotta take his full measure and blow his cracker ass back to his Mississippi plantation."

FEETS

"After they tried to sucker us, Posse made sure that we were ready that night. They returned back and snuck up on us in the middle of the night. If we hadn't made that dummy camp, they would have trapped us up next to the road. We made a false camp with Posse rolling up blankets around the campfire to pretend that we were sleeping. We set up a trip cord on the ground. Posse roped it to his banjo. Rebs came in the dead of the night wanting to torment our asses," blurted Feets. "Posse circled and outlined the fake camp with some old gunpowder, turpentine, leaves, anything that would burn. Then, we bundled blankets and twigs and slept outside the circle, away from the natural approach and behind a small creek. Eggplant and her mom were with us! We sent them south to Memphis for their own safety." He shared the story with his mother after she admonished both him and herself.

"Never should let you go up there with that man, didn't ever trust him no how! Some reconnaissance parties found your camp. 'Least ways, that was what they told us down at the fort," said Mother Roche.

MEMPHIS

"Mom, I have a question for you. You know dat medallion that I have worn since my twelfth birthday?" he continued without pausing for an answer, "I think I found another, just like it!"

"Oh!"

"Yes. I found it at Fort Pillow."

XIX

Memphis

She stopped her movement now, studied the look on his face for a moment, and returned to the ironing she was doing; as she put her hand down, her eyes locked on his face to discern the depth of his knowledge. "Found it at Fort Pillow" was what he said. A searing pain shot through her hand before she realized she had paced it at the angle at which the iron and board met.

Now she spoke out loud, ignoring the pain vocally, but gently massaging the back of her hand, "Found it how?"

FEETS

"It was burned. We, me and Posse, found it around the neck, under a swarm of flies."

"A swarm of what?"

"Flies mom, a swarm of flies. They were all over the place, almost like locusts. They scattered when Posse poured whiskey over the body. I think the rebels had cut off one foot an—"

"Oh my god. Let me see it—the other half, let me—"

She took the medallion in her hands, looked upwards, and broke into sobs, each becoming louder and longer.

"Mom. Mom," Feets implored as he rubbed her shoulders, but she was abandoned to her tears. At sunrise she prayed.

It seemed like nowadays she was always ironing, but at least she had some help with the washing, and the clothesline out back always fluttered with a barrage of winged shirts, bits of union or confederate rags, and bedding. They flipped and flapped

heartily as the wind grew, ignoring the temperature, hot, cold, or just plain warm.

He felt for the medallions in his pocket. Grabbing
both halves from his pocket, he surveyed the parts
and fit the two pouch-like pieces into one. Taken
apart they functioned singularly, each having an
"R" that mirrored the other. Feets examined the
"S" seam that divided the two parts, serpentine like
a snake.

Millicent knew that Feets' medallion was more
than art. It functioned as a way to keep families
knowledgeable about relatives: a brother sold, a
sister stolen, an uncle hung. Black folk spoke in
double entendres all the time, the blues being the
most conspicuous. For many slaves, getting the
Union blues was the greatest thing going in life,
an opportunity to strike a blow against slavery, a
chance to look evil in the eye, a time to tussle with
the definitions of a racist culture. She also knew
who wore the other half and her grief, furious at
first, became more solemn and dignified with the
weeks. Her questions voiced her emotions, "Who
buried the bodies? How many bodies did you see?
Are you sure that you saw only one foot? Why did

they stop you from examining and burying the bodies? Where are the graves? Are they protected, safe?"

Only the passage of large amounts of time, time in which she heard nothing from Penny's and Feets' father, would she finally believe that the burnt, chained body Feets had seen at Fort Pillow was that of his father.

"I could slap myself for letting him go to that place," and she could feel the eyes of her mother, father, great-grandmother, great-grandfather looking over her shoulders, studying her decisions, leaning to see how this adversity would affect her, how she would handle it. She could feel the slaps of generations sizzle across her cheeks, whispering, "Good thing he did go! If'n he hadn't, he never woulda known what happened to his daddy, never been 'spired to carry on with the fight, never seen the terror of slavery up close and personal." The slaps fell across her face in a thousand snaps of playing cards, making her shudder on both sides of the issue: hope versus truth.

"Deeper slavery!" The phrase haunted and teased

MEMPHIS

Feets. The ridiculousness of life at the mercy of anyone else, the new shanties that had embellished the already dilapidated contraband stood within a stone's throw of mansions lining the streets of downtown. "Deeper slavery!" He processed the thought again thinking, we all knee deep in slavery, both slave and enslaved, and it mostly dredges up ignorance on both sides. He knew that he was lucky and made a personal commitment now to make every second count, every glorious second that he was allowed to live would be to serve the cause of freedom.

Earlier while still manacled, Feets was led to a room that had a small desk in front, a bench on which he sat, and a picture on the sidewall. Foremost in the picture were tented coves of stacked rifles, a large big top tent, and a wide expanse of soldiers gathered underneath, invisible to the photographer. He examined the photo carefully, waddled backwards and sat down. "Damn, this is the farthest I've ever been from freedom."

"Boy, don't you look like a mess!" exclaimed his mother, gazing raptly at him as she strode towards Feets. He bent his head in shame. "We prayed for you every night," she whispered softly and planted a kiss on his cheek.

"Good to see you, Momma," he answered back bashfully. "Ma, we got a window of opportunity," informed Feets.

"What you thinking, boy? Knew something was on your mind. Staying out late, coming in here at all hours of the night!" retorted Mother Roche.

"Ma, Lincoln has freed the slaves. We can just pack up and git," begged Feets.

"Git to what? They riding up north, guerillas all over the place. You got a good job. That helps to hold this family together," explained his mother.

"But Lincoln has stuck a stick in slavery's bear trap, sprung it open in a yawning position. That stick is straining to close, moaning, groaning, waiting to clamp shut," countered Feets.

"Hush boy! I have lost my best friend and you lost your daddy. That's enough losing for awhile," Mother Roche explained.

MEMPHIS

"Now, I…" stammered Feets, raising his hand to rub his temple, "…is this it? Is this what our lives, our freedom, is going to be about forever? This home, us hoping and scraping, our plans for the future? Is that what it's all about? You working for the Hightowers, me running somebody else's business. Haven't you sacrificed enough waiting for this Hawk, this man you say is my father? Why are we here? When are we going to leave? My friends are volunteering to fight! Their mothers and sisters drive oxen to Ohio! They be lined up at the fort all the way down Front Street, ready to get their blues, get their rifles, and start pointing 'em at pecker-woods!"

"Feets! Look at that medallion. Wasn't made so that the whole piece would die in the same summer; it was made with a hope for life. How the devil you gone be any good to anybody, if you dead or help-less from mutilation? Your daddy made it so a part of him would always be with you—living!"

"Momma, we are suspended between sides like a pair of pants hanging on your clothesline with no breeze, like a roach cannibalized in a corner, trapped in this damn cracker's spider web," complained Feets.

FEETS

"Boy, don't you curse in this house, you know better!" scolded Mother Roche. At her wits end, she drew out a pen and a large piece of paper similar to the one she had engaged with Mother Bickersdike. *Me and my son, we got to work through this now; we can't let our vision and hopes be scarred under this pressure; we got to think and work this through.*

She sat down, drew lines and ordered her son, "Take a seat, young man. Men and women, whether young or old, got to think now. If you think you are man enough to fire a gun, then you had best think through what you intend to do after you fire that first shot. Now I done taught you about the Golden Rule. It certainly ain't been used against us. If you gone take something you can't give back, then that is something real special that has earned its way to the discussion table."

Memphis

FEETS	MOTHER ROCHE
Momma, I think Posse was honestly trying to track a runaway for the bounty. I don't think it was for anything other than money. I knew that our dad was a blacksmith, but you never called him Hawk! I wonder though, if he had known that the man was me and Penny's father, would he have claimed him?	Feets, I don't know if he would have even brought him back alive. Your daddy was such a proud man. He headed up north on one foot! Either way, hunting for bounty being a slave for money is no better than being a slave for man.— either way, you a slave.

FEETS

Ma, I know that my trip was dangerous, but, I got to do something that helps us to buy, fight, or fly out of this mess. Even now we see flocks of plantation refugees, heading up north as far and fast as their feet will take them.	Feets, I understand how you feel and all. "Revenge is vain" says the Lord. "Thou shalt not kill." We gots to stay together Feets. Hawk would have wanted it that way. Now if you think you just got to fight, I want you to see the maimed and injured we deal with every day at the hospital.

"That trap gone snap shut if the union loses, bam!" while Feets brought his fist down hard on the table, "and ..." His eyes became misty, neck taught, veins exposed, "... most whites don't think we'll fight, stand up, and kill for freedom. Ma, if they wanted us up, we would never have been down in the first place. I'm thinking about soldiering for the Union, git my blues."

"Right now boy, you ain't doing no such thing. Those poor soldiers coming back from Shiloh have been mutilated with every kind of wound imaginable. Ones shot in the face, missing arms, legs, even their guts. You want that?"

"Momma, Hawk, my father, is dead. I couldn't put one shovel of dirt on him. The papers are saying that this thing at Fort Pillow was a massacre, the Union effort totters at Chattanooga. If the Union loses, no telling what happens to black folk. I see black men signing up at Fort Pickering. We could be the difference in this war. No one man, even that Wizard Forrest can keep us down if we put one shoulder to the Union wheel!" Feets declared.

Weren't nothing the Bishop could do to put you and daddy back together even though he tried. Maybe if daddy had been here in Memphis, he wouldn't have had to run like a fugitive; he really be a fugitive from injustice.

Well, your food is waiting! I feel better now that we talked without screaming at each other. Eat your dinner and take a bath. I will run some water for you and you can make my rounds with me in the morning. I don't want Penny to come, so don't say anything to her about it. You almost a man now and I understand your thinking, but I don't agree with it!!!

FEETS

Sleep-eyed and nosey, Penny eases up to Mother Roche, putting her arms around her mother. "Mommy, I'm sleepy. Whatcha doin'?" questioned Penny.

"It's okay, baby. Your brother and I are just talking about our family."

"But, it sounds like you're arguing," countered Penny. "Feets loves you Penny. He loves Mommy, too. He wants to make sure that we get our freedom," explained Mother Roche.

"Hi, Feets. We missed you while you were gone. The sign said, 'On Vacation.' Was that soldier really your father?" Belle quizzed as she passed Feets on the way to the shop. They chatted briefly on Front Street. "Oh, Posse told the authorities that the Whitworth—you know the one with the telescope—was your gun. He said you earned it? Anyway, it's in the kitchen. Come over for a sandwich and I'll get the gun to you."

Feets remembered the high trees around Fort Pillow. Sharpshooters had climbed those trees and took out the officers first. They attacked the brains of the fort. He back-flashed, quickly at first, and then with more focus on the crows and the single, high-flying red-tailed hawk that circled high above the smoldering brush and blackened trees of the site that looked like an open grave. A trained hunting hawk, Posse's hawk, was a new revelation for him; it would take time for him to appreciate its power and left his understandably numb.

"I've seen gunsmiths," offered Posse before their ill-fated expedition, "use pre-gauges to check the high spots in the barrel. Tell you what, I'll make up a list of repair supplies now, if you will help me spell it."

Feets foraged the shop and found the old list of supplies. Squads of cavalry and infantry muddled past the shop on their way to the west. Infantry was in the rear and was composed of what was left of the 59th Colored Army under the command of Colonel Bouton.

Posse had dictated a list containing a trundle lathe, pin gauges, vise (which he already had), square, and a hacksaw. Feets wondered about the Whitworth, "What will he use? Why did he give it to me? Why hadn't he been released, or had he?" All those questions popped up in Feets' mind. However, he said nothing except, "Yes, ma'am."

He had put the news clipping in his pocket. It quoted a military log. On the Ripley road about 11:00 pm:

> My men being in rear of the column were attacked at early dawn on the morning of June 11, some five miles from Ripley, when they formed and fought, using ammunition that had been thrown away by the troops in advance and picked up in the dark. They repulsed the enemy and fell back, fighting in this way for an hour, and falling back a mile until relieved by cavalry, when they moved on to Ripley, picking up every round of ammunition they could get. At Ripley, I attempted to fully reorganize my brigade, but had hardly commenced when the enemy charged into the lower end of the town, breaking the line of cavalry formed to hold them in check, when my men were …

MEMPHIS

On June 9, 1864, a Union force of 10,000 men
approached Booneville, Mississippi from the
west. This command included a large contingent
of African-American soldiers verbally committed
to the massacre at Fort Pillow. General Forrest,
considered a "genius of warfare" with no official
military training, was quoted as saying, "Their infantry, separated from the advanced cavalry, will
be tired after marching in the mud and we'll walk
right over them."

XXI

Memphis

The African-American soldiers garrisoned at Fort Pickering were anxious to help Feets with his marksmanship when he stopped by the park to return fresh shod horses or return the end products of the miscellaneous outsourced chores he performed each day. On occasion, he had read portions of Butterfield's *Camp and Outpost Duty for Infantry*. Most of them could not read the papers, but the words fascinated them when Feets read aloud. For instance, he had read, "no man is to remain behind or quit the ranks for any purpose whatsoever, without permission from the captain or officer commanding the company." They would repeat the sentence back, and time permitting, copy the sentence in phrases on pieces of paper. Of course, the spellings were atrocious, but many caught the pronunciations quickly. They liked words like "abatis," a fence-like structure with pointed sharp edges and "lunette," a two-or three-sided field fort with its rear open to interior lines. He read proudly as he was cheered on and was amazed by their curiosity.

"Sturgis would not let the niggers have any of the ammunition that got trapped in there. We scrounged for the throwaways in the wagon while it was dark, but best we could manage was to help cover the retreat. Sturgis was stupid for letting his infantry get so far from the Calvary. Bouton tried to get ammunition for us but Sturgis denied the request. Sure wish we'd had Thomas that day! Whenever we could, we clubbed with muskets and poked with bayonets!"

The paper stated: "Those boys ran like rabbits at Brice's Crossroads, flat out hauled ass over the country side." Who did the paper quote? Not Bouton, not the colored combatants. By most verbal accounts and military diaries, the colored fought heavily and ran out of ammunition. Sturgis self-imploded and dumped ammunition along the way to lighten his wagons and make a speedy pathway back to Memphis.

"Hey man," another voice piped in, "not only did he discharge ammunition to lighten his wagons as we hauled ass back to Memphis, niggers rear-guarded Sturgis' stupid ass all the way. Our ears were flat back and flapping in the breeze. Damn near another massacre! Now that makes two! Y'all understand that the first attack was to remind niggers not to rear up against 'massa.' The truth be told, if Forrest had any black soldiers at all on horseback, Sturgis would never have made it back to Memphis."

To that bit of fantasy, chuckles and long guffaws erupted around the little campfire. "I got to go!" Feets explained, heading for the main gate. "See you later guys."

Feets had very little problems getting back into his old routine. Oddly enough, a few old newspapers at the parsonage had detailed accounts of General George H. Thomas at Chickamauga. He placed his two large railroad ties in the wall across from his anvil, hung the report of Chickamauga, and read as he hammered horseshoes into their final shape.

"...the breech in the Union line at Chickamauga was penetrated by Longstreet. Union troops under Sheridan, armed with Spencer repeating rifles, fought brilliantly, but found themselves abandoned when General Rosecrans fled the field and retreated back to Chattanooga. General George H. Thomas, henceforth known as the 'Rock of Chickamauga,' gathered scattered troops and almost single-handedly kept the Union troops from annihilation by his heroic stand at Snodgrass Hill, allowing the defeated army to retreat to Chattanooga."

"Morning," he aimed the greeting at Mr. McLemore, the apparent leader of the group of rubberneckers.

Belle brought the Davidson scope, wrapped in a woolen blanket, to Feets' shop shortly after the lunch hour. "I want to be sure that you get this. Posse asked to powwow with some of the syndicate members about his fees. They balked, didn't want no public truck with that Fort Pillow stuff. Spies are all over Memphis, so watch yourself!

There's a fair amount of discussion about you being mixed up with the Union. The guerrillas and home guard have targeted Union-friendly businesses," Belle cautioned.

After passing a good part of the day in the shop with a variety of repairs, Feets headed over to Belle's Biscuits to retrieve the rifle. On the other side of the street, he stopped to watch a conga drummer ply his trade on the nearby street corner. The hemiola in his pulse seemed to gain additional bite when a colored soldier, decked in Union blues, passed by. He quick-spied the group of syndicate members as he gently closed the door and headed to the kitchen to find Belle. He expected someone to advise him that he was supposed to use the rear or black entrance. No one did! He grabbed a fistful of runaway posters, sliding them into his waistband.

"Hey Feets," shouted Boss Noland. "Come on over and have some breakfast. Heard you was up at Pillow with Posse. Paper says things got kinda rough for your African brothers! I hear tell that one of those soldiers was your daddy! Shore am sorry to hear that! Posse still holed up in that there

FEETS

Union brig, least we can do here is buy you some breakfast!"

"I better pass on the breakfast," said Feets tipping his cap ever so politely. "I do appreciate your kind thoughts and will pass them on to Mom and Penny. Posse is real pissed about being in the brig!" *But he knows his ass is a lot safer there than outside where you folks can kill his ass,* he thought without speaking.

Belle met him at the door of the kitchen, placed the gun in his hands, stuffed some biscuits in a large handkerchief and draped the bouquet of biscuits around the rifle's muzzle. As Feets walked out the door, he added, "Oh, Posse say you Cotton Syndicate folks still owe him some money for supplies and such, even though he knows he doesn't deserve the bounty fee. He be right joyful, if you folks would ante up. I'd be happy to take the money down to him!" Hearing his voice trumpet those words surprised him.

Nolan rose and pointed his large frame in Feets' direction. "Well, honestly, son, that is a right thoughtful thing for you to pass on. Take Mister Posse this note and read it to him. Now since you was in cahoots with him, you being his ace-nig-ger-in-travel at Fort Pillow, and you being on the Union payroll and all, then that means we got to watch both you and Mister Posse. Take him this note and read it to him. Read it real slow!"

Feets took the note, added it to his poster menag-erie, and slipped out into the street. Belle hurtled out the door with a jug in her hand, "Feets, be careful. Carry one or two of these biscuits down to Posse when you see him. I will give you anoth-er batch for him later this week. You a good kid, Feets. Bless you."

He walked up to the corner where the drum-mer played and listened. Suddenly the drumming ceased. "You be Feets, the blacksmith. The boys at the Fort be mighty sorry to hear the soldier who got burnt was your daddy. They be taking up some money for you and your momma." Feets looked around to see who was speaking.

"Damn it boy, its me. Now don' look at me, just listen! Got that, just listen! I play white on the left and black on the right. If you hear two like this, and the blind man played duple rhythms like dis, den that means that white—the guerrillas—is coming up the street from the south. If 'n I play triplets, like dis, and the man switched into triplets with his right hand, dat dare means that the blacks is coming from de north. And if I play both together, dat dare means that everything is just fine! I be pickin' at Pickering all the time of day wid my congas or my banjo. Drop a penny in my cap and God bless!" The man added, "Course, you know better than anybody that price of triplets have gotten high lately."

The haphazard clutter of horse hooves on cobbled stones countered with the drums' mellifluous croon. Feets fisted the rifle close as he entered his shop; seated next to the anvil was Bishop Hightower.

"Hi, Bishop," he asked, "You need something?"

"No, Feets. I was just thinking. It's a lot more peaceful in a bed that is warm and indoors than outside bivouacked by the bears, cold, stars, snakes, possums, and the groans of the dying all around, ain't it?"

"Well, Bishop, as you often say, any peace is purchased at a price. I am thankful that I did not have to pay the same price as my daddy and very thoughtful to learn the truth with my own eyes."

I am thankful that we do not have to pay the ultimate price and very lucky to learn the truth with my own eyes.

"Things are good at the house?"

"Yeah. Mom's not crying as much."

Representatives of the syndicate were surprised to see Posse outside the walls of Fort Pickering; they tested his mood and politics with a new offer. "Posse will look over these posters and further speak—pass on the breakfast today—until we meet again say, in a week or so, for final proposal."

He rose and said, "Good day, gentleman."

Never one to be flamboyant in speech, Posse had carefully considered his situation: bounty hunter for the Rebs, counterspy for the Yanks. Of course, he had to align himself with prevalent power, especially since his effort to angle with loyalty met with blanket refusal to materially acknowledge his effort. Hurlbut finessed the counterintelligence arrangement as a necessary prerequisite for his release. Posse hated doublethink, loved being in business for himself and resented this new indenture; the adventure of hunting for bounty appealed to him much more than feeling caged, either physically or strategically. He felt trapped.

As Posse left, he paid for the coffee and headed for the blacksmith shop. "If they go south on Tennessee, one set in triplets, but if they go north, then in duplets … this one picking up at Pickering." The conga drummer smiled broadly, "Posse … that you?"

Posse headed eastward towards the shop. As he entered the doorway, Feets handed him the note, as if expecting him. "Bonjour, petite frère."

Feets smiled, saying, "Came from the syndicate; no booty, no bounty!"

XXII

Memphis

June 1864

Late in July, Feets accompanied Mother Roche to the hospital to observe the wounded colored soldiers. To validate her position, she said, "If you still want to join the Union soldiers, you should know what you are in for." Feets knew that soldiering would be a huge and possibly life-threatening challenge. One black soldier he struck up a conversation with said, "Least, I came out breathing … can't walk … but I can breathe. If you gonna join up, git with the General Thomas. He knows what he's doing. He makes 'em practice target shooting, read to understand orders, and takes questions from our people so that they know how to handle each situation in a crisis. He really plans a campaign."

Another soldier, missing his arm, spoke furtively, "Git your mom and sister, git a big ass wagon, a rifle, a revolver, and lots of ammunition to head towards Canada. Fuck this Union! Say goodbye to Memphis and head north little brother. Do it while you can!"

Feets didn't quote him to his mother. Actually, he had problems with the word contraband and preferred to call the hordes of feet heading northward daily, refugees. African-American refugees from a Confederacy of Slavers, to be precise.
Runaways and fugitives ran even more rampant upon the return of Sturgis' expedition from Brice's Crossroads.

"Took us nine days to get over there and thirty-six hours to haul ass back to Memphis!" commented a begrimed, foul-smelling black private. Feets had seen many of them days before; the entire company appeared shock-ridden, horse-whipped, sleep-deprived, and glue-mouthed as they straggled into Memphis.

MEMPHIS

Their frustrations were well founded. Apparently the colored soldiers were denied a request for ammunition. Commanding Officer General Bouton had approached General Sturgis for obviously unused munitions; Sturgis denied the request and trashed the ammunition to lighten the load of his retreating wagons. Even as they fought tooth and nail to fend off a relentless pursuit by Forrest, Sturgis had refused them ammunition. Forrest had rolled out his wizardry with canister shot loaded in a cannon. The ultimate humiliation of a hand-pushed cannon had "cracked and splattered Union troops all over North Mississippi," commented one smoked-Yankee.

"Calvary was whipped-up like homemade butter at the front. Bouton begged Sturgis for ammunition that the white infantry threw away to lighten the load of drawn wagons. Those wagons had overturned in Tishomingo Creek. Sturgis refused the request, even as Forrest performed a double envelope on Union troops that outnumbered him. Sturgis wasn't letting any niggers have that ammo." Feets noticed several of the USCT troopers were jet black from the dust and mud.

FEETS

"Wagons stuck in the mud and overturned on bridges! Brutal hand-to-hand combat had reduced our Federal ranks severely!" The survivors trembled and prayed just talking about it.

"We had to search and thrash through the wagons at night to get that ammo, what a fat fool!"

Eggplant promised to walk him to the Fort on her way back to Camp Dixie. "Hi Feets! You been practicing your shooting?" asked Eggplant. They heard the rattle of the drums, even as they set up to practice on the rifle range, kick into a slow lilting ceremony; it was a gift not lost to future generations of slave descendants, even though muted from white paranoia. It was a ceremony which did not forsake the contributions of all and improvisations of each. It was a lamp which retro-fired improvisation, at impulse, on cue, in the moment for each individual. The pulse was slow, and the women who inhaled its magic, stopped what they were doing, heading to Fort Pickering, usually on a Thursday night, to see the show.

With every imaginable kind of drum—tenor, snare, and congas of every shape and size—the smoked, newly minted black Yankees of Fort Pickering formed a circle, a drum squad. They whined harmonies like the singers in blues bars; they strutted like the big-hipped, red-lipped ladies of the night who earned their living on their backs or their knees. The first tune they broke into was "Stoop Down," 'cause men away from home think about the things they miss most about being at home.

The sun was set low in the sky; the sound of the ensemble was soft and sweet. Belle had just dismounted her buckboard, dressed in a fashionable white dress with large dark blue polka dots. Many a black soldier would wonder about her ancestry, as her hips, thick ankles, and general hourglass figure gave the impression that there was black in her blood. Only her lack of incisive rhythm gave her away. *Stoop Down* was one of her favorites, and she knew more verses than anyone sober on Beale Street. The drummers kept the volume low as if to invoke first the spirit of the song, prior to any words being sung. The instruments stewed in the harmonic juices of a low tessitura. On cue, her words grew out of the spirit of that invocation. At first they stuttered forth in an emotion out of step with the rhythm, but then a lyricism trumped the beat. Belle's words would tease them into a living remembrance of how they made love before they left to challenge fate, runaway, and join the Union Civil War effort. Belle broke into song against a slow beat that at once was funky, fierce, and re-pressed: *"Stoop, stoop, stoop down, baby; lay your love down low …"*

The magic of music caused Feets and Eggplant to turn in their tracks, mesmerized by the captivating sensations created by both words, whines, and pulse.

"Stoop down, baby, let your daddy see … ooooooooh …"

Darkness embraced the bluffs of Memphis, now dimly lit by small campfires lacing the lowlands of the riverbank. The gathering crowd hooted, "Go on, baby, sing it." The dancing drunk pranced and weaved. Everyone clapped on the upbeats.

"Stoop down, baby; lay your love down low; stoop down, baby; let your daddy see …"

Belle had taken off her wide-brimmed straw hat now, and used it to slap her ample thighs as she let her voice cruise over and around the beat like a hawk winging into the darkness. Feets and Eggplant snapped their fingers to the infectious rhythms. The circle of drummers smiled and hummed, trapped in the joy that seeped up through the crowd, rocking the onlookers with a message that was understood even within the hovels of shanties that bedecked the hilly bluffs.

"You got something down there worrying the hell outta me!"

Still the dancer never spilled a drop. The large crowd hooted, howled its approval, and clapped when Belle had finished. She took three graceless bows and walked over to a pipe-smoking O'Reilly and asking, "You seen Feets and Eggplant?"

"Yeah, Miss Belle. That was some kind of performance! They are right over there. They were practicing at the range as you came in. Guess you didn't see 'em. Real good kids," and he pointed out to here where they were standing.

The circle of drummers segued into a faster pulse now, each taking a solo improvised to impress the crowd and best the former soloist. They competed with one another recklessly and with unabashed showmanship.

"Let me give you guys rides home; no way I can go right to sleep after all that excitement!" offered Belle.

"Gosh, Miss Belle, I would never have known you could sing like that!"

"Feets Roche, we all got our stories. As darkness descended, the evening glided forward with the soft caresses of a feeble breeze; the bright lights and high-pitched sirens of fire engines seemed to approached the fort, but took a quick detour. They momentarily chatted with the "Dancer of Drunk," as some called him along the streets. Feets had yet to witness a spilt drop from the man's bottle of whiskey. He was charmed by the horrific contortions the man made, even as his body seemed to move as if his head were almost magnetized to the air; even now, as the day grew closer to sunset, the dancer still sang, "Stoop Down, Baby" as he glided down the corridor of Beale Street.

MEMPHIS

Further down the street, members of the Cotton Syndicate, joined by home guard guerillas, sat outside eating sandwiches, smoking cigarettes, and chewing on cigars. They watched gleefully as the "Prince of Stupor," their own name for the marionette, came within view.

"Oh yeah. The guys down at the fort tease me, but I'm getting better. How'd you learn to shoot like that?" questioned Feets.

"Oh, my papa taught me. Went all over Mississippi, well almost all over, with that man. He said he always wanted me to be able to fend for myself," she countered. "That was a lucky shot on the expedition. Just the same, you want to be cool and relaxed when the pressure is on." Eggplant and Feets listened to the stories of the colored soldiers returning from Brice's Crossroads; they listened to learn.

"You ain't seen hell until you tried to fight canister with no ammunition; a hail storm of horizontal lead coming every which way but from the sky. Like nails blown through the teeth of the Devil hisself!"

FEETS

They then collapsed, sleeping in their uniforms for several days; nobody dared asked about the wounded. Black veterans made regular stands to cover the retreat; surplus wagons had twisted up in the Tishomingo Creek. Another soldier recalled, "Grierson had been pinned down up front and Forrest's cavalry had hauled ass down both sides of the road. They pushed cannon right down the middle of that road!"

"*Bertie, cheerie libertie*!" The moans of "the buck" pockmarked the slosh of waves.

Feets reflected on the situation, thinking about the hawk-like swoop, the speedy gallop of horses necessary to accomplish such a feat! "Double envelope," said the first black soldier as he awoke momentarily, "damn double envelope."

"Double envelope, my ass! Felt like we were in a sealed envelope, licked, surrounded, and sealed!" mumbled another. "It's a wonder Grierson got out of it alive. Feel sorry for those caught niggers. Maybe they played possum, stayed buried in the mud. Heard they gonna investigate, see if Sturgis had hit the bottle. One thing for sure, ain't no niggers going to fight under his command again. Everybody was out of position."

The tired combatants rummaged through vivid images that issued forth from their colorful and frightening recollections of the engagement.

"Good thing old Posse jailed up. He might justa thought he coulda capture a bounty jumper or two."

But he ain't, thought Feets. "Damn fool!"

You could almost set your clock by the arrival of Feets and Eggplant to the Fort Pickering firing range. Usually, it was in the late afternoon, a little after five. It was a little warmer today than at the identical time a few days before. With the onset of August, Feets approached his work and enterprise with a vigor and intensity far beyond apprentice-ship. He measured his steps to work, and measured the time it took for him to get there; he was gra-cious to those he passed on his way and took a few moments to answer questions about his work.

"I've got a mold," ventured Feets, "for the Whitworth

to start making some ammunition. Hurlburt says that he'll let me buy some iron bars at the Union rates if I supply ammo locally. Got a mold that works for both the Enfields and Springfields. Whitworth really takes a different one. Got me a trundle lathe, too. Got it to do some minor repairs, little polishing and calibrating. One thing for sure, always some extra repairs to do," Feets informed.

"Mom, Eggplant promised to bring some posters down to the shop today. I'm headed for the fort for some practice after work. If you save me something to eat, I'll be most grateful. Don't wait up though, cause I'll probably be late." Feets said.

"Hi, Feets!" Eggplant shouted towards the end of the afternoon. "I saw Posse earlier today. He gave me a boatload of posters. He calls them his 'Carnival of Slaves' collection. His posters got slaves of every conceivable description."

Feets stood beside her as her fingers raced through images, drawings, and photographs. "Can we use these for target practice?" asked Eggplant.

"Oh sure. Posse said he's through with the bounty

business. He got real pissed off with the Cotton Syndicate when they renegotiated on his bounty reward money. Says he'd not going to fool with it anymore," Feets informed.

Feets wiped his hands on the blue apron embossed in gold with an eagle. "Sure be fun to put some holes in the scourge of slaver, sink the slavery ships," he chuckled. For a brief moment, there was a silence that grew into a reaction of a joyful meeting of their eyes. Eggplant tiptoed up to him and kissed him on the cheek. Swiftly, his arm went around her waist firmly and when he let go of her, his arm brushed against the long sleek flank of her heart-shaped rump. As they strode towards the Fort, Feets asked, "Eggplant, is that your real name?"

"Nah, that's my nickname," answered Eggplant.

"Okay, so what's your real name?" Feets asked.

"Vivian. Yep, Vivian" replied Eggplant.

"Your mom says I should stay over with her to-night rather than return to the camp this late," informed Eggplant.

FEETS

"Good. I think she likes you. Where did the name 'Eggplant' come from?" asked Feets.

"My daddy thought my smooth skin and dark hair were prettier than an eggplant. In school, they called me Vivian," explained Eggplant.

"Oh, I like both those names," uttered Feets in split attention, his vision scanning a nearby news clipping.

"That's pretty, do you like it?" questioned Feets.

"Of course, I save it for special occasions and people!" while she laughed merrily.

While laughing and chuckling, one of the older soldiers also handed some old posters to Feets adding to his "Carnival of Slaves." Feets took the stack of unused posters, bound them together and wrapped them with heavy cord string in quartered sections. Eggplant tied and Feets held the posters with his fist.

Memphis XXII

A rearranged shop held the bellows and hearth at one end and machinist tools, ordered outlined, and cataloged at the other. Despite the contradictions, the grime and smoke of blacksmithing and the precision and exactitude of gun-smithing, the shop reflected two distinct parts of his personality; he treasured both the reckless creativity of blacksmithing and gunsmithing's orderliness and found both stimulating. The reorganized and improved venting system made the shop operate more smoothly and efficiently.

During the afternoon, he worked in the shop on both rifles, polishing the muzzles and crowns of barrels, tuning the barrel bores inside with pin gauges, and freeing the triggering mechanisms. When he visited the firing range at the fort, he practiced drop firing; he practiced hanging the rifled instruments from overhead timbers with wires; he practiced slow breathing and worked to squeeze, not jerk, the trigger. Feets Roche practiced trigger squeezes, kneeling; trigger squeezes, half kneeling; jogging, feet close, feet open, inhaling slowly, drop firing, live firing, trotting, cantering, and running to change his position and pace. And his marksmanship got better, even as he wondered about the meaning of the groans of that black buck with the fingers of his hand ripped to nubs.

"*Li-bertie*!" Someone had mentioned that the cries of the jailed murderer sounded like a foreign language, maybe a tribal tongue.

Eggplant, Feets, and Posse felt jubilant about the camaraderie they shared. Their sense of purpose escalated and the renaissance of the shop instilled pride and joy. With Fort Pickering close by, all of them felt that their enterprise was protected and felt joyful in their hard work and sense of independence. Union sympathizers championed their focused activity. When their work for the day was done, they walked down to Pickering, waved their passes as they eased pass the guards, and commenced target practice at the shooting range.

"Look at this one, Feets," smiled Eggplant. She passed over a poster to Feets who was officially adorned in a blue Union apron. He read from his bench next to the furnace, "Comely black wench and unfaithful concubine, left Alabama plantation in June of 1860, sought by her sovereign masters."

"Hee-hee, whose heart is aching now," snickered Eggplant. "Here's another: Buck Slave, six feet, one inch tall, yard and a half wing span, tooth missing in upper front, missing from Mississippi plantation, August 1860."

Feets and Eggplant thumbed through their posters and newspaper cutouts, while murmuring. Feets read out loud while the girl fastened her study on faces, markings, and moods. He was not aware it of at first, but he found himself frustrated by the lack of feet in those posters. His thoughts spoke to him, *The story of these people is*

FEETS

written on their feet just like the horse hooves. Are the nails
brittle? Is the skin cut, lacerated, perforated, keloid-crusted?
I need to see the feet!

"Told that silly, dumb sucker to stop hunting for
bounty! He just sits and say, 'money is real good or
got to do what I'm good at! Told that guy—Indian,
Creole half-breed to stop. Stop chasing niggers all
over yonder and beyond, stop bounty hunting!"

Belle sauntered in sipping a large glass of lemon-
ade with who knows what in it.

"I need to see the condition of the feet to really
know what these people felt; feel the bones hard
and soft spots," responded Feets sidestepping discussions of Posse. He suspected that Posse had
cut a deal with the Yanks.

"Well, you sure-nuff ain't going to see feet in these
drawings, " replied Belle. "Might as well get use to
it and get over it! When you going to Pickering for
that practicing of yours anyway? Wonder he didn't
get killed a long time ago. Did all I could, even
cuffed and bound him, so he know what it's like to
feel enslaved and owned, bound, nailed down to

a damn spot. No good, no good! All I got for my trouble was 'I need the money.'"

She paused for a minute, glancing at the news head-lines: "Congressional Investigation finds Signs of Massacre at Fort Pillow." She rolled the crumpled paper into a baton and parked it under her armpit. "Fool's in jail now without bond. If he had the money, wouldn't do him no good." Belle rose and paced the middle aisle of the restaurant.

No, he ain't, thought Feets.

"I got to say," said Feets "that I never would have learned what I did if it weren't for Posse. Could have been a long while in jail for him, military arrest is different from civilian."

"I understand all that," said Belle interrupting, "but it could have been avoided. Spies, syndicates, cheaters, and hustlers all around. Don't help none that he didn't even get paid on that last half-ass round up y'all was on."

"Tell you what," spoke Feets, "come down to the fort after you close up and use the range with us, sharpen up your shooting. The posters are interesting. We got these from that old trash bin. Look at this one: AUCTION SALE. This day at 11:00. Location North Exchange Building. Run-away Negro by the name of Mosses. Said he belongs to Major Balls of Helena, Arkansas."

Rising, he took Eggplant round the waist and nodded to Belle. Going door-ward now, he thought saying to Belle, "Come on down to Pickering if you feel like it, you can get in on my pass."

"Um," replied Belle half-heartedly.

"What you going to use for bullets?" spiked Eggplant, still leafing through a fistful of flyers and posters.

"They going to let me use some Union ammo. I made a swap deal! I'm going to read instructions, write letters, and sketch some topography for the Memphis Garrison, the 59th artillery, for payback. Can get all the ammo I need."

"Look at this one," cried Eggplant. "What it say?"

"Girl, we gone get you started reading yet, get you some cards just like Posse's! It says," and Feets reads, "'Freedom, Protection, Pay and a Call to Military Duty,' issued by the Secretary of War, the 21st of July 1863! President Lincoln issued another call for volunteers. Lotta my friends have already signed up, Mom knows it. Up North, the Abolitionists agitate for arming the slave; Douglass has repeatedly asked for slave volunteers. If I join I'm free. Mom and Penny are free even if I'm killed. Heard this song about getting the blues the other day. Lots of folks think the blues is about sadness. No, the blues is about hope!"

"You seriously thinking about getting blues? I made nurse's round with your mother a few days," continued Eggplant. "Saw her nursing on some folks had been shot something terrible. Rather see you eat horseshit than to go fighting in that old war. You think you want to learn to shoot? Fine, this day and time, everyone needs to know how to protect self. We will use these posters for target practice, use the posters and these boot outlines!"

"Halt!" shouted the gate guard. "You got to show that pass Feets, you ain't legal yet! Oh, and by the way, they changed the hours on the range, extended them to ten o'clock. You can read and write can't you?"

"Oh yeah, why?"

"Well, I got this friend at home, wants to send him word about me here in Memphis. Lots of these guys want to get word down home. They'll pay for it."

"Count me in," replied Feets. "Be fairly easy to draw some pictures of y'all, write some notes to your people. Tell you what, we can trade favors. Be great if some of you could help me tidy up the shop. You know, redo the door and replace some shingles."

"Depends on what we got up. Word is Sherman wants Forrest out of commission, rack him up anyway we can. Between these three generals we got right here in Memphis, one of these clowns will be assigned that task soon. Until then, we are glad to help you. Get your lumber and it's a cinch."

MEMPHIS

The black guard smiled at Eggplant, offering, "Mornin' m'am," as an offhanded introduction.

Once they had outfitted the shooting range, Eggplant perused more of the posters while Feets loaded each of this three weapons. He had cleaned and calibrated each rifle. He wanted to run accuracy tests himself from varied distances. Look at those feet! Size fourteen, I bet," commented an onlooking soldier. "He getting better with that Whitworth."

"Hey sonny, mister size fourteens, give you eighty bucks for that Whit!"

"Not for sale, and the name is Feets. Lots of sentimental value" back-barked Feets. As he flashed on Posse, his face became compressed, fist-like, *"You would think that the fool would have made some financial arrangements with that slave syndicate, down payment, a pay schedule, something written down. He didn't ask enough questions, document enough facts."*

"Put one right there against the dirt mound," Feets instructed. He marked off fifty paces and squeezed off three shots, one each with each rifle.

FEETS

"Okay, Feets, that's pretty darn good. Getting a lot better! Can you tell which is which?" applauded Eggplant.

"I'm getting more drift from the Enfield. The Whitworth is quite an instrument, not much drift, the bullet marking is unusual too, see?" Feets demonstrated, "O'Reilly says the 'Figure of Merit,' the accuracy, of the Whitfield is much higher that the Enfield. He repeated at 150 paces and 250 paces. As he performed the experiment, the gaslights were priming up at the edges of town to blossom into the scarlet darkness as if it were an approaching musical note. "You wanna shoot?" Feets offered Eggplant.

"Sure! You're gettin' lots better," she confirmed.

Eggplant clawed through the flyers saying, "Lets start with Moses first. See if you can blow off his neck chains! You know, Miss Belle weren't none too pleased with Posse's predicament. Seems like she is a fair-minded person, but she gits kinda emotional 'bout Posse!" The song-like groans of "Bertie" had limped sorrowfully from the brig, even as they made their way to the firing range.

MEMPHIS

"I ain't really sure about Belle," answered Feets, looking down, checking the barrel of his Whitworth. He took his shirttail, exhaled heavily on the telescopic lens and wiped both ends dry. He walked to the target area with Eggplant. "Emotionally, I think she's fine, but I think the business end was nonsense to her."

"She's still mad. You think she got feelings for Posse?" questioned Eggplant. They walked over to the ordnance counter, "Can I check out some ammo?"

"No problem," answered the range officer. "Sign here and leave your pass as collateral."

He checked out .45 and .55 caliber rounds, and gave the .55 caliber rounds to Eggplant, holding the .45 caliber ammunition for himself. Eggplant wrapped her braids horizontally, around the back of her head imitating a turban. Feets paced off some distance, aimed, and squeezed the Whit's trigger, firing shots, which went inches to the right of Moses' neck. Eggplant placed her shots squarely between the neck chain and the mark of Feets' effort. Laughing, she teased, "You getting better, but blowing too hard can throw off your aim."

She held a sliver of paper close to his lips as he fired again, less wide than before, but wide nonetheless. "See," she repeated, "breathe easy like this," and she magically squeezed the trigger, becoming one with the bullet that exploded the chain link on the poster. "And I told you she had feelings for Posse!"

"My goodness girl," Belle's voice broke across octaves. "I believe that you can out-shoot that stupid assed, bounty-hunter-slave-chasing-fool that calls himself Posse." She was mesmerized by Eggplant's accuracy and continued, "I ain't gone stay long, but I thought you kids might need a ride home. My buggy is outside the gate. Take some more shots while I go check the brig on Posse. Looks like he gets even dumber while he waits on the tribunal for his sentence."

"Look!" said one of the guerillas, an odd looking sort wearing the requisite red-bandanna and scruffy beard, "Look over there." He repeated, pointing to the sky. The wings of Posse's red-tailed hawk locked into its sides. Arrowing downward, it sailed into a stunning elliptical dive. A uniformed gasp of silence seized the living, freezing speech. Even breathing seemed ceased! The arc through which the hawk passed took only seconds; the bird passed through its completed swing like a guillotine on a pendulum, leaving the dancer's neck pummeled with his own blood. Shattered shards and fragments of glass were preceded by the pungent smell of alcohol. The vacuum of air through which the bird had cannoned seemed greased by olive oil, the kind used by Belle in her biscuits, transparent and slippery. His sorcery against gravity rudely abated, "Drunk Dancer" broke into a full gallop.

He ain't there, thought Feets.

"Look at that sum' bitch run!" shouted the guerrilla. "That clown went from 'Stoop Down' to 'Swoop up' in seconds." As the bird swung around and sloped downwards again, the guerrilla unholstered his pistol, firing several shots at the bird. All but two missed.

From their position at the firing range, Feets and

FEETS

Eggplant thought the shots were echoes of their practice firing. "Even echoes don't last that long," commented Eggplant. "Where'd those shots come from?"

"At first, I thought they were echoes of our own shots, but now I think they from up near Tennessee Street." They resumed their practice after lighting a lantern to help them see more clearly. Streaks of black and dark purple clouds sliced across the humorless sky, pushing the sun downward past the horizon. A deep crimson flushed the countryside with sloshes of blood. At the top of the Memphis bluff, the sky jokingly mirrored the sunset, aping the shrouded arc now seeking slumber in eastern Arkansas flatlands.

"Anybody seen Feets?" blared a stentorian voice.

"He was here a minute ago!"

"Feets, Feets, come quickly! There's an emergency at the shop!" were the words Feets and Eggplant had *seen* articulated, but not understood, probably because Belle spoke so quickly. When a squad of soldiers rushed in with the same words, "Feets,

Feets, come quickly," the words took on additional meaning and developed into "There is a raging fire at your shop, the blacksmith's shop, at Fauk's place! Soldiers from the Fort, along with the fire volunteers are trying to douse it."

"Oh, Feets!" Eggplant passionately murmured. He was startled by the warm, fresh ocean of Eggplant's breath and the increased curiosity of her fingertips. Feets embraced her long enough before hearing, "Your shop is on fire!"

Belle frantically added, "The wind and draft from the river are throwing embers down Union. It might set my restaurant and some close by buildings ablaze!"

They raced towards the halo of flying embers, past a lieutenant barking orders, and the "clang, clang-clang" bells of fire wagon bells.

"*Ber-tay for l' homme noire! Eh-ber-tay*" spurted forth from the bars of the brig, castigating all who passed. The words whiplashed the horse drawn buggy to a faster pace. Feets noticed the clenched face and fists of Belle who drove them frantically towards the chaotic fire scene. He smelled the faint odor of kerosene blended with the pungent odor of burning wood and metal. Timbers started to fall, kicking the fire into an even more ominous groan as the sizzle and crackle of wood, gunpowder, and shop materials of assorted types exploded past the licks of burnt orange flames, and sent showers of embers wayward.

"Damn" was the only word he could muster. He clutched his rifles and pressed against the crowd.

"There's Feets now!" several onlookers noticed. The line of water-bearers continued their frantic and stalemated assault on the fire; townspeople looked on, the bright glow of the fire reflected in florescent apparitions in their faces.

Feets raced full throttle toward the inferno, only to be tackled, forced to the ground, and placed in a chokehold by one of the Fort's sergeants who recognized him. "No, no, son. You can't go in there!"

Blackened and blistered timber, crisp and weakened by the intense heat, fell to the ground. A tenacious huff of smoke whined through the heat, smoke, and charred refuse of the blacksmith shop; it bleated, belched, and yawned in the face of the crowd, causing it to retreat. More citizens rushed to newly arriving wagons, eager to assist in subduing the fire with the train of buckets that sloshed water on the feisty flames. When the Bishop and Mother Roche arrived, their amazed gazes were met by the swinging, burnt skeleton of what later turned out to be the dancing drunk. He had been hung from a rafter which now struggled to stay aloft, finally succumbing to a death-rattling yawn similar to the final choke of a ship sinking.

"Oh, my God," voiced mother Roche as she witnessed the dancing puppetry of the skeleton. Bishop Hightower added, "Oh, my God!"

Hymn 13

John Newton

The Bitter Waters

Bitter, indeed, the waters are.
Which in this desert flow;
Though to the eye they promise fair,

FEETS

They taste of sin and woe.
Of pleasing draughts I once could dream,
But now, awake, I find,

That sin has poisoned every stream,
And left a curse behind.
But there's a wonder-working wood,
I've heard believers say,
Can make these bitter waters good,
And take the curse away.
The virtues of this healing tree
Are known and prized by few;
Reveal this secret, Lord, to me,
That I may prize it too.
The cross on which the Savior died,
And conquered for his saints;
This is the tree, by faith applied,
Which sweetens all complaints.
Thousands have found the blest effect,
Nor longer mourn their lot;
While on his sorrows they reflect,
Their own are all forgot.
When they, by faith, behold the cross,
Though many griefs they meet;
They draw again from every loss,
And find the bitter sweet.

XXIV

Memphis

"He talking like he on Clementine cordial lately; maybe he'll calm down a little." The young pair hitched a ride to Feets' house, dropping off Eggplant at the church to join her mother.

"Shit," said Feets as he got around to crowbarring some of the burnt lumber from the shop site. He shaved, peeled, sledge hammered, and wheel barreled burnt timbers away from where the fire had been. One of the contraband in the engineering brigade helped him remove some of the salvage. Where his motions had been awkward and tentative on his return from Gideon Pillow's Fort, now he was focused in movement, efficient in organization, and reluctant to talk about or share his thoughts.

"Why you so quiet?" was put to him by Penny, Mother Roche, and Eggplant. "She thinks you are thinking about joining the Union, thinking 'bout what happened to Daddy." To all his answer was, "What's there to talk about?" and invited them one and all to haul timber, hammer nails, sweep dirt, and hinge doors for the rebuilt blacksmithing shop.

"What can I do without the shop? Not shit. If the Union blue is what it takes for me, Mom, and Penny to turn the corner, then the blues it is. If I stay here now like this, if something happens to the shop, no pay from the hunt, no stake out from Hawk, I got no dignity either."

Bishop Hightower had stopped by sometime after Brice's Crossroads and was awestruck at the rebuilding job Feets had accomplished in such a short period of time." Ain't God good?" said the Bishop, even joining Feets in a prayer. "For good providence and magnanimity in Memphis."

MEMPHIS

He didn't say who should be magnanimous.
Should it be the black or should it be white; should
it be Rebel or Federal? Three hundred sixty de-
gree abstraction always seemed to piss Feets off.
Arguments floated towards heaven without the
practicality of gravity. Feets thought, "My muscles
sure could use some magnanimity and lots of lini-
ment rub, since they ache and squeal regularly."
But even the spasms could not mute his hammer
or damper his resolve. It was as if his body had
made a decision and his mind cantered proudly
through nails and wood.

A choir voiced his mind's biggest problem: *Who
burnt your shop and why? Because your mother works for
the hospital? Because you work for the union making horseshoes, because the man thought to be your father volunteered
for the Union? Because your work as a blacksmith helps the
Union? If you didn't work and your mother and sister were
unemployed, then you talking prostitution and theft. "Feets
have 360 degrees but wings got the Universe,"* he thought
to himself.

"Don't worry about ammo and don't worry about
help for rebuilding," Eggplant sided up to Feets.
"I kept the old posters you brought down. If

you want to go through all those and select some targets!"

"The quartermaster left the outlines of feet he made to order shoes and brogans. 'Here they are,' then he trashed the outlines. He just traced a soldier's bare feet right on this paper." The playful chime in her voice was music to Feets. "Ain't nothing beautiful, but it gives us something to shoot at. Leftovers from the commissary where they pass out boots."

"Wow Posse, you're becoming quite a speller. I recognize everything you wrote down," complimented Feets. Posse made three copies, one for each person, and said good night. "Can I borrow your buckboard Posse to take Eggplant home?"
"No problem, lad," retorted Posse. They had not really talked since Posse's release from the guardhouse. Feets thought he felt a sheen of reserve in his friends demeanor, but his level of trust in the man did not waiver. Belle obviously did not know about the deal he had struck with the Union.
Bishop Hightower received half of Feets' profits. He gave his mother twenty-five percent of his earnings and bought rifles, an Enfield and a

Springfield, with his savings. Additionally, he bought pin gauges, a vice that was slightly used, a T-square, and a hacksaw. Sergeant O'Reilly taught him how to customize the rifles, check barrels for tight spots, refine the crown, and make bullets from molds. He also watched the soldiers in their drills, timing their reloads and memorizing the bugle calls, which spurred standing, kneeling, and prone positions. "Make your finger squeeze and don't pull. Squeeze and don't pull," he silently reminded himself.

"Squeeze and don't pull, Feets," reprimanded Eggplant.

Belle extended a challenge. "See that plank out there. Raise it two feet each night with some bricks. Fire from on top of those planks. Test yourself while you are planted on those planks. See if you can shoot the center of a foot or a face planted on those planks. That's what happens in the chaos of battle. See if you can hit the broadside of a barn under crazy circumstances!"

On August 21st, General A. J. Smith had recently pushed deep into the Mississippi Delta to keep

FEETS

Forrest away from the supply line that supported Sherman's "Push to the Sea." Sherman's men pushed, screaming their way to Charleston, South Carolina, to "make the rebels howl."

Forrest, unable to counter the 18,000 men of A. J. Smith in Mississippi, struck in Memphis with a force of 1,500. On his way, he laid waste to assorted contraband camps prior to masquerading in a heavy four o'clock morning fog, as a Union party returning with prisoners. He sought to capture three generals: Buckland, Hurlburt, and Washburn, that were quartered in Memphis. "Fall of Memphis" dispatches were sent by Forrest's men to Cincinnati and St. Louis.

His raiders also attacked the Irving Block prison to release Confederate soldiers captured by the Union army. After butchering extraneous Negro sentinels and pickets, he retreated to the city's outskirts to bargain for trade in prisoner release after the Fighting Iowa had foiled the raid. General A. J. Smith was forced to return to Memphis in reaction to the chaotic situation. Memphis was threatened, but far from being captured.

MEMPHIS

"Man what a bold son-of-a-bitch," mentioned one of the evening smoking crew as they gathered around a mess tent for gossip. "Rode through the lobby of the Gayoso Hotel, cut telegraph wires, knifed sentries, terrorized contraband camps! Sent messages, too, sent them to Cincinnati and Louisville. Memphis is in Confederate hands. Washburn just barely made it back to Fort Pickering."

"Barely is right. Made it in his drawers. Rebs stole his uniform!" Thighs were slapped, catcalls proliferated, and impassioned laughter combed through the darkened outer ranges of the campfires. The laughter that rose on the banks woke the ghosts of the Chickasaw Indians chiefs.

"Son," Mother Roche spoke softly at Feets' bedside early on a September morning, "I know what you are thinking, about your father and such. I couldn't say much about his plan because I didn't want you and Penny to get your hopes up."

Tears welled in her eyes. He saw fresh crow's feet; touches of gray rimmed her hairline. "I don't want you," she stammered, "I don't want my memory of the love between me and your daddy, my living memory," and she brought his head to her bosom, "snuffed out like a used campfire, like a burnt candle. Make my rounds with me today at the hospital. I want you to see the colored hospital, Camps Chelsea and Dixie. I want you to talk to wounded veterans, look at their wounds, their charred legs, broken arms, shot out eyes, and see if you still want to run off and fight."

"Mom, you have work there and it's personal work," he replied, "meaningful work that helps the Union. I can get my freedom and freedom for you and Penny. Daddy tried, and now the mission is left to me. My friends have volunteered to fight. We know that the fight is about slavery, no matter what fancy words politicians use about the Republic. You carry linen and carry baskets of water to help lift spirits and care for the soldiers confined for recuperation. If I end up in the shape they are in, I pray that I have a person care for me as beautiful as you!"

XXV

Memphis

"This is your boy, Mother Roche? Big boy, looks like you, too."

"Your mom tells us you thinking about joining up. Decision every man got to square with his own conscience, but I tell you, I seen men shot up every which way but loose. Loose from their eyes, legs, guts, bones, feets, and arms, loose from their asses." He leans over into Feets ear, and whispers, "Loose from their dicks!"

"Well," answered Feets, "I figure my body can be slashed, amputated, owned, and ravished by slave masters in the good old Confederacy. Or I can be maimed by my own freewill, with my feet pointed towards freedom. I lose a piece of my shoulder or rear end, then so be it! Right now my private is in tact and my feets pointed toward where I want to go, sho nuff. You want a drink?"

Even in the thick humidity of mid-July, Belle's voice rang crisp and clear. "I know what you up to," said Belle. "One damn fool around here is enough. You think you going to join up and fight in the war?"

"Yes, but it might be a key to help me make sure that I live respect myself," chirped Feets. If I can add my verse to the poem, pitch into the battle, fire some well-placed grape, the Union might be to be able to use me when Forrest gets cranked up again."

"You planning on taking him single-handedly?" Mother Roche shot his way, hoping to get a read on the temperature of his commitment.

Mother Roche avoided philosophical banter with Feets after Nathan Bedford raided Memphis. She had seen black refugees and civilians indiscrimi-

nately slaughtered in Memphis streets. General
Sherman had called Mother Bickersdyke to Atlanta
in support of the campaign. If Feets had asked her
if she felt safe and secure in Memphis, her answer
would have to be a resounding "no."

"A rifle doesn't make a man," chastised Mother
Roche.

Part II

XXVI

Nashville

The hooves of horses are similar in character to human toenails. They wear horribly if not protected by the iron shoes hammered to their underside by farriers. Nashborough, the genesis point of Nashville proper, clamored with the sounds of stevedores, armed soldiers, loaded wagons, and shouting teamsters as Feets disembarked from the gunboat which ferried him and fellow smoked Yankees up the Mississippi and down the Cumberland from Memphis. He wore his army issue boots proudly even though their rigid leather caused a tenderness in his heel. Their warmth was comforting. Common to the Nashville black population were feet populated with coarse calluses and raw bunions. The bullet-punctured carcass of a huge black crow, long since dead, floated down the river before him, talons curved up against the once majestic body.

"Damn Yankees are grabbing everything that even looks like a horse," complained a short Irishman crossing the street. Close behind, steering a large two-wheel cart, jogged a powerfully built black male.

"Use to be a slave, now I got my own hollering business," crowed the man as he jockeyed past the Irishman towards the docks and down the cobble-stone street aligning the wharf.

"Umph, umph, umph. Posse is probably still low profile," thought Feets, nibbling what was left of Belle's gift of traveling biscuits. The Irishman had paused long enough to ask, "Where you from?"

Feets had responded, "Memphis." The toothless buck replied, "Niggers pouring out of Memphis like pepper, must be kinda hot down there!"

NASHVILLE

Feets smiled inwardly, "Yeah," thinking, *They done gone from slaves to contraband to African-American refugees to soldiers,* but continuing, "it's real hot!"

Many of the black soldiers brought from Memphis with Feets to Nashville still lamented fellow comrades lost at Pillow and Brice's Crossroads. Some of the older veterans from Mississippi remembered the speeches launched by General George H. Thomas at Corinth.

"Seen where they got Pap Thomas soldiering right here in Nashville. Remember him talking to troops in Corinth 'bout blacks in the army, 'bout how it made sense to use niggers in the war on the Union side, 'specially since the Rebels was using slaves to build forts and cart around them heavy-assed cannons!"

Church bells at First Presbyterian segmented the hours at Nashville. As Feets studied bare black feet and faces held high in pride, he noted keloided backs, broken veins, plantation tattoos, smashed toes, and amputations in stoned silence.

"Used to be a slave, ever been branded?" as more

questions peppered him. He climbed the cobblestone and strode past St. Cloud Hotel. Signs decorated the streets and bold headlines dominated the headlines: *"Union Uber Alis"* and *"Libertie, Libertie, pour l'home Noire"* splashed in bold black letters, draped against side of a brick commissary. *What language is this*, he thought, tracing the word with his finger, slowly attempting a barrage of pronunciations.

"Change the 'ie' to 'y' makes it LIBERTY!" Immediately he flashed back to the black buck in Memphis. "It's French," added the passerby.

"Hey there pilgrim!" squealed an alto voice catching him in mid-stride. "You with those rifles thrown across your shoulders. I need a helping hand once you get finished gaping at the streets signs. You read French?" Standing at the doorway of the street market, a tall angular face under a black turban motion curved her index finger, beckoning him. "Need you to help me with these groceries. Sign says 'freedom for the black man.' Lift these packages onto my wagon for me. My house is a block down the road. I can spank this donkey into action if you can ride in the back and keep those packages from bouncing about. Where you from?"

"Memphis," Feets paused, examining the woman carefully: black turban, long black officer overcoat, and short broad heels. "My sister and mother are there still; my freedom comes with this uniform. You free?" He continued, "Would feel good to touch real freedom, hold it, fold it, bring it to fruition in life!"

"Of course," responded the woman. The small wagon jostled and bumped as he rode in the back, his hands on the packages. Street vendors hawked fruit and gawked. The woman added, "I draw you a map of the city when we get to my place. The Cumberland stretches on top of Nashville like the wide-brim of a woman's straw hat. The Confederate line rims her chin and round face with the Union and Rebel lines staring at each other. Negley is her left eye. When the shooting starts, the ball opens and the dance of death begins. This house was once an Underground Railroad, or at least that's the rumor, not something seen daily. Interesting history. You hungry? Once we get those things in the house, I'll show you a wall sculpture, a tapestry of carvings by runaways. You can put those packages right there inside the door. You got a trade?"

He slipped into the questions and said straight out, "Blacksmith." Against the landscape devoid of trees, the three-story house seemed small and beaten by more than weather.

"Like the way you carry them boxes," teased the girl seated at the table. "The boys just keep marching along," chimed in another. The first said, "Oh yeah, boys in blue."

"Girls listen. This here is Feets from Memphis. He headed to Fort Negley, just making his pilgrimage to Nashville. Hands off, ladies!" Madame Sable commanded. Feets unloaded the packages. The first girl, called Sugar, added, "Don't make no treats with Feets! We just so happy to see him back here with your packages."

Madame Sable: "Stop playing ladies and clean this sty up. Slovenly is bad for business."

"I better be going," said Feets demurely.

NASHVILLE

Madame Sable: "See there. Done scare off my little helper. Sugar do like her sweets." Pointing to Feets, she added, "Your sandwich is right around the corner, so just hold on, not so jumpy! That fort ain't going nowhere!"

The girls, scantily clad in robes and oversize tee shirts, put away the bagged items as Lady Sable eased herself into a chair, motioned to Feets, and sliced bread. As she spoke, water in the teapot began a sizzle. "Feets, I have information, very important information, that I want you to carry up to the fort. Sugar, slice some tomatoes. Feets, take off your jacket and rest your rifle and hammer sack. Sugar stood by the doorjamb, looked at him wistfully, and parted her linen robe just enough to reveal the pear shape outline of sugar colored breasts. She sliced two tomatoes, warmed two ears of corn, poured tea, and grazed his shoulders, placing the plate before him. "Excuse me" she said just within earshot barely moving her mouth. She tossed an unboiled ear of corn to the donkey outside.

"Sherman marching on Fort Wagner," the newsboy outside shouted.

FEETS

"Oh, Oh, here we go again with that hall of wings!"

"Ladies," shouted Lady Sable. "Ladies, it may not be important to you, but to me, those artifacts, the 'hall of wings' as you call it, the story told by that art is fascinating. Feets, finish that sandwich. The tea is yours, too. I will be back in a moment." Sugar follows Madame Sable through the door, flapping her elbow as if she were in flight. She spoke breathily in Feets' direction, "You ever made yourself a man for a woman?" and flew right into Feets lap. She jumped up quickly as Madame Sable re-entered the room, minus her coat and with a lantern in her hand.

— XXVII —

Nashville

Madame Sable, lantern lit, followed the meek, wobbly light along a dank, earthen underground trail. The smoky residue of the turpentine, combined with clay, teased his nostrils. The soft footfalls echoed less as the trail emptied into a dome-shaped convexity, tasseled with the images of birds. "Watch out for spider webs!" she announced, waving the light side to side, hoping to burn away whatever preceded their path.

He recognized the swallows that played along the riverbanks of the Mississippi, the feisty mockingbird that policed the yards of Poplar, the broad wingspan of the hawk rising to a ridge, a squirrel in clutch. His eyes hopped from one hieroglyph to the next, ravished by the sight of flight. "Just don't back-step!" caught him off guard as he clockwised, then countered, to watch the image flutter alive in the shadowed flicker of lantern light. His heart hammered his ribcage, now taunt with the long inhale his lungs refused to release. His gaze was fixed against the rich fresco that charmed the brownish-reddened sky; his precious medallion, motioned by his steps, plumbed vertical, its pendulum silenced.

"Sugar, hold up this lantern so our pilgrim can see. I'll be back in a bit."

Sugar replied with a smile, "Delighted!"

Feets back-flashed, hearing the crunch of dry leaves at Fort Pillow, smelling the crusty kerosene, watching the winged wonders writhe and squirm in the flickering light, searching for the flight that frees them from gravity.

"So natural," he said as he reached upward to touch the earthen ceiling, finger the sculpted wings, pointed beaks, and rounded eyes before him, "So natural and almost real."

NASHVILLE

"And so delightful," added Sugar with a breathy snicker. "They used these chisels and hammers— some of them—others just used knives. Nashville is full of this kind of limestone and rock. One day a wall was just a bare, ugly surface, and then the next, a shape would start to spurt out at ya. Kinda like, 'peek a boo.'"

Beneath her bared shoulders, her breasts seemed to inhale. Arms raised, their pear-shaped contours mimic flight. Feets recalls the "s" shaped pattern of his medallion. The buxom eyes of her nipples pout, pink with tenderness before her own flapping imitations shadowy apparitions of flight. Sugar had placed the lantern on the ground. Morphed into, indeed transposed into flight, her caped apparition surprised her, startled him, causing a series of back stumbles, with both landing on the ground. Breaking the silence, Sugar laughs adding, "This ground is cold." Sugar inspects the medallion around Feets' neck.

"You be better off flying outside then inside. If you try inside again, be sure you got some wings and not just that piece of housecoat."

FEETS

"Tell me about this medallion," as her fingers toured the black shield, finding metal and meat, abdomen and taunt chest. "What does it mean? Where does it come from?"

Feets put the medallion's face to the flickering candlelight. "Look closely and you can see the crack where I had to join two pieces together; some welding here and there, no solder. It's a hawk, some say a red-tail, and it was designed to remember family. It was made by someone who loved me."

Sugar placed herself between the light, tracing images of wings on Feet's chest, periodically touching the embossed image on the medallion. The tips of birds' wings flared upwards still, animated by the gleam of candlelight; the warmth of her fingers and his abdomen, conjoined so that their skin felt as one. She put her finger on his lips continuing, "So what if you die? What if you are killed trying to secure freedom for your people? Wouldn't it be a shame if you never knew the joy of a woman, mister pilgrim?" Now her fingertips were in flight. He gasped as the buttons, grown rigid against the firm hardness of his manhood, erupted in fluent succession.

NASHVILLE

"Brown cannon balls owned by pilgrim Feets." The thought and the teases froze in his mind. It was not the anger that engulfed him when crackers, angered by the merest hint of a question, challenged his words; it was not the rapture that he'd felt when viewing a well-rendered painting, or hearing the bass line of *Ezekiel's Wheel*, or the flood of satisfaction when he won some trumped up sports challenge. This was different; it evoked a deeper pleasure than he had known.

In the shadow, he half-saw his arms, the backs of his hands against the wall, the rim of her skull semi-detached to his thigh. The long inhale he managed at the sight of bird in flight faded and shriveled in comparison to the vacuum he felt tearing at the underside of his testicles. Her fingers seemed to burn against the ripples of his abdomen; his nose congested with the scent of her hair, the ripples of light against careening images, and the soft, gentle strokes of her fingers dimmed resistance, and focused his sense in a way he had not known possible. Taking her right nipple first between his teeth and then his lips, he became lost in the rhythm of the warm wave rushing over him; lost in the pulse that focused his passion lower, then lower in his body.

FEETS

He thought *run, stand, rollover,* but he could not move, feet and mind frozen; *stem to stern, starboard to aft.* His body jack-knifed into a perfect heave, spouting a trail of honeyed phlegm.

"A perfect comet!" she sighed.

His dreams rambled past the hung carcasses that mocked their entry to Fort Pillow, tip-toed through the crunch on leaves that decked the brown carpet, gradually turning black in color, glimmering in the sheen of glossy sparkles that is known only to maggots and tiny waves in brilliant sunlight. Later that night, she had mounted him, placing her nipple in his mouth and pleading with him "suck harder my pilgrim," and her chant became his spiritual mantra, for his spirit or whatever kept the trunk of his manhood as rock rigid as this, desperately sought relief. The reason of his travel, itself almost a distant apparition, sailed past the eye of his mind *"need to get to Negley"* and fell asleep.

"*Was it a dream?*" he thought, awakening to the dim flutter of one candle smoldering in the darkened room. His unbuttoned pants suggested another line of thinking. The dampened sounds he'd heard from the kitchen, suggested another. He thought he heard a deep, rich voice, the voice inhabited by an educated black man. He edged closer to the sounds. They had responded, "Forrest, in Murfreesboro?"

He read the following note: *Dear Pilgrim, if you die in purchase of your freedom, covet it well; if you live, embrace life like a flower full of passion only if it can be fifty-fifty, damn the forty-nine!*

XXVIII

Nashville XXVII

At the cock's crow, Madame Sable brought a plate of scrambled eggs, speaking softly with focused diction. "Bring this sealed note directly to General Thomas. Place it in your underwear so no one is granted access to those parts, which give you great pleasure. Drink your coffee while yet hot!"

He looked up at the regal black woman, "Why do they hate and despise us? What is it about their psyche that needs slaves?"

"Oh Feets, do not waste more time. Eat your breakfast. Sherman will have reached the ocean by the time we answer that question." Feets packed his gear, grabbed his rifle, and stepped past Madame Sable.

"Thanks for breakfast and showing me the room, that hall." Madame Sable kissed him lightly on the cheek. Questions with no answer sparkled in the daylight as Feets made his way to Fort Negley.

General George Thomas, dapper in his full dress, studied the morning sky. "You sure enough spit polish this morning," said his Negro manservant. The general's horse nodded in agreement as the fifty-seven-year-old veteran gingerly mounted his trusted bay. He smiled greetings to the parade of grimy soldiers and mud-clad laborers on his way to survey his troops and the broad expanse of territory known as Nashville, Tennessee.

The Union high command felt that Hood would leapfrog Nashville hoping to join Lee in Virginia. Thomas, so far not joined by A. J. Smith, rambled through his strategic options: meet Schofield in Franklin, attack Hood between Franklin and Nashville, retreat to the north side of the Cumberland, attack without cavalry when Hood reached Nashville. Schofield had been ordered to shadow the movement of Hood and became trapped at Spring Hill. He had engaged Hood spectacularly at Franklin, delivering a crushing defeat to the rebels.

General Thomas peered through his binoculars, tugged at his homburg, hand patted the bay, and carefully scribed notes on his battered military notepad. The red-tail hawk carousing above especially captivated him; he thought momentarily of his sisters who had disowned him subsequent to his decision to fight with the Union. As a young boy he had realized the humanness of the slaves on his plantation. He knew firsthand that the Nat Turner rebellion, from which he and his family had narrowly escaped, was a scream against the inhumanity of slavery. His men adored, nay idolized him, for the extensive defensive measures he undertook on their behalf: the dugout trenches, reconnaissance, intelligence, and strategic parries emboldened their resolve. Thomas had hijacked the odds against neophyte troops and his plea for training black soldiers had finally been honored. Now all he needed were horses, Spencer repeaters, and for A. J. Smith and his troops to show up.

FEETS

Shoes for civil war soldiers were more of a problem for the confederacy than the Union. Feets had almost broken in the brogan he received as regulation issue at his enlistment.

"Show your papers, soldier," greeted him as he reached the limestone archway marking the entrance of Fort Negley. From the knees down, few of the slaves swinging picks and shovels sported shoes that covered the veined ankles, broken toes, scratched heels, and calloused rims of their dirt covered feet.

"Feets Roche reporting for duty, sir," he said and saluted smartly. Feets showed his papers, quickly surveying the pitted frost like keloids that covered the backs of many of the male refugees; soft smiles, quiet stares, and quizzical looks bore down upon him, much like the rays of sun that poured upon him that day Posse had placed that miracle shot, only vastly multiplied. The stares beamed upon him from beneath sweaty brows.

"Where you been all this time? Your crew came in yesterday? You been watching cows? Your squad

came in late last night, nigger. Raise your hands!"
Feets followed the order, knowing the fort was on
high alert. He tongued-wagged a blurt past tense
lips, "I have a message I need to deliver to General
Thomas. Where shall I find him, sir?"

"Were you ordered to speak? I will deliver whatever needs to go to General Thomas! We got
Wilson running round like a chicken tryin' to get
cavalry ready, and his help, cow-watchin' all over
Nashville!" The sergeant threw his papers down
responding, "Wait here. The shop is up that hill
and next to the first bastion. Wilson trying to get
his cavalry ready and needs all the help he can get."
Feets remained silent.

Whispering voices rose higher; commanding voices
barked orders. "Whoa. giddyup." Donkeys, horses,
and mules, anything capable of pulling wheel vehi-
cles, strained against large burdens. Feets thoughts
traveled to the envelope strapped inside of his
long johns. His memory suddenly flooded with a
bottomless, gut-wrenched feeling of helplessness.
With his hands in the air above his head, he pictured Pillow, the snap of twigs, the cold blanket of
crisp wind, the desolation of death lurking behind

shadows. The banjo next to two workers jostled him past his jangled nerves. He smiled, feeling the pendulum of the medallion that still decorated his neck.

"That your token?" quizzed the sergeant. He eye-marked the coin around Feet's neck. Closer to the fort, the road had changed from pebble brick to macadamized earth, sleek and hard.

"Roche reporting, sir." The man behind the gate remained silent at his desk. "Feets reporting, sir," he barked again. The eyes gradually looked up and said, "You a blacksmith?"

I got all the qualifications sir. I'm black and I know a heck of a lot about smithing, Feets thought. He said, "Yes, sir! Farrier, sir."

Soldiers moved all around him from the Colored Infantry, 14th USCT. They had been raised among teamsters, cooks, servants, and camp follow-ers in Gallatin, Tennessee under the command of Thomas J. Morgan. Morgan had been a firm supporter of forming armed colored regiments. Unlike many other colored regiments that had been raised for garrison duty, the 14th was recruited to be a fighting regiment receiving intensive drill and training to that end. They were commonly held up as examples of a high level discipline and ability that could be achieved among former slaves.

Anxiety now flooded Feets' spine, froze his limbs, paralyzed his knees, and planted his body in its spot. His mouth dried shut. Beams of sunlight, castrated by spinning wheels, flared in frozen slices, casting fragmented flashes that reminded him of the sparkles thrown by the sabers of the home guard. He back-flashed; *hoodlums holding him at gunpoint, his face sprayed with the spittle of stale whiskey and splattered with globs of tobacco-laced phlegm.*

"Damn nigger boy."

He remembered. The daguerreotyped vision came back to him, haunting and inflammatory. It eclipsed the column of sunlight, punctuated by the bloodied vest of the squirrel. The hawk had dropped its prize; the prize had crashed into the mirror. Now his pants were dry and free of pee but the tint of home-guard hatred remained.

"Roche reporting for duty." Feets delivered a smart

salute in the direction of a lanky Scot sergeant. His fingernails scrubbed the bill of his Union issued cap, his elbow parallel to his eyeballs. Some of the workers who were close by slowed the clump and thump of their picks and axes. The silent drama caught the undivided attention of every living thing close by, becoming a study in stone, a picture of silent, underground war. Even the eyes and pointed ears of the mules, not to mention the black teamsters' focused faces, beamed their attention in the direction of the encounter. The Scot motioned in the direction of the young private for his papers mumbling, "You make one more nigger too many. That gunboat came in yesterday!" Feets, maintaining his steady salute, focused forward, a stone picture of stalemate, said nothing.

"Step over here, private!" boomed the loud voice, laughing boisterously. What Feets did not know is that there was also racial tension at Fort Negley. The men of the 14th Cavalry became involved in a racially motivated riot on November 14, 1864. The riot had started during a disagreement with an Illinois Artillery Company. As the men of the regiment defended themselves, shots were fired, and when the affair ended, two white and one African

American soldier were dead and three men were wounded.

Feets took a deep breath. "My orders are to report to the blacksmith's shop after delivering this message to General Thomas." He took two smart backward steps.

"Step over here, Private! Thank you for your diligence, Sergeant!" barked the toothy brown skinned regimental captain who spoke in commanding terms. He slowly obeyed the directive, stopping short of the man's rigid salute.

"The name is Bama. Stand at ease!"

Feets was impressed with this black named Bama; his in-charge manner was uncommon in his Memphis experience. The lanky Scot scratched his fingernails against his blues and quick-rolled his eyes upward.

"I help to manage the colored troops," proffered Bama in a distinct undertone, and who seemed to rummage the papers just a little too quickly. Bama bellowed fortuitously, "You look a helluva lot better today than your drunk ass did last night," adding for the onlooking crowd, "vomiting all over the infirmary! Was it was the beer or the hardtack that gave you the shits? I'll check your papers for you. I got him, Sarg!" The Scot, slightly dumbfounded by the unexpected brassiness of the commander some called Bama, moved his lips but said nothing.

"What your name, boy?" quizzed Bama in a whisper.

"Feets. What's yours?"

"I get to ask the questions, sonny! "

"Bama." his eyes sparkled as he added, "You sound like you from behind the cotton curtain! Grab your britches and fire up your nerve. This ball gone open up here real soon. Dollars to donuts this here fort will be crawling with Confederate flies before too long. I'll take you on up to the blacksmith shop."

"Came up yesterday," commented Feets. "Thanks for your help with that. I got a note I've been directed to give only to General Thomas."

"You owe me for that lie I told!"

"Easy, bro. We report to the blacksmith shop first. General Thomas is out mapping up Johnny. Believe me, he will find you. In the meantime, I won't ask you where the hell you been. Wherever you were, a repeat performance might not be in your best interests."

"What do you do around here?" probed Feets as he thought, *Nigger here might be shit, might be hot shit, might not. Not a whole lot of options right now, so act trusting and follow.*

"Thank God you just a black slave. You been white, you mighta been shot as a damn spy. I help these officers understand slave language especially when it comes to learning firearms and such. These here boys can't read so I repeat the officer's word, bark them for hearing."

Here comes the houseboy speech, thought Feets.

Bama continued, "Y'all inside boys think y'all smart. Look at that mess of shit you just stepped in. Might as well been downwind of the cavalry after Thanksgiving or just walking through yonder shit pile. Been fights around here betwixt white and colored. Lot of these pale faces ain't seen niggas afore this dance. Don't believe coons can count, read, learn, fight even. My job is to even up the odds, spin the bottle a bit! You houseboys ain't heard tribal language, ain't heard black folks speak in the old tongue. Yeah, even up the odds just a bit."

Bama took out cigarette papers, finger-tickled loose tobacco into a row, licked it, rolled it, lit it, and took a long drag, handing the stems to Feets.

"Listen over yonder," smiled Bama pointing in the direction of warm harmony pitched by rich, low voices. "Dese boys just like that Jacob Ladder. You listen to the words, dey cut two ways, East or West, North or South. Could be liquor, could be fighting, could be loving. Depends on what you listening for. Depends, too, on the color of the listener."

Just as they rounded the next bend, Feets pulled Bama away from a fresh field biscuit still steaming in the row. Noticing the pine board ahead, Feets walked up to it, scanned for information, and found his name under "Blacksmith." He noted that he was assigned as a munitions runner. Bama eyed the hieroglyphics now, looked away, and added, "What did it say?" At that moment, Feets realized that Bama couldn't read. He made no comment other than to say, "I got me two jobs."

Bama took him by the arm. "This way, pilgrim," and led Feets up the circular ramp to an attachment of the blacksmith's unit. Wagons carrying limestone bricks squealed, clamored, banked, and rumbled upward toward the high bastion. Posted inside the fort, bombproof bastions connected by tunnels allowed artillery and infantry to move to fire-protected points unobserved. The command was under orders to minimize campfires, saving the lumber cut from felled trees to maximize clear fields of vision. Slave laborers sang work songs and artillery units drilled for precision in open areas around large cannons.

"Private Roche," spoke the Scot sergeant, his brogue easily identifiable from their earlier confrontation. "Private, I understand you have a letter for General Thomas. He don't give no audience to niggers, but if you give me that 'telligence, I'll make damn sure it gets to him directly."

"Intelligence, Private Roche?" smiled Bama, overhearing the conversation from nearby, "You have intelligence for General Thomas? You said nothing to me about that." Turning to the sergeant, he barked, "Sergeant, you are dismissed!"

"Roche, Roche the farrier! Boy, you have just got to learn who your friends are! Now I don't have no truck with those intelligence boys, but if you got some important intelligence to share with General Thomas, you'd best meet up with them. I will pass on the word. You report to Hotel St. Cloud at 1700 Friday. St. Cloud Hotel at 1700 sharp, soldier!"

Feets toyed with his uniform buttons humming "Jacob's Ladder." Bama thought out loud, "We gone be bait, farrier Roche, fighting bait, but bait just the same. We ain't gone have no Spencer repeaters, but we the anchor. Wilson be the hammer, if'n he find horses, and we be the anvil, brother Feets. We can make freedom happen. Not even a squirrel, just damn worm bait!"

NASHVILLE

From the sky-high purview of *buteo jamaicensis*, also known as the buzzard hawk, the troop demarcations before December the 15th vividly demonstrated the operational plan of commanding officer General George Henry Thomas. Squarely in the center of the circular fovea of our red-tailed hawk was Fort Negley, neatly nestled below the cocky straw hat of the Cumberland River at Nashville, Tennessee. At 12:00 is north; 1:00, Edgefield Calvary barracks; 2:00, Lebanon Pike; 3:00, Mursfreeboro Pike; 4:00, Nolansville Pike; 5:00, Franklin Pike; 6:00, Granny White Pike; 7:00, Hillsboro Pike; 8:00, Harding Pike; 9:00, Charlotte Pike; with the Cumberland River at 10:00.

Thomas followed the path of a red-tailed hawk as its trajectory sailed towards the horizon. He had served on the jury at West Point that had condemned Schofield's academic behavior at the school. The incident had almost resulted in Schofield's dismissal from the Academy. What irony it was to have him now under his command at Nashville.

XIX

Nashville XXVII

"Mornin', General," pitched a passing soldier, his toothless jabbering almost hung in his mouth. "Bless you, Pap," commented another. Thomas felt honored and adored by his men. They knew instinctively that he cared about the survival of each and every one of them. They treasured his leadership. The papers had called his stand at Snodgrass Hill one of the most spectacular acts of heroism in any war. His response on that fateful day prevented a complete rout of the Union army. The memory of that stand blended into the distance, as he now jotted down more notes, more incidentals in his preparation to meet Hood.

FEETS

Trenches had been dug, intelligence sorties planned, mobile command posts established, hospital ambulances readied, and ferocious attempts at training black refugees in military command attempted. He needed a hammer and he had none. Without the horses necessary for swift movement, even the Spencer repeaters could not guarantee him a victory. Every step of his preparation emphasized the philosophy of the defensive perimeter. He needed two things: for A. J. Smith to show up and to match the speed and firepower of Nathan Bedford Forrest with more horses.

Schofield grinned to himself aware that Updyke, not himself, was the hero at Franklin. Air bloated and nervous, he clamored inwardly for strategic command and sovereignty over the Army of the Cumberland. Fresh from implied victory at Franklin, he envied Thomas' position and the hallowed respect given "Old Pap" by his men, qualities that eluded him even as the glow of victory lit his path to Nashville. Thomas, outfitted with the strategic vision of Sherman and an unmatched sense of defensive preparedness, carefully thought out his options with the patience of Moses.

NASHVILLE

"Slow Trot" Thomas tugged at his black homburg and began to write, carefully scripting additional notes on a hopelessly beat-up military notepad carried in his vest pocket. Fascinated as he was by the military scenario, he was especially captivated by the red-tailed hawk, which easily espied the terrain on which the battle would be fought. It challenged his imagination to develop a foolproof plan that would deliver victory to the Union army at Nashville. A makeshift configuration of refugee African Americans, former slaves, ignorant laborers, cooks, and unproven militarists. *Where is A. J.?* he thought privately.

He and his sisters, who now disowned him, had narrowly escaped death at the hands of Nat Turner in 1831. At the outbreak of civil war, George decided to stay with the Union. At least his push for training black solders had been honored. He hoped time and time again that he would be getting the horses he needed to form a cavalry. Troopers mounted on horseback with Spencer repeaters would form an arc swinging from right to left to turn the left flank of Hood. He was oblivious to the psychological machinations of Schofield. The thought to watch the actions of Schofield would come later at the urging of his commanders in the field. This bizarre drama threaded its way throughout the entire campaign of 1864 at the Battle of Nashville.

Part of this cast of great warriors trained under his tutelage included the names of Hazen, Steedman, and James Harrison Wilson. Thomas had sharpened his intelligence network for war throughout the course of his career. Speculating on his troop numbers, he wrote: Hood: 44,000, Steedman: 5,000, A. J.: 15,000, Schofield:18,000, Wood:15,000, and miscellaneous cooks, laborers, slave refugees: 3,000. He had smiled at the thought of USCT soldiers the other night, spinning the bottle to decide who would be in the small reconnaissance mission. *At least they all have shoes,* he thought. Shoeing the Civil War soldier, especially in this bitter cold, had always been a problem for the feet of slaves. The Rebels hadn't solved that problem for either the slaves or themselves it appeared.

Feets took time to inspect his treasured rifle, developed by Sir Joseph Whitworth of England in the 1850s. The unusual bore was hexagonal in shape and patented in 1854. It had found its way into the hands of Bedford Forrest's men at Fort Pillow. Once the prized possession of Posse, it was now his. His rifled memento of Fort Pillow was used primarily by Confederate sharpshooters. When outfitted with a telescopic sight, it had the effective range of 1,500 yards. Early in the war, this instrument had helped Rebels, with the aid of superior cavalry, dominate the battlefield The twisted hexagonal bore imparted a steadiness of flight to its 45-caliber bullet and made this rifle a Confederate favorite.

"That's a beautiful rifle you got there. You get loaned out to use it?" Bama asked.

"Loaned out? Why you think I get loaned out to do anything?"

"Well, you gots that token around your neck! Where I come from, that's your safety ticket, your identification. You might just get sold or whisked off by some jack-legged plantation owner, or even a bounty hunter, and be a slave to three or four different owners. Means you be a slave in this life and the next. Shit, maybe the one after that too!" At the thought, he roared backwards in laughter. "You just a black slave! If "n you a been white, you might have been shot back down there as a damn spy!"

Nashville

"How these white officers gonna teach gun fighting and soldering to this many Africans?" asked Feets. "I did some teaching in Memphis, but teaching this many, in a short period of time? Lotsa these fellas can't read or write."

"That's where you house boys come in," smiled Bama. "Y'all gotta get 'em up to speed quick on the soldiering part. Some of the smart niggers reads from the manual out loud and the new recruits jus' repeats what dey say; you know, repeats it right out real loud. Makes some of the house niggers feel real uppity. Guess you could say their education keeps away from the dyin' part. Too bad, cause I ain't seen an uppity nigger worth dying for," and he fish-eyed Feets before spitting. "I been actin' as a relay for reading, especially when it comes to learning of firearms and such. These here boys can't read so I repeat the officer's words, bark them out for hearing." Bama smiled again.

He *just loves that houseboy shit,* thought Feets. "You know how to shoot and all, so you can take me over to the practice range, time permitting," Feets volunteered. "Find Thomas and get to that blacksmith shop—quick."

"See those niggers out there? They be spinning the bottle to see who gonna do night patrol. Thomas sends out reconnaissance every night. They report on every activity. Sometimes they strip the dead of cartridges; money, too, if they can. This here circle pretty much outlines the battle lines so far. Ain't no Jedediah Hotchkiss, but it's pretty much how things stand. How many men are Union soldiers? They say Hood had 44,000 before Franklin. Thomas is waiting on Steedman from Chattanooga and A. J. Smith from Missouri. Right now we're a little under staff, bro. You ever killed a man, pilgrim?"

NASHVILLE

Feets inhaled the question, back-flashed on the burnt turpentine smell of his last defensive perimeter, and shot back after the thought, *More houseboy shit. When is this dude gonna try a different angle?*

"That's a real good question for my rifle. You sound like you think killlin' is something to be proud of. You ever brought back anyone from the dead, Bama? Maybe it's better to never take something you can't give back!"

Bama tongue-launched a wad of tobacco towards the pot that would have been hot if it weren't for the ban on fires. "Kill or be killed in battle, my Memphis pilgrim, ha-ha," blurted Bama. "I got scout detail in an hour," he added softly. "General Thomas sends us out in night squads. We develop Johnny's positions, find food, check spiral reports, telegraph lines, defensive perimeter protected. Check out the cvilians, too. Keeps us on our toes. You ready?"

"Let me get my pencil and paper out, letter writing stuff, too."

"Who gonna read it when it gets there?"

FEETS

"No idea, but whoever does, can look at the pictures."

"Can you draw my face?"

"I'm not the greatest artist, maybe a sketch."

"So draw my face, my hat, my gun, draw Bama. That's the blacksmith shop just ahead."

Feets smiled inwardly as the smell and sights of familiar tools came into view. The burly soldier sweating over hot irons shot them both a quick glance, adding, "Hope one or maybe two of you young laddies came here to bust some iron. Another good hand or two, and we could have them Rebels running home to their mommas in quick fashion."

Feets pulled his upper body and heels to rigid attention, saluted, and hooted, "Feets Roche reporting for duty, sir!"

December 1st

It was now the first of December. Hood, with the total force of 44,000, wanted to minimize the magnitude of his defeat at Franklin. After the "dance" at Nashville, he claimed to have only 22,000. He busied himself laying out infantry lines southeast of Nashville, in broken country called Brentwood Hills. Thomas, with the force of less than 50,000, plus 10,000 armed civilians, found Hood in a double line of entrenchments and fortifications. Smith's 16th Corps and additional Missouri regiments making a force of 15,000 had arrived at last. Now they were within Union lines. Feets was given a dual assignment: help with the blacksmithing and training as a munitions and ordnance runner.

The Union morale at Nashville started to flex muscle. Steedman's USCT 14th, determined to make Nashville by any means necessary, had contended with Forrest along the Nashville-Chattanooga railroad to arrive on the night of December 1st.

"You ever laid eyes on Captain Baker?" Bama asked, "They say he fought like a tiger against Forrest. They callin' him 'The One!'"

Conga drumming encircled Feets during his break. He gazed at the Nashville panorama through the Davidson telescope on his Whitfield rifle. Wagon wheels bumped along on the bumpy grounds in sharp contrast to the tight counterpoint of African rhythms. Teams of laborers dug trenches and built head rails and skid posts. A crudely drawn battle-field map on the wall of the blacksmith's corral showed Nashville as a wide brim southern belle's straw hat, her pie face covered by trenches. Fort Negley marked her left eye. Schofield troops had fallen back to the heights immediately surrounding the city. The 10,000 men of A .J. Smith's 16th Corps had been in Western Missouri chasing Confederate General Price. After picking up additional Missouri troops on the way, they arrived in Nashville on the night of November 30th, less than twenty-four hours before Hood's arrival at Nashville.

Smith's command would occupy Thomas' right, resting on the Cumberland River. The 4th Corps, General P. J. Wood temporarily in command, held the center, and General Schofield's troops, the 23rd Army Corps, occupied his left extending to Nolansville Pike. The cavalry under General Wilson was directed to take a position on the left of General Schofield, which would make secure the interval between his left and the river above the city. General Steedman's troops, having fought their way to Nashville, took up position at about a mile in advance of the left center of the main line and on the left of Nolansville Pike.

After three years of war, no commander in the western theater was about to make the mistake of taking Forrest lightly. General Wilson, now exercising command in the field, had only about 3,000 mounted men. The attrition rate in horses, necessitated by the fighting retreat to Nashville, had been exceptionally severe. This attrition lay at the foundation of Thomas' concern for mounted cavalry. Colonel Horace Capron's brigade, 1,200 strong at the start of the campaign, was reduced by a third, 411 men and 267 horses, by November 30th. Wilson drove his subordinates hard to speed up the process of re-equipment.

XXXI

Nashville

December 2nd

"You are authorized to seize and impress horses and every other species of property needed for military service in your command."

—Secretary Stanton

"Wilson has parties out now pressing horses and I hope to have some 6,000 to 8,000 mounted in three days time. I do not think it prudent to attack Hood with less than 6,000. Under Forrest, the enemy has at least 12,000."

—Thomas

FEETS

"Feets, get over to Edgefield today and help get some more of those of horses shod. Wilson's boys are supposed to be armed with Spencer carbines. The cavalry is the hammer, and the hammer must have shoes." Armed with these words from his superior, Feets made haste across the Cumberland bridge; his route took him past the St. Cloud Hotel. After parking the mobile shop, a smaller lightweight version of the central blacksmith shop, he disembarked and came to attention before the armed guard stationed outside the hotel.

"What your business? Have you spoken to your commanding officer about this so-called intelligence? General Thomas is a very busy man. The general will be here somewhere after 4:30! Come back then!" barked the guard.

The wide expansive panorama of Nashville, especially the clear brisk air, invigorated Feets. Along the river, while a brass band played "Eternal Father," gunboats guarded river crossings, re-enforcing the picket lines. A large, multi-decked hospital boat sat docked in its three-story splendor right at Fort Nashborough. The sight sparked a tinge of homesickness. *Could sure use some of mom's home cookin'. Wonder what Penny's up to?*

Edgefield was the feather at the left side of that cockeyed straw hat. He spent the day shoeing horses, repairing wagon wheels, and strengthening chains that had frayed during combat.

"If toenails were talons, it sure would make these hills easy to climb," chirped Bama as he slid up to Feets at dinner that night. "Show me that map sketch, Feets! We unloaded a whole crate of Spencer carbines this afternoon. Folks say you load it on Sunday and it fires all week! Sure wish we could get some of those for the 14th, the 59th. Just bait, lil' brother! Anvil bait!"

Feets replied, "I got my Whit, so I'm good! My biggest problem will be having the strength to lift it after working in the shop all day. That work is never-ending. My muscles ache just talking about it."

Somehow, he thought he knew the face. Where before it had sparkled with a mirth that glittered underneath the serious face, now it seemed occupied with matter very serious.

FEETS

It mouthed phrases that seemed almost intelligible, but he could not understand the words. The room was painted all in white. He remembered the smell.

City Point, Virginia
December 2, 1864
MAJOR-GENERAL THOMAS
Nashville, Tennessee

If Hood is permitted to remain quietly about Nashville, you will lose all the road back to Chattanooga and possibly have to abandon the line of Tennessee. Should he attack you, it is all well, but if he does not, you should attack him before he fortifies. Arm and put in the trenches your quartermaster, employees, citizens, etc.

—U. S. Grant

Thomas replied with factualness and cool temperance to Grant's needling telegram. He made it clear that he had collected an adequate force of infantry to go over to the attack, but that he could need more cavalry. In a second wire sent December 3rd, he expressed the hope that he would have 10,000 cavalry, mounted and equipped, within a week, and would then be ready to take the offensive.

NASHVILLE

Your two telegrams of 11 AM and 1:30 PM are received. At the time Hood was whipped at Franklin, I had at this place but about five thousand men of General Smith's command, which added to the force under General Schofield, would not have given me more than twenty-five thousand men. Besides, General Schofield felt convinced that he could not hold the enemy at Franklin until five thousand could reach him. As General Wilson's cavalry force also numbered only about one-fourth of that of Forrest, I thought it best to draw the troops back to Nashville, and await the remainder of General Smith's force, and also force of about five thousand commanded by Steedman, which I ordered up from Chattanooga. The division of General Smith arrived yesterday morning, and General Steedman's troops arrived last night. I now have infantry enough to assume the offensive, if I had more cavalry; and will take the field anyhow as soon as the remainder of General McCook's cavalry reaches here. It must be remembered that my command was made up of the two weakest corps of General Sherman's army, and all the dismounted cavalry except one brigade, and the task of reorganizing and equipping has met with many delays.

—General George H. Thomas

FEETS

For the following three days, Thomas had only Hood and Forrest to contend with. A virtual barrage of telegrams from Grant resumed on December 5th. His wire of that date expresses concern over the possibility of Forrest getting behind Thomas and crossing the Cumberland below Nashville. It ended with a mild admonition. On December 2nd, Grant suggested to Thomas that authority be given to Wilson to impress horses to mount his troopers. Stanton wired Thomas, "You are authorized to seize and impress horses and other species of property. "Wilson has parties out now pressing horses and I hope to have some 6,000 to 8,000 mounted in three days time. I do not think it prudent to attack Hood with less than 6,000. Under Forrest, the enemy has at least 12,000."

Grant replied, "If Hood is permitted to remain quietly about Nashville you will lose all the road back to Chattanooga. Should he attack you, it is all well, but if he does not, you should attack him before he fortifies. After the repulse of Hood at Franklin, it looks to me that, instead of falling back to Nashville, we should have taken the offensive against the enemy where he was. You will now suffer incalculable injury upon your railroads, if Hood is not speedily disposed of. Put forth therefore every possible exertion to obtain this end."

Feets studied feets: the massive bunions of the unshod feet of slaves, their broken and misshapen toes, hardened bunions and calluses, and mangled ankles. He checked his thoughts, but they outflanked him, imagining the irons and restraints that could have caused these bruises and keloids. His mind calculated the miles that most had added to the markings, new insults to old injuries. *First thing freedom grants is shoes. All God's chillun got shoes!*

"Young man," a voice sounded behind him in baritone, "I understand you have information for me!"

He looked, scrambled to erect attention, saluted from behind his apron, and saw the same likeness he had seen back in the offices of Generals' Buckner and Washburn in Memphis. He did know a general's insignia.

"General Thomas?"

FEETS

"Good morning, Private. I understand that you have been quite helpful here. Your superiors seem to be quite pleased with your efforts. I understand that you have a package for me?"

"Yes, sir! Madame Sable asked me to give you this package!"

"Oh, Madame Sable. Quite a sense of humor that Madame Sable. Provides good information. I trust your visit to her establishment was of sound purposes. Thank you and carry on, son." Some said later that the note suggested Hood was addicted to the then popular pain reliever Clementine cordial; others would say it mentioned the possibility of Forrest being detailed to Murfreesboro.

Feets took deep, long breaths to arrest his excitement! "Just think, General Thomas!" He felt pride and pleasure in finally getting to deliver the envelope.

Bama showed up shortly after the general had left the shop. "Was that General Thomas? You get him that espionage you was talkin' bout? What did he say?"

NASHVILLE

The pulsating sound of hammer and chisel against bricks of limestone pranced within earshot. Feets smiled at Bama adding, "I just met General Thomas!"

Bama bent, pulled over an empty crate used for assorted munitions, and flutter-shuffled a deck of cards. "That's what I figured. That token, what you call a medallion, did you weld that back together?"

"Yeah. It fused together pretty easily, better than I thought it would. Found half of it at Fort Pillow and the other half was mine long as I can remember. Mom said my dad made it for me."

"And you been calling it a medallion all this time?"

"Yep. Mom said my father made if for me from his! Cut the whole thing in half, so if I got lost or he got sold, or whatever, we could always hook up with family, always know where we was from!"

"Damn! And you found it at Pillow?"

FEETS

"Well, it's almost as if it found me! It was burnt into the skin of a corpse, maggots all around. I didn't realize what it was until I got back to Memphis. My mom showed me the way the piece I found fit mine. I never have called it a token. What the hell is that?"

"Well, a token is like a safety pass, a chit to guarantee your safe passage to and fro. Back home, black folk gits stopped when they can be jus' moving 'round, minding their own business. So, in that case, you have to show that there token. Lets the authorities know who you are and what master you belongs to."

Feets took a boxing stance, shadow-boxed against the limestone wall at the back of the 'smithin corral, and fist-threw punches in the air. "We gone knockout some Rebels bye and bye, knock out some Rebels and be free! Be FREEEEEE!"

Bama half-cocked his head upwards, eye-casted a long look in his friend's direction, and added, "Freedom may be a long time comin'; these Rebs got mean hearts; they gone do everything in their power to snatch freedom back! Keep black folk chained to slavery every way they can. Don't be thinking you gone get schools, legal rights, votes, business, and such. Naw! Ain't gone happen soon iffn ever! Can you shoot?"

General James Harrison Wilson and his men acted with no light hand to round up horses for cavalry. Wilson personally seized Governor Johnson's carriage horses. His troopers rounded up streetcar horses and all the private carriage and saddle horses they could lay their hands on. Delivery stables, farms, and circuses were stripped of horses. Secretary Stanton received this angry telegram: "The general impressments of horses by the military is here so oppressive that we cannot think it meets your approbation. Horses are taken without regard to the occupation of the owner or his loyalty. Loaded country wagons with produce for market are left in the road. Milk carts, drays, and butcher's wagons are left in the street, their horses seized."

Within seven days of Stanton's order, 7,000 horses were rounded up. John Bell Hood, commander of the Confederate forces, rested at "Traveler's Rest" with the Overton family before the fight. He was not in good shape mentally or physically; he had lost a leg at Chickamauga and had a useless arm after Gettysburg. Now somewhat prone to drink or opiates, the thirty-three-year-old took opiate-based painkillers to fight physical agony.

"Oh, so you here to pay back old General Forrest! How the hell you gone do that? You ain't never even shot nobody, never kilt a damn soul."

Feets had given him a full display of the sharp-shooting skill he developed over long practice hours at Fort Pickering.

"Sharp shooting ain't nothing like killing. You want to meet killers, check out them Ohio tigers, Opdykes' crew! They just sidestepped old Forrest at Franklin! C. W. Baker bear-hugged him at Mill's Creek, too. Mark my words, Thomas ain't gone do shit until he can match Forrest speed for speed! He gone find some hoof speed, first and foremost! After that, you might get your chance, mister private sharp-shooter! You ain't gone be shooting at stationary tin cans and beer bottles when the time comes."

Feets telescoped his targets and "Whittled," picking off the two beer bottles that Bama had just missed with his Engfield. He foot shuffled twice in celebration and cupped his ear towards Bama, taunting him to repeat the judgment he had just made.

"You shuffle twice like that on the battlefield and you be one dead nigger!"

"You sound like old massa, talking 'bout what somebody can't do. Why don' you concentrate on developing what you can do? If you hawkeye the target, take a deep, slow breath, you won't jack your rifle when you shoot. Had to get by that experience myself. Take my word for it, take a slow breath." Feets said recalling Posse's lessons.

"Ain't no plantation in Alabama heaven, seen my share of Alabama plantations, witnessed my share of death firsthand. Tennessee ain't no better. You think Forrest learned to whip those West Pointers in a monastery?"

Some of the soldiers sang "John Brown's Body"

and drank soupy gruel as they retired to the tents. A brass band in the distance slipped into taps.

December 3rd

"Last night the enemy made quite an advance and constructed a line of breastworks in front of the entire division of this corps and extending beyond the right and left of it. In front of Streight's brigade (Beatty's 3rd Division) the enemy got position of a ridge about 600 yards from our works, and along the crest of it for about one regimental front, they have thrown up strong breastworks. Our artillery has kept up quite a steady fire upon the enemy all day. The enemy has not yet replied with artillery.

—General of the 4th Corps

Thomas reread the lines of his telegram: "It must be remembered that my command was made up of two of the weakest corps of General Sherman's army and much dismounted cavalry. In more than a few days I shall be able to give him a fight."

In his room, George Thomas patted his foot to the harmonies and rhythm of the post band playing outside. The after-dinner serenade drifted past mounds of card-playing soldiers festooning their stories with trills, oompahs, and cracked notes. An out-of-tune tuba seemed just around the corner. Hymns, marches, and ballads defined the concert menu. "The Battle Hymn of the Republic" drew the largest applause, cheers, and a husky-voiced chorus. Few knew the words to "Eternal Father."

"Feets, they say Thomas' kin sisters disowned him when he remained true to the Yankee cause. Turnt his picture 'round to the wall."

"Where you found all this shit, Bama?"

"Say he taught niggers in Virginia to read."

"Well, he seems like a fair man to me. I ain't got but one sister, and if we fell out, I'd feel pretty bad."

"His body servant is that old black guy, looks like a damn preacher up close! Like one of them guinea preachers."

Feets smiled, retorting, "I've seen lots of preachers

in Memphis. Most of mine been piss-in-the-pal-ions! Though ain't none been brown. Do you ever have bad dreams?"

By December 3rd, Thomas had positioned his infantry in entrenchments that stretched across the south of Nashville and touched the Cumberland River above and below the city from right to left. Thomas's line was occupied by General Smith's troops; Major-General Thomas J. Woods' IV Corps; the XXIII Corps led by Schofield; and Steedman's amalgam of troops. Wilson's cavalry had crossed north of the Cumberland to Edgefield to refit.

Feets flashed on Cajun Posse, sombrero bouncing like a target on a turtle's back, and rimmed with a cloud of cigar smoke. How in the hell could he smell turpentine in the mist of that blue smoke? He remembered the words, the twang of his speech. *Build a defensive parameter; dry fire tomorrow!* Without thinking, he grabbed a pencil, straightened out some paper, and wrote:

Dear Mom and Penny,

Things are quiet in Nashville. Me and my friend Bama

practiced shooting today. I have been assigned to the black-smith shop and ordnance detail. We are ready for battle; we also see newspapers from other cities: New York, Chicago, Cincinnati, etc. A few days ago, I met Gen'l Thomas; everyone here respects him and the morale among the men is real good. Also met Emerson Opdyke; he tells me that this is a great battle for human rights, and that the black soldier must never despair. He quotes Frederick Douglass from memory! A huge hospital boat looms nearby on the Cumberland. I hope I do not see it from inside. Say a prayer for me and I hope to see you real soon. Love, Feets

He traced his foot on the bottom portion then folded the paper, slid it into an envelope, and addressed it to Mother Roche and Penny.

XXXII

Nashville

Sunday, December 4, 1864

No change in enemies or our lines today. We have been firing at the enemies' lines with artillery during the day and he has not yet replied. It is supposed he has not much artillery ammunition with him.

Whipple

General Thomas was especially cheered by the presence of Smith's men who were some of the rare victors in a contest against Forrest at Tupelo. Unbeknown to him, the espionage from Madame Sable that Feets had delivered to Union

FEETS

General Thomas became a stealthy reality. On December 4th, Confederate General Forrest headed to Murfreesboro with two cavalry divisions and one of infantry. Military historians are still confused by Hood's decision; they consider it a military blunder. Forrest successfully attacked blockhouses at Laverne and Overall Creek thus protecting the railroad between Nashville and Murfreesboro; he was stalemated at Fortress Rosencrans, but did manage to tear up several miles of track.

Bama studied the decks of playing cards he had now whitewashed, dried, and transformed to cards of study. They sported the alphabet, several basic words common to newspapers, and the names of several prominent battlefields.

"Who taught you how to clear and calibrate guns like that?"

"Told you, I was a blacksmith's apprentice in Memphis and he loaned me books. Fort Pickering had a gunsmith's shop. I apprenticed some there, too, and read some books. Mainly, I watched! I made some casting trays to make bullets for the Whitfield; some just use regular shaped bullets, but they actually need to be hexagonal to perform as designed. Oh, I had an old female teacher, too." He tossed his own sense of humor a quarter-smile, "She taught me squeeze, not pull!" *Eggplant! He knew he had left out something in his letter!*

"Somebody scouting our sector today seen rats! That hawk you talk about gave chase, don't know if he got him though. Them hawks is smart. Knew some Rebs that trained 'em to chase people, track down runaway slaves. Get betwixt that diving hawk and whatever he's after—you 'd think stink was heaven! 'Magine it's like getting smacked by a bullet! Don't know what hit cha!"

"I got assigned to run munitions for Wood; think I saw where you assigned to Steedman and the 14th!" He had spoken without betraying the stutter of his thoughts. His thoughts stammered through "Rebs trained to chase slave runaways." His mind raced backwards! *Posse's hawk was trained for that! The hawk was with them, the same hawk, from Memphis to Pillow! Posse's accomplice!* He spoke more slowly now, scaffolding his words with weakened resolve, "I hope the hawk got it. Those trenches are infested with rats! If you lucked out and got the 14th, wear your brogans so you can swim past the rats."

"Feets!" barked the blacksmith. "Be sure you triple-check the yokes and chains for your wagon. You don't want that axle to freeze up on you with all that firepower at your back!"

"Yes, sir!" Feets replied, moving toward the can of grease automatically.

"And check the shims on each wheel. Put a cannon ball in there for old Nathan Bedford. Scratch an NB on it! Don't want him to pull no magic out of that hat of his. It's way too late for us to start back peddling our asses across the Cumberland."

Bama gave a nod as he said, "I'd better get going. Thanks for checking this rifle. I feel a heck of a lots more comfortable knowing that it will shoot the ways I tells it to. Might even have to pluck off some of these Rhine rats before this dance is over. They so tough and cold by now, bullets probably bounce off them like cast iron. Jus' think, me all the way from Alabama and you from Memphis, jus' to take potshots at cast iron rats."

"Bama, you are crazy! Hold on. I'll walk you to your tent! Boss, I'll be right back—gone walk Bama back to his regiment!"

"Okay, Feets, but make it snappy. I want the linch-pins on every wagon that comes through here double-checked!"

They walked down the ramparts and eastwards toward the Etowah encampment, the sound of their boots pounding the cold ground in unison.

"Feets, you ever kill a man?" Bama broke in, eye-searching Feets deeper for truthfulness.

Feets responded slowly, "No, I haven't to tell the truth. I almost did, but couldn't."

"And you lived to talk about it," replied Bama. "Well, can't be no hesitation now. It's kill or be killed. Those boys that lived through Franklin say that was the bloodiest fighting they had ever seen. Old Frederick Douglass be agitating for us to put the African shoulder to the Union plow; he sent his own sons into battle for this cause. Lots thinks we in this for keeping the Union together, but it's more than that now. We fighting for our freedom, pure and simple!"

"What about you? You ever killed a man?"

"Well, I shore as hell have fired in the direction of one. Didn't wait long enough to know if I hit 'im. But I'm taking my pistol along, just in case I need to repeat a shot real fast. My guess is that second chances will be real hard to come by." As his voice trailed off, the music of chains clinked as the wind caused the wooden gate to rock back and forth. Neither soldier thought deeply of the seconds as they ticked way, creeping closer to the hour of battle.

Monday, December 5th

"No change in the enemy lines today except that his works may not be so full of troops as they were yesterday. We still keep up our artillery firing and had been making observa-

tion to see whether there is a point in the enemy line that we can attack with a chance of success."

—Thomas

"It seems to me," General Grant wrote from City Point, Virginia, "that Hood should be attacked where he is. Time strengthens him in all probability, as much as it does you."

The thoughts and hopes that sparkled in the imaginations of these men were to be buried or nurtured by the decisions of chance. The nerves and psyche of Feets, ground raw by the focused concentration of each trooper, caused his moments of rest and sleep to be populated by unusual combinations further enriched by the unfamiliar sights and sounds of Nashville. He mentioned the strangeness of his dreams to no one, lest he be thought unstable.

"You had lots of books to read when you grew up didn't you, Feets?" asked Bama. They had taken practice at the firing range and now walked to mess tent for the endless portions of oatmeal fortified with pork and designed to sustain the high alert of their battle stations.

FEETS

Feets responded, "You can say that Bishop had a good full library. I always had books to read. I love to read!"

Bama added, "You get books for Christmas? I ain't never got a book for Christmas," he added continuing, "Hell, slaves need shoes whole lot more than they need books. You seen the broken toes, bunions, callus feet, manacle marks on their feet?"

"Shit yeah, but rumors has it that lots of Hood's boys ain't got shoes. Their big chance to trudge across the Cumberland on the backs of bluecoats and their shoe leather worn plumb out! Barefoot in the wintertime. All skin and bones. If you look at the rebel honeycombs, they got graves that put a little pep in your step. Yeah, to go the other way."

Bama retorted, "You ever seen anybody hang a rat? Rat be bouncing all over the place, wriggling, curling up, whatever it can manage, biting even, to get free—racing with itself to outsmart that rope. Usually ends up outsmarted by that dumb old rope. Mostly male rats, female rats too valuable for breeding."

"You letting this thing get inside your head. Let's get practical. If I get out alive and you don't, what do you want me to do with your stuff?"

"Feets, I done talked to you probably more than anyone about what we gone have to do to get started in life after this; no education, no money. A mule and acreage—pipe dreams. The onliest thing we have is the ghost of good spirits, the inspiration of good conversation, belly laughter, and the relief of good friendship. Jus' remember Bama. What about you? What you want me to do with your stuff?"

"Well, Bama," replied Feets, "just two things: teach my sister how to shoot with this here Whitfield and take this medallion—I ain't calling this no token— my medallion, and give it to my mother."

Schofield's envy of Thomas rose as the temperature at Nashville dropped. Was it vengeance? Jealousy? The soldiers loved and honored Thomas. Many thought the ambition of Schofield was boundless and his military career to be a failure except, of course, for Franklin.

FEETS

Tuesday, December 6

Nothing of importance today; the enemy is still strengthening his works. We still keep up our artillery fire. The enemy replied with a few shots from two guns opposite the knoll held by Colonel Streight's brigade. Major General Couch assigned to the 23rd Corps today; leaves General Wood in command of the 4th Corps.

—Thomas

Attack Hood at once and wait no longer for a remount of your cavalry. There is great danger of delay resulting in a campaign back to the Ohio River.

—Grant

I will make the necessary dispositions and attack Hood at once, agreeable to your order, though I believe it will be hazardous with a small force of cavalry at my service.

—Thomas

NASHVILLE

… records show that 22,000 cavalry horses had been issued at Louisville, Lexington, and Nashville since the 20th of September.

-Halleck

"Look at this noose, Feets. Gone catch that fool rat tonight," barked Bama.

"Looks like that hawk might be trying to beat you to the punch," replied Feets.

.

"What hawk?"

"The one perched up on the other side of the river, up on top of the bridge. The wide wingspan of the hawk cause it to glide easily."

"Look through the scope," added Feets.

"A little cheese on hard tack, a mighty morsel to make a food magnet for that fat sucker!" grinned Bama. "You want to be rat bait?"

"Rat bait? What do you mean?"

FEETS

"Well, if the Spencer's cavalry, and A. J. be on the west end, and we be on the east end, the African is the bait, mate!"

Feets flashed on the dead at Fort Pillow, the crawl of iron filings rinsing maggots across his father's dead body. The slow waddles of buzzards, the hammer-like thrusts of crows seemed to eviscerate the spine of his fortitude. He wipes his hand downward across his face to shield his eyes, to make sure that they were still in place, ungouged! His thoughts spun recklessly, passing the fire at his shop, and landed on the weirdness: the bizarre ghosts that wove through the pictures that haunted his dreams: Mother Roche, dressed in a nun's habit, General Thomas reading from a newspaper, Eggplant hunched in corner praying, and Penny polishing her Sunday shoes. He gritted his molars to see if he could taste dirt.

XXXIII

Nashville

The Napoleon chest slid smoothly on the wagon floor. Bama spit through his teeth, rolled up his shirtsleeves, and peered towards the logistic plan wall, tacked by the ordnance officer.

"Spencers on horseback," sparked Bama, "Fire all week, you ever fire one?"

"Naw," replied Feets, "but Opdyke's boys love them. Say they floated Sheraton at Chickamauga and felled Cleburne at Franklin."

The casual low-flying grace of the red-tail hawk burnished the afternoon, with a rustic elegance.

FEETS

"Reb set up a flag of truce at midday."

"Yeah, I heard about it! Said they want to make a prison exchange."

General George Thomas had sent Rebel prisoners north some time ago.

Wednesday, December 7

The enemy is moving a force to his left, opposite General A. J. Smith's command and he is constructing works extending in the same direction. 2:00 pm, General Thomas directed General Wood to discover, by observation or pressing forward, our picket line, whether the enemy is yet in strength opposite us. Division commanders report that the enemy yet occupies the works opposite our front in the same strength as yesterday if not in greater. This fact is reported to General Thomas. Observation had been made today to find some point in the enemy line of works that we can assault. An assault will be made by the 4th Corps as soon as the troops can get ready— within a few days.

Whipple

NASHVILLE

Just after dinner, Bama located Feets counting munitions crates and stacking them on wagons.

"This fort is huge!" exclaimed Bama, "wagons lined up all over the place!"

"Take off your jacket and work off some of those beans, Bama," replied Feets. The mission depot was located halfway between the rail tracks and Fort Negley.

"Them Rebs been up to no good, Feets. They been building abatis, redoubts, trenches, too. Got slaves working for them … slaves! Damnedest part is that we gets them horses we got to horseshoe them up real fast. Those Schofield boys workin' on getting Thomas fired, relieved of command, saying that Thomas moves too slow. Schofield boys been sprouting that crap! Opdyke was the hero at Franklin, not Schofield Ambition is a bitch … even white on white! How do you know about the success?"

"Prisoners and Reb deserters we caught told us."

"Could be lies, Bama,"

FEETS

"Ain't no lies. All the liars hanging out at the telegraph office with Schofield, pecking at Thomas, lying to Grant."

"You go out with that reconnaissance party?"

"Yep, did that defensive parameter circle, reconnaissance party bit thing regularly...it tells us what the johnnies are up to!. No real problem, Brother Feets. Here, let me give you a hand with those."

Feets was restless during his sleep that night. An angel appeared to him with a book to read. He couldn't make out her face, but her voice sounded familiar. Behind her stood General Thomas reading a newspaper. As the General started toward him, he awoke with cold sweat on his neck.

Earlier that day, Thomas had informed Halle of the receipt of a dispatch from Major General Russo at Murfreesboro on the afternoon of the 7th. Melroy succeeded in getting on Confederate General Bates' flank and completely routed him. *You will note this fight took place 36 hours before the start of an ice storm.*

NASHVILLE

Thursday, December 8

"Last night the enemy extended his lines to his left, a short distance beyond the position he held at dark, and construct-ed there a line of breastworks. 12:15 pm, the enemy forced back the scrimmage line of the 23rd Corps just where it joins the scrimmage line of the first division of this corps. This caused part of our scrimmage line on our left to fall back a sort distance. The enemies' scrimmages follow up closely, but they were driven back and our original scrim-mage line re-established at 3:00 pm. It had been decided to attack the enemy at daylight on the morning of the 10th, and the assault would be made by the 2nd division of this corps upon that part of the enemies' lines opposite Streight's brigade, 3rd division, just northeast of Hillsboro Pike. The 2nd division will be supported by the rest of the corps, save one brigade to be left in our works. General A. J. Smith will follow-up the assault and cover our right flank, and the cavalry will follow-up General Smith.

Whipple

Dear Feets,

Penny and I are cheered by the news of the Union victory at Franklin. The misery of war injuries surrounds us yet in Memphis; the agony of amputation and death leaves many grief stricken. We pray daily for your safe return to our family, and have faith that death is not the price you pay for freedom.

Love,
Penny, Eggplant, and Mother Roche.

The sharp crack of a fire rifle bullet missed the heavy, elongated shape of a red-tail hawk lifting a mouse up over the Cumberland River into a cracky bed of fieldstone on the north side of the river. Feets smiled as the bird lost its grip on the rodent, banked smartly, and angled off into the distance. Through the scope, he could see the prize smack into the rocky ridge for a later meal.

General Jacob Cox penned in his diary, *"freezing sleet and snow covering the ground with ice and making movements impracticable."*

"I had nearly completed my preparations to attack the enemy tomorrow morning, but a terrible storm of freezing rain has come on today, which will make it impossible to fight to our advantage. I am, therefore, compelled to wait for the storm to break and make the attack immediately thereafter. *Admiral Lee is patrolling the river above and below the city, and I believe will be able to prevent the enemy from crossing. Hurlbut informs me that you are very much dissatisfied with my delaying attacking. I can only say that have done all in my power to prepare, and if you should deem it necessary to relieve me, I shall submit without a murmur."*

George H. Thomas

On the day these messages were sent, namely on December 8th, Thomas received a report from Wilson. After confirming it with his division commander, Wilson stated that the cavalry could not be assembled and made ready for an active attack offensive until three days thereafter, that is, until December 11th.

"Cannon fodder or not, every black toe in this line will kiss the breeze any second now. All ya'll been prayed over through and through. Ain't no telling how many voodoo dolls been poked, rabbit foots been wrapped and tied; belts, Bible, and buckles be clinking right along with us when that second arise," Captain Baker, noted for heroism when Forrest attacked the 14th on the way to Nashville from Murfreesboro, barked at his troops.

Bama muttered, "Damn tooten! These here tents and stacked wigwams and burned-ass pots will be damn cold and breezy while we gone."

"Ain't no great big old thing, shit. We gone have us some Confederate stew and butter biscuits after we done pumping musket balls into Johnnys."

"You can have all that stew to yourself. Folks tell me that damn Johnnys are skinnier than Abe Lincoln, freezing from the ground up, and stench like those skunks we ran across in Chattanooga!"

"Urghgh! Those were the funkiest skunks the devil could have imaged. Check, check your ammo, pack a pistol, and 'member Pillow."

"Feets!" exclaimed one of the Minnesota troopers, "Somebody said that you were looking for a Davidson scope to attach to your Whitworth. I found this scope at Franklin. The glass is still good, but one of the screw nuts is broken."

"Wow," answered Feets, looking through the cross hairs of the scope. "How much you want for it? I see Davidson right on the side."

"Not to worry. Take it. It's yours."

Friday, December 9

Owing to the severity of the storm raging today, it is found necessary to postpone the operations design for tomorrow morning until breaking up of the storm. I desire, however, that everything will be put into condition to carry out the plan contemplated as soon as the weather will permit it to be done, so we can act instantly when the storm clears away. Acknowledge receipt.

—Major General G. H. Thomas

The slopes in front of the line were a continuous glare of ice so that movement away from the roads and broken past could be made only with the greatest difficulties and at a snail pace. Men and horses were seen falling whenever they attempted to move across coun-

FEETS

try. A man slipping on the hillside had no choice but to sit down and slide to the bottom, and groups of men in forts and lines found constant entertainment in watching these mishaps on the hills and rolling country about Nashville. Maneuvers were out of the question for nearly a week.

—Jacob Cox

Bama rolled papers around some loose tobacco leaves, licked the papers, gently folding the edges to seal, and put fire to its end. Inhaling deeply and exhaling smoke, he spoke, "You can slide all the way back to Memphis on that slick shit."

Feets shot back, "Or to Alabama if you want those Johnnys to slit your dick, yank off your brogans, and hang you up by your nuts."

"Might be a better position than old Thomas finds himself in. He got Schofield and Hood after his ass. White folks do that to him, you know, they gone fish fry a nigger!" countered Bama.

Feets swished the point around in his brain and muttered, "The end of that smoke could get you seriously bushwhacked. Put it out, we need you breathing tomorrow."

"You think that token around your neck makes you a general or something? Ain't nobody promoted your dark ass yet. You best pray rather that spout out orders."

XXXIV

Nashville

Your dispatch of 10:30 am this date is received. I regret that General Grant should feel dissatisfaction at my delay in attacking the enemy. I feel conscious that I've done everything in my power to prepare, and that the troops could not have been gotten ready before this. And if he should order me relieved, I would submit without a murmur. A terrible storm of freezing rain has come on since daylight, which will render an attack impossible until it breaks.

—G. H. Thomas

When this wire reached Grant on the morning of December 9th, it ignited instructions to Halleck to "telegraph orders relieving Thomas at once and placing Schofield in command. A proviso was added that Thomas was to report to Schofield for duty. Halleck held up the order temporarily and wired Thomas, "General Grant expresses much dissatisfaction at your delay at attacking the enemy. If you wait until Wilson mounts his cavalry, you will wait until Doomsday."

"Well, no matter what Schofield boys think about Thomas, they got to obey protocol."

"Protocol? What the hell is that?" said Bama.

"Protocol means an expected diplomacy of military rapport in exchange between two individuals in a military organization, or any organization for that matter. A discussion of orders, for instance. It's a good idea to speak to a horse's ears and head rather than its romp mainly cause the ears are equipped to handle information."

Bama interrupted, "Like when you came to the gate. That Sergeant hassled you trying to get you to explode by crossing you up with that jackass protocol that he put on you."

"Yes, indeed. You got it!" added Feets.

Bama went on, "Thomas will have a war council before the ball starts and the protocol will be for him to listen to all his commanding officers and then explain his decision to them. That Sergeant didn't want to listen to anything you had to say. He wanted to establish personal sovereignty over you, bro!"

Feets interjected, "Thomas will have a war council before the ball starts, probably when things warm up, when the ice thaws."

Bama conjectures, "You looked like a damn pilgrim when you came out of Sable's place. What happened down there anyway?"

Feets thought for a moment, then answered, "I learned I want to live, and I want to live like a free man. I didn't experience love, but I did get some gratification that was new to me. I also learned that history is important, and I was inspired by the art of our people. This fight is about the freedom of black folks, and this thing around my neck is not a token, it's a medallion carved out of the sacrifice by my father for the freedom of my family!"

FEETS

Saturday, December 10

Nothing of importance occurred along our lines today. There has been much picket firing. The day has been quite cold. There is no apparent change in enemy's lines this morning. The same force appears to be opposite of us, and the enemy is still working on its parapets to strengthen them. The snow and sleet that fell yesterday is yet on the ground. It is almost impossible to move over it either on horseback or foot."

—General Thomas

General Wood received a note from General Thomas. "What is condition of the ground between the enemy's line and your own? Is it practical for men to move about it with facility?" 3:00 pm

General Wood replied to General Thomas's note stating: "The ground is covered with heavy sleet which would make the handling of troops difficult, if not impractical. From the condition of the ground, an offensive movement would be feeble. The enemy is working on a new and interior line of work this evening. The line appears to be almost parallel to the first line and a about half mile in the rear of it."

NASHVILLE

"Muffins, muffins. Get your red hot muffins right here." trumpeted the young woman touting a head basket holding fresh muffins on top of her turban. "Right here ... muffins made for the Union man! Extra energy! Chaplain blessed! Muffins, cornbread, and wheat muffins, five cents. Muffins, five cents apiece," chanted the bakery girl.

"Gone be some shooting soon," said Bama. "Wish we could get us some of those Spencer's."

"Damn an Enfield if Forrest is on our right. I got my rabbit's foot, voodoo doll, and a prayer to get ready. Might be a damn sight better in a tight spot!"

"Ain't nothing constructive or strategic about either one. Whoever got the best plan will win the fight."

"Damn it, you know less about mules than women, and mules don't scream. We got some horses today. If our cavalry can't cover our flanks, we gone get rolled up like Hooker at Chancellorsville."

FEETS

On December 11th, when temperatures hit ten below zero in Nashville, Grant who was in Virginia, telegraphed Thomas. "Delay no longer for weather or reinforcements."

Thomas could only reply, "I will obey the order as promptly as possible, however much I may regret it, as the attack will have to be made under every disadvantage."

The bass line of "Eternal Father" drifted westward, slowly caroling through his ears and heart. Maps, spread out and drawn open, sketches of troop positions, and a plethora of scribbled notes, decorated his shiny wooden floor. General George Thomas drew a crude staff of music ledger lines, tacking notes one through five on each of its lines. He targeted lines, from the bottom up, one through three with Steedman, Schofield, and Wood; four with A .J. Smith; and five with Harrison Wilson.

The stanza, "Whose arm has barred the restless waves," caressed the brisk Nashville air. Now in closed chambers, Thomas slowly, past his pursed lips, pitched his plan of attack and took a vote of his war council generals. Wood, Smith, Wilson, and Steedman approved the plan with the exception of Schofield, who vaguely responded, "I'll obey orders."

His trusted manservant stood by the room window and studied the oblique reserve of Schofield while polishing his shoe tips on the back of his trousers. He clenched his snow-white teeth and flashed on the telegram recently received from General Grant.

"If you delay attacking longer, the mortified spectacle will be witness of a Rebel army moving for the Ohio, and you will be forced to act, accepting such weather as you find."

The St. Cloud Hotel was a far distance from City Point, Virginia. The servant had tagged Schofield as the Judas undermining Thomas in Washington with telegrams of disapproval. According to Wilson in post battle reports, "General Schofield states a deliberate falsehood when he says that as the ranking officer next to the Commanding General, he waved his right to speak last and promptly sustained Thomas."

FEETS

Sunday, December 11

There is a meeting of corps commanders at General Thomas' headquarters. It is decided that we cannot attack the enemy with any show of success until the weather moderates and the snow and sleet now on the ground thaws. The ground is yet covered with a cake of ice, and it is very difficult to move over it. The weather still continues very cold, below the freezing point. There is no change in the appearance of the enemy's lines, except that he is working on his exterior line—the new one he is constructing. Considerable picket firing today; no artillery firing. General Grant has been insistent for several days that General Thomas must attack enemy. This will be done as soon as the weather will permit.

—General Whipple

The truth is that General Schofield did not speak at all until the other generals had given their opinions, and then only said he will obey orders. General Thomas knew three days before the battle of Nashville that Schofield was playing the part of Judas by telegraphing to General Grant at Washington disparaging suggestions about the action of Thomas, saying in one dispatch, 'it is the opinion of all our officers with whom I have conversed,

NASHVILLE

that General Thomas is too tardy in moving against the enemy.'

—General Wilson

Freezing weather still hung on, fuel was consumed at a great rate, but although Thomas had woodcutters out every day, there were no big fires for the soldiers to warm themselves. Only fires for cooking were allowed. No day was complete without a nagging telegram from Grant.

Thomas sent Halleck an amplified version of this message. "I have the troops ready to attack as soon as the sleet has melted sufficiently to enable the men to march, as the whole country is now covered with a sheet of ice so hard and slippery it is utterly impossible for troops to ascend the slopes or even move over level ground in anything like order. I believe an attack at this time will only result in useless sacrifice of life."

Thomas' corps commanders gathered at the St. Cloud Hotel for a strategy session as doom cloistered the room. Each general mind-wrestled with the situation: a straight-jacket of ice and sleet locked the face-off between Hood and Thomas. The hammer of Thomas' cavalry was cocked, aimed at the bell of Hood; some thought that Hood's "antifreeze" was the narcotic laudanum. The voted majority opinion of the commanders was that the attack was impossible.

Bama and Feets collected combustibles for cooking fires. Thomas had shared the order from Grant "to move regardless of the weather," and restated his determination to attack only when the weather was favorable. He did ask them for their opinions. Wilson, Wood, Smith, and Steedman all agreed that an attack was impossible. Most accounts leave Schofield silent or vaguely concurring. The Negro manservant immaculately coiffed in a vest, starched white shirt, and slick black cordovans, stood at the room's icy window in the St. Cloud Hotel. Silently, he considered the psychological circumstance of his charge: This methodical warrior, considered to be the finest general in the Union, is ordered to attack under ridiculous circumstances by a general more than a thousand miles away.

Lips pursed, teeth clenched, and tongue roof-lashed, he almost thought out loud. "The cavalry is north of the Cumberland, the bridges are completely iced, most of the cooks, teamsters, and impressed laborers, now arranged as 'soldiers' have never fired weapons; the majority of Negro troops can neither read nor write." A knock on the door interrupted his chaotic thoughts. He patted the pistol under his vest, opening the door for General Harrison and Steedman.

"Evening General," they spoke as one. Harrison continued, "We are done refitting most of the horses. We hope we don't mutilate both the horses and the men by trying to cross these damn icy bridges before the weather breaks."

General Thomas responded slowly, staring out the window, his manservant standing at the window side facing the room and frisking his mustache, "The author of those telegrams to Grant is Schofield."

Steedman and Jacob Cox wrote orders directing Brigadier-General Cruft to reconnoiter the enemy position. This reconnaissance, made by a brigade under the command of Colonel J. G. Mitchell, documented that, owing to the whole surface of the country beingcovered with ice, it was almost impossible for men or animals to move over the uneven ground. The steep slopes to be ascended in approaching the position of the enemy was difficult duty, but it was accomplished; the position of the enemy was developed.

Monday, December 12

The sun shines bright this morning, but it is yet very cold. The enemy is digging and throwing up works in our front and is constructing trenches for body reasons in front of General A. J. Smith's works and rear of his own flank work. Batteries placed at this point will command the Hillsboro and perhaps the Harding Pikes.

3:00 pm

After an urgent session, core commanders at my headquarters decided that we cannot move to attack the enemy or to demonstrate until the ice and sleet diminish. It is a wet cover and there are ground fogs. Considerable picket firing today and no change within the enemies' line. General Whipple, our intelligence, told us that Forrest was directed to Murfreesboro and Cleburne was dead. We are poised for

NASHVILLE

victory in the west and even the weather cannot deter our destiny.

—General Thomas

Thomas reflected on the situation and reflected on what he had promptly written to General Grant. An attack under the present conditions with the terrain covered with a perfect sheet of ice was impossible. Troops could not move on level ground. General Whipple, who was Thomas's Chief of Staff, began to declare someone was sabotaging the wire to undermine his commander with leaders in Washington. Thomas sent for Steedman, an accomplished veteran of Chickamauga, and asked if it could be Governor Johnson. Steedman did not think so. He had talked with Johnson and knew him to be trustworthy at least. Grant, en route to Washington from City Point, was met by the wire from Thomas announcing readiness to move and designating the time of his movement.

General Thomas, a forty-eight-year-old Commander of the Department of the Cumberland Brigade, and General James Harrison Wilson, a twenty-seven-year-old Chief of Cavalry for military division of the Mississippi Valley, sat huddled over supper at the Nashville St. Cloud Hotel on the night of December 12, 1864. "The Washington authorities treat me as if I were a boy. They seem to think that I am incapable of fighting a battle," Thomas lamented.

While Thomas worked to get his cavalry across the Cumberland River, sparsely clad Confederate soldiers tried to stay alive on the hills overlooking Nashville. One federal soldier recalled the plight of his enemy as he looked out at the Confederate line.

The Rebel soldiers are not as well supplied in winter garb as the Union soldiers are. I saw Rebels frozen to death; I feel uncomfortable rejoicing at this suffrage.

The unsettling winter storm continued. It caused Thomas to wire Halleck on December 12th.

Monday, December 12

It has taken the entire day to place my cavalry in position. It has only been finally effective with eminent risk and many serious accidents resulting from the number of horses falling with the riders on the roads.

—Thomas

The cavalry withstood the extremities and managed to cross the river on the 12th. Warmer temperatures began on the 14th. It finally began melting the ice and snow.

Forrest in Murfreesboro, thought General Thomas. *Sable sent me that message—accurate!* Hood had feared reinforcement to the federals; additional troops from Chattanooga had bolstered his right. Thomas was glad Steedman made it; his troops were green but anxious. He thought "Green Blacks" while he chuckled to himself. Outside, he watched black jack-legged preachers, "sambo" the new soldiers and old laborers. Then he reflected, "Thank God! A. J. made it and that definitely changes things.

Reconcile yourself with God. Repent before the great battle. If you do die in our great fight for freedom, die with your feet facing victory!

FEETS

The rubble rags of bed coverings, sheets, curtains, pillowcases, shirts, and robes covered the feet and shoulders of the ragtag Union contraband. The ruffled sound of a single trumpet and drums accompaniment strained "Jacob's Ladder" closer to the docks of downtown Nashville while it drifted up toward Fort Negley.

XXXV

Nashville

"Pray for victory, fight for freedom!" commented Bama while grinning. He strolled with Feets along the Union interior line. "Every round go higher."

"Higher? Niggers don't know shit about rounds," Feets thought. "Rounds don't go higher, but they go deeper, deep into the bone, the gut, and the brain."

"Indiana boys said this is probably the first time blacks would be a strategic force in a Union battle." Bama said.

Feets pondered and thought about it. "A slave

one day, then a soldier for the Union and dead the next."

Bama took a long swig from his whiskey flask and offered Feets a drink which he refused and continued on with an open hand. Bama uttered, "Half of these suckers will never enjoy freedom and see their children free and have a place of their own. Oh, I saw Madame Sable earlier today and told her you got her message to General Thomas."

"Really?" inquired Feets.

"Yep, she told me to wish you the best and added something about making feets wings. Said you would understand," Bama jabbered. Feets smiled.

"Let me taste that rat gut you tossing," Feets solicited while licking his chops.

Thomas smiled and thought, *Forrest may have speed but he could not line up wheat.*

Tuesday, December 13
No change today. It is quite cold but the wind is from the southeast.

NASHVILLE

5:00 pm
Growing quite warm and the ice is thawing. Usual
picket firing today. The enemy's second or interior line
appeared better. Manning with more troops than he
could afford.

Special order #149

To: Major General John A. Logan, United States

Volunteers will proceed immediately to Nashville. Report
by telegraph to Lieutenant General Grant from Louisville
upon arrival at Nashville.

From: General Grant

General Logan sent by Ulysses S. Grant is on route
to Nashville to relieve General Thomas of duty.

Feets cleaned, calibrated, oiled, and reassembled
Bama's rifle. "You ever killed a man, Feets?"
asked Bama, "You been ducking and dodging
that question like a prime cock fighter in training or that red-tailed hawk over yonder. It ain't
easy to take what you can't give back. It's not like
that plantation yard shit where shooting enough

bullets causes obedience. A death cannot be erased."

Gun boats moon-patrolled the Cumberland heights of Thomas's make-shift army. The defensive scheme of Thomas was designed to dissuade Confederate forces inclined towards leapfrog tactics to gain Ohio via the Nashville route.

Feets eye-scanned the darkness, spun, and recounted the chambered rounds in his pistol. He and Bama sidestepped guards making the rounds on night watch. Feets crumpled the map in his pocket as wind-spun clouds ghosted past the full moon. After a quick re-examination of the battlefield map, Feets chose another way to venture on his route to support the sector in which his troops would be engaged. In the dark, he made crude notes of areas rocky in nature, of areas with frozen tree stubs, and of ground that could be difficult and muddy. The few dwellings that remained standing cast eerie shadows bleached by the moonlight. He soft-stepped beyond the fallen timbers and fieldstones while creeping past half-walled tunnels and drew his pistol. The small white flag they saw fluttering in moonlight seemed a cross between a handkerchief and a large person's over-sized underwear. Bama and Feets halted movement, their backs to one another, their eyes peeled for the unexpected. So far their reconnaissance patrol had been un-eventful. The words were not clear at first, but the color of the uniform was anything but blue, even in the moonlight.

"I will shoot the shit out of your partner if you so much as breathe hard!" the voice of the Confederate gunman muttered in a hoarse south-ern drawl.

"God damn, niggers! A man can't even surrender with pride! I sure as hell ain't gonna surrender to no damned niggers!"

Bama felt the cold steel rim his neck. He stood stone erect, his body stiffly silhouetted against the Nashville skyline.

Feets fingered the flask he'd put in his pocket, fingered it and teased close the metal cap over its contents. Working it loose from his pocket, he flipped it backwards against a group of stones recently added to his list of things to avoid. The can rattled against the rocks and ripped loose the concentration of the desperate rebel for a split second.

Feets pistol rocketed to position, rang out against the bleary silence, "Niggers," the voice screamed. "Niggers on the—"

KABOOM! KABOOM! KABOOM!

The echo of shots blurted over the field. In its wake, the excited voices of Union troops could be heard, followed by telltale pounding of horse hooves. The voice clothed in butternut maintained a stony silence, perhaps before hitting the ground. A smoky residue hung about the air, thinning into gray, smoky wreaths.

"You okay? We better get outta here, fast!" Bama, stilled stunned, broke into a stride that matched those of Feets. After a distance they slowed, pointed in the direction of their tents. They jogged northward, alternately scampering like antelopes on a perpendicular course, due-north path straight to the Cumberland.

NASHVILLE

"No need for epithets and these old stale black codes," voiced Bama, gasping for air as they neared their tents. Feets glanced his way and nodded, "Be careful tomorrow," and they separated, each to his own bivouacs.

In his tent, Feets ears perked to the sound of funeral music filtering in from a downtown church. He sat for a moment on the dirt floor and silently recited a brief prayer. His instinctive reaction had been efficient and effective; it had been downright deadly. He would honor his allegiance to the Union. The bout with that redneck almost seemed like a distant dream now.

Feets inhaled deeply of the crisp December air. He sniffed the pistol and inhaled the fumes of residue left behind by, not one, but three fired bullets. Sliding into a doze on his bag, he reappeared as an unclothed black buck, manacled with iron shackles around his ankles. Clouds ripped away the tent covering, and sweat mingled with the frigid blast of cold air. A moonbeam lit the face of Nathan Bedford Forrest, clothed in the body of a red-tailed hawk. Its winged tips grasped a scythe that ignominiously sheared the feet of a regiment of colored soldiers climbing a ladder. He startled, awakening vertically to blink, then ducked fully clothed as canister and shrapnel exploded all around.

"I dreamed … "

Unamused, with pistol at one side and rifle at the other, he slipped into the unconsciousness of sleep. Headless blue coats appeared filleted, sliced, and diced. While still in uniform and wet with sweat, he saw himself float above the Cumberland in a pirouette.

Raptors have a region of the eye called the fovea. In fact, this area includes both a deep and shallow fovea which are specialized areas for perception of sharp visual images. The vision that allows the red-tail hawk to see at eight times the acuity of human beings is enabled by the telescopic nature of the fovea.

XXXVI

Nashville

Feets arrived at the post and quickly changed his shirt to a sweatshop garment for comfort. He put on his apron and banged away, bending horseshoe iron into rounded horseshoes. The fire flagged a bit so he pumped the bellows hard to achieve maximum speed in readying horseshoes. The rhythms of Memphis sang through his body, his arms, and into hefty pounding on both down and upbeats.

Thomas spoke to General Harrison, "We have taken every precaution, Jim. The Washington authorities treat me as though I was a boy. I am sure that the Africans will fight." Neither of the men knew that Grant's order relieving Thomas was being held up in Washington D.C. by telegraph operator Ekert. The actions of Grant were opposed by both Stanton and Lincoln.

Wednesday, December 14

The ice and sleet have all disappeared this morning. The ground is very muddy and there is heavy fog.

11:00 am

In regards to the heavy fog, nothing can be seen of the enemy's line this morning.

12:30 pm

Proceed with the preparations to be made for movement as previous arrangements.

General Wood, Meet me at my headquarters today at 3:00 pm.

—General Thomas

From City Point, Union General Johnny Logan was ordered by Grant to proceed at once to

Nashville with instructions to relieve Thomas upon his arrival if the attack on Hood had not been made. Thomas was spared this humiliation. Logan was met at Louisville with the news of the Union victory at Nashville and proceeded no farther.

Thomas's wire of the 13th to Hallick stated:

There were signs of break in the weather.

His wire of the 14th said flatly:

"The ice has melted today. The enemy will be attacked tomorrow."

Unfortunately, the wires were down from being over weighted with snow and ice and that message would not reach Washington before December 15th.

The knock on General Thomas's door was bolder and more business like tonight. The Negro man-servant patted his vest for the Colt revolver. His touch confirmed the presence of a loaded gun. His eyes met those of General Thomas before opening the door. James Harrison Wilson saluted smartly and spoke, "Evening, General. We are ready."

"Good, Jim," replied General Thomas with a salute in return. "Look here at the map. General Steedman is in position. I am holding back Schofield in reserve. Your men should strike after Steedman's demonstration on our left. I have confirmed that Forrest is in Murfreesboro. The ammo train will trail your horse holders. Can you think of anything that we have missed?"

"No, General," replied Wilson.

"Very well," replied Thomas.

Grant himself said that he was met by the dispatch from Thomas. Thomas announced his readiness for the interchange and designated the time of his movement. "I concluded to wait until that time," said Grant in later interviews on the subject. Other accounts conveyed that the Nashville victory news reached Grant when he disembarked a steamer at Washington where upon Grant decided not to go to Nashville.

NASHVILLE

Bates, a dispatcher from the telegraph office, told still another and most circumstantial story of a conference at the war department on the evening of the 15th attended by Grant, Halleck, Stanton, and Lincoln via Grant's insistence. Pending his arrival at Nashville, Schofield would be placed in command of preparation. That order was effected despite Stanton and Lincoln's strong opposition of handing the order to Eckert for transmission to Nashville. Eckert pocketed the order for an hour while other messages were being exchanged with Nashville. At 11:00 pm, the arrival of the first report of Thomas's victory at the War Department devolved to the subsequent suppression of the order with Stanton and Lincoln's approval. It was indisputable that Grant did not proceed beyond Washington.

Half frozen with mud and slush under his boots, Bama's weight shifted haphazardly while trudging along the fieldstone and boulders. He had been lucky last night and hoped his luck would persist. The phrase "Freeman's Castle" ricocheted through his gait as he scanned the limited view along Murfreesboro Pike. Fog rose in miniature clouds from the ground; the easy camaraderie of the former morning had vanished, replaced by the efficient and harsh preparation for battle. Bama marched as a skirmisher with the 14th Colored Troops followed by the 17th and the 49th USCT. In the distance, ordnance lobbed by Admiral Fitch's gun boats in the Cumberland punched at the enemy's position. "When the order of fire, is given," trumpeted Captain Clarence Baker, "be sure to alternate ranks."

Bama quipped, "Come on boys! Nathan Bedford is waiting for us to pay him a visit in all this fog. If we feint with tympani, we could make them Rebels skedaddle before lunch time and dance on their hind-pots!"

The comment drew no laughter from his comrades.

Commanded by General James Harrison Wilson, the Union cavalry of 9,000 men—3,000 of whom could not be horsed—rode around Hood via his left flank. These men were equipped with Spencer repeating carbines. It was the shortened version of the Spencer seven-shot rifle. The carbines added speed and firepower to dismounted cavalry fighting as infantry. Once behind Hood, they were to focus on sealing off escape routes. Fitch focused his gunboat armaments on several predetermined Confederate positions. The men of the cavalry did not really move into action until afterward.

Thursday, December 15

10:00 am

Having thus disposed the troops as directed for the protection of the city, fully commanded all of its approaches and rendered the public property and surplus in securing against sudden attack from either flight, I moved out in obedience to the orders of Major General Thomas.

—General Steedman

Thursday, December 15

6:00 am

Very foggy; cannot suitably form the troops yet.

6:30 am

Morgan unit moves in three lines parallel to Murfreesboro Pike. At first, Shafter's unit faces apparently a mound of logs. However, they found out it was a lair, a lunette. They were ambushed with grape and canister as soon as they passed it.

General Smith has a long distance to swim around before we can advance. His troops are forming slowly.

12:30 pm

Our right is now moving slowly and conforming to General Smith's movement. General Beady is ordered by General Woods to assault the works on Montgomery Hill. Colonel Post's brigade selected to make the assault.

1:00 pm

Colonel Post assaulted Montgomery Hill and carried it out handsomely. We captured quite a number of prisoners. Our losses and kills along with the wounded are not large enough for success.

1:30 pm

General Thomas sent word that he had sent General Schofield to General Smith Wright to enable the cavalry and to go around the enemies' left flank. He wishes General

NASHVILLE

Woods to march his troops against General Smith's left. Our reserves were once masked in that direction.

2:00 pm

Visited General Smith on his line. Our whole line now swings up toward the enemy's operations.

2:30 pm

General Smith carried the left of the enemy's operations. Quickly a word was sent to the division commander of 4th Corps to push forward.

3:15 pm

Generals Elliot and Kimball advance.

3:25 pm

Generals Kimball and Elliot occupy high ground but not very near the enemy's solid works. Council's brigade provide cover for Steedman's troops which form up."

—General Thomas

FEETS

On December 15, General Thomas telegraphed General Halleck from Nashville:

"I attacked the enemy's left this morning and drove it from the river, below the city, very nearly to the Franklin pike, a distance of about eight miles. Have captured General James R. Chalmers' headquarters and train, and a second train of about twenty wagons, with between 800 and 1,000 prisoners and sixteen pieces of artillery. The troops behaved splendidly. I shall attack the enemy again tomorrow, if he stands to fight, and, if he retreats during the night, will pursue him, throwing a heavy cavalry force in his rear, to destroy his trains, if possible."

XXXVII

Nashville

Bama had marched out with this group and met the hailstorm of Granbury's brigade. Granbury's Texans sent out devastating volleys throughout Shafter's ranks. African-American troops fell like ten-pins. This brigade was part of Cheetham's troops that dueled with Thomas at Chickamauga. This portion of Thomas's anvil was devastated, Bama included.

Early on the morning of December 15th, General Thomas had checked out of St. Cloud Hotel on Church Street and strolled among the gas lantern lit Fifth Avenue. His manservant saluted General Thomas and smiled. "Nothing like the sound of cannon thunder," the General mused, even though he was still angered at the telegrams received from the distant Grant. "Since when is City Point, Virginia Petersburg or Washington, D.C. Nashville?"

A distant voice barked general orders, "Bayonet any deserters. When the order to drop is given, drop as fast as that hawk flies. The rear ranks will fire over your heads, just like our drills. Our artillery will soften up positions as we approach. They are to send volleys over our heads into the rivers."

General Whipple writes on the morning of the 15th of December:

The weather was favorable. The army was formed and ready at an early hour to carry out the plan of battle. Propagate in special field order of the 14th. The formation of troops was partially concealed from the enemy by the broken nature of the ground and also by dense fog which only lifted towards noon. The enemy was apparently totally unaware of any intention on our part to attack his position. Especially, he did not seem to expect any movement against his left flank. To divert his attention is still further from our real intentions.

NASHVILLE

Major General Steedman had on the evening of December 14th received orders to make a heavy demonstration with his command against the enemy directly east of the Nolensville Pike. He had accomplished the assignment with great success. However, he did incur some losses due to attracting the enemy's attention. Part of his lines induced him to draw reinforcements from his center and left.

As soon as General Steedman had completed his movement, the commands of General Smith and Wilson moved out along the Harding Pike. They commenced the grand movement of the day by wheeling to the left and advancing against the enemy's position across the Harding and Hillsboro Pikes. A division of cavalry under Johnson was centered at the same time to look after the battery of the enemy located on Cumberland River at Bells Landing, eight miles below Nashville. General Johnson did not get into position until late in the afternoon when in conjunction with the gunboats under Lieutenant Commander Leroy Finch. The enemy's battery was engaged until after nightfall, and the area was finally evacuated on the morning of the 16th.

FEETS

General Steedman writes:

In this assault, the troops behaved well by carrying a portion of the enemy's works, as they were exposed to a destructive fire. The enemy rapidly reinforced that part of his line and my objective was to deceive the enemy as to the purposes of the commanding Major General. I withdrew this force and immediately reformed it for an attack. Utilized a force occupying an earth segment east of and within short musket range of the range house. This attack was made at 11:00 a.m. and resulted in my troops getting possession of the range house . This attack was made at 11:00 am and resulted in my troops getting possession of the range house and other adjacent brick buildings.

Bama's group, the 14th USCT, had marched across the open field east of the Nashville and Chattanooga railroad. The open field was ablaze with frenzied musketry, bugle calls, and belching cannons. The assault was received by Cheetham in the forenoon of the 15th. Granbury's brigade had been placed by the corps commander in a lunette with a section of Turner's battery. Lieutenant Colonel Grosvenor's brigade assaulted the salient angle of this field and claimed in his official report that one of his captains with one hundred men gained the interior work.

"However, the 300 strong men of Granbury's brigade reserved their fire until the assaulting column was in short range. The volley was terrific, and to escape the bombardment, part of Grosvenor's force undertook cover of a ditch in front of the field work and were there killed. No attempt was made to gain possession of the interior work," recounted a later published Confederate report regarding the beginning of the Battle of Nashville.

It would have been an impossible undertaking. It was held and defended by a body of trained veterans who possessed a capacity for successful resistance against five times the numbers they met. Given the reported numbers, had it been attempted, there would have been no survivors. Additionally, there were no federals killed inside the works. Cheetham's entire line was well defended, Granbury's were well entrenched, and no military impression was made of their position. No loss was sustained by its defenders except from Union sharpshooters.

Colonel Morgan commanded the two colored brigades and reported that his line advanced very close

FEETS

to the enemy line. His troops did come forward as if on dress parade. The massing of the troops made them easy targets for Granbury's sharpshooters, located as they were behind a lunette, disguised as a mound of logs. Steedman anguished over the decision made early on December 15.

Our Rebel men had never before encountered them on the battlefield. We were amazed at the soldierly bearing of the blacks. There was no cover to conceal the advance, and it was difficult to restrain our men from mounting the works to witness the novel and imposing spectacle.

—A Confederate general

Morgan's line was permitted to advance very close, but when a volley was delivered, it was a race between the poor deluded blacks and their officers for a place for safety.

Lieutenant Colonel Grossman cited:

The troops were mostly new conscripts, convalescents, and bounty jumpers. On this occasion, they behaved in the most cowardly and disgraceful manner. The enemy seemed to be hesitating and wavering. They fired a heavy volley and stampeded the whole line and nearly all the men fled from the field. The hillside in our front was covered with the Federal dead and wounded.

One of the Black survivors remembered:

We loopholed the Rains' house after the 14th got wasted. General said some penetrated the rebel positions but I ain't seen that. Look to me like they got bushwhacked from behind that moon-shaped barricade. Africans seen jumping into the railroad underpass. That's what I seen. Ain't seen no artillery popping close to that lunette neither from Fort Negley. Where were those Fort Pickering artillery boys when they were needed?

Steedman indicated:

I was deceived as to the character of the work built by the enemy on the 14th. If I could have known the exact nature of the work, the troops would have carried it out by direct assault from the north side. Perhaps less would have been lost than what was sustained. During the night of the 15th, the enemy retired from our front. Granbury's brigade had sent out devastating canister and musketry throughout Shafter's ranks where men fell like ten-pins. The curtain of logs turned out to be an entrenchment of fallen trees.

Twitching ordered the day of December 15th, both

pre-and post-feedings of oats. The team of horses and mules sensed extra electricity from Feets. They twitched! Feets swung himself low atop his buckboard with his sleeves rolled up, ears perked, pistols packed, and Whitworth wrapped around his torso. He twitched! Private Feets Roche snapped the reins at 5:15 am, accompanied by raucous chatter. His team lurched forward as red-fanged tongues of cannon fire pierced the fog.

The munitions officer pointed at the new Confederate lines drawn by Hood and received the call for renewed munitions supplies from General Steedman.

"Roche, watch for my signal." Woods troops attacked. "Re-doubt 1, 2, and 3 and stay inside our entrenchments."

"Move out, Roche!"

"Yes, sir!" was accompanied with a snappy salute by Pvt. Feets Roche.
Friday, December 16

History will do me justice!

—General Thomas

NASHVILLE

General George Thomas destroyed his personal papers, thereby leaving no trail of his thoughts, communications, strategic and logical determinations to uphold the Union. His sisters died in Virginia at the turn of the century, bitter about what they viewed as his betrayal of the South.

Friday, December 16

6:00 am

Whipple writes:

The enemy appears in our front and in considerable force. Scrimmaging commences at 6:30 am. We drive the enemy's scrimmages and advance toward the Franklin Pike.

8:00 am

Gain possession of the Franklin Pike. Driving back the enemy's scrimmages. They retreat down the pike southward. It is supposed that the enemy has been retreating in this direction during the night toward Brentwood.

As he cooled down trying to rest, sweat rolled down his neck. His arms smelled funky, his apron stank, and

FEETS

his suspenders were soiled. As the weather broke clearing the fog, Wilson's men attacked ripping through abatis on the left flank of the Confederates. "Abatis, abatis!" The word reverberated, repeated as if a chant. Syncopes of the drums shot past the ears of Yankees into their hearts, punctuated by sounds of rile and pistol fire. Feets reflected on the night of the 15th. Gunboats cruised the Cumberland by dim moonlight, guarding the flanks of Thomas' makeshift army.

McArthur's division of General A. J. Smith's command, on the left of the cavalry, participated in several assaults.

Indeed, the dismounted cavalry seemed to compete with the infantry as to who first gained the works. As they reached the position almost simultaneously, both units claimed artillery and the prisoners captured. Finding General Smith had not taken as much distance to the redoubts as I expected. I directed General Schofield to move his command from position in the reserve to which it had been assigned over to the right of General Smith. It enabled the cavalry there to operate more freely on the enemy's rear. This task was rapidly accomplished by General Schofield and his troops participated in the closing operation of the day.

—General Thomas

NASHVILLE

Friday, December 16

1:00 pm

In obedience to an order from Major General Thomas that my command is formed in conjunction with the command of General Wood. My troops would unite with General Wood in assaulting the enemy who was strongly posted and fortified on Overton Hill. In this assault even though it was unsuccessful, the troops engaged in exhibiting courage and steadiness that challenged the admiration of all who witnessed the charge. The concentrated fire of musketry and canister from the enemy's line forced them back with severe losses. When Wilson's 7,000 cavalrymen reached redoubt "five," he had his men dismount and fight, learning that from Forrest, the master titan. Armed with deadly Spencer carbines, the shortened version of the seven-shot repeating rifle, they charged the fortification of failed heavy artillery exchanges.

—General Steedman

2:45 pm, Shafter writes:

The larger portion of these losses, amounting in aggregate to fully 25% of the men under my command who were taken into action, under observance, fell upon the colored troops. The severe losses in this part of my troops was in their brave charge on the enemy's works on Overton Hill on Friday afternoon. I was unable to discover that color made any difference in the fighting of my troops. All white and black courageously did their duty as soldiers. These events projected cheerfulness and resolution such as I had never seen excel in any campaign of the war of which I have borne a part. In closing, I feel that justice compelled me to mention several officers who distinguish themselves by their energetic courage and unremitting efforts to secure success. To be sure, Captain Baker in reality commanded the 14th US Colored Infantry in the Battle of the 15th and 16th and acquitted himself with great credit. He is cool, brave, and untiring thus he deserves a promotion.

Feets had been assigned to the USCT 2, and had indeed memorized the strategic plan of the battle-field movements. Wilson to redoubt 5, A. J. Smith to redoubt 4, Woods to redoubt 3, 2, and 1. He wondered, *Is the thundering earth I feel cavalry or cannon? The ground shook momentously, as he proceeded in the rear of the troops before him. Fog shrouded the battlefield, made soupy by the bluest of cannon smoke.*

— XXXVIII —

Nashville

"Stay behind the tunnels and trenches," he repeated the phrase over to himself. The team of mules moved with stubborn grace, in accordance with his guidance.

"SNAP!" He heard the crackle of gunfire slightly different from the broad belches of cannon and also different from the Spencer's cackling on his right. "Snap, snap!" The reports were familiar to him in a strange way. Waves of blue smoke both anticipated, swirled, and trailed him. A field of Union blue, situated at an angle of about forty-five degrees, cheered "huzzah, huzzah," raising their flags and steering prisoners across crunchy half-frozen mud. His munitions wagon lurched, groaned, bumped, and buoyed over the fieldstone and rolling terrain.

Swirls of butternut and gray peppered and reddened the charging blue that threatened Overton Hill with grape and canister. The panting and bloodied nostrils of engorged horseflesh snorted and whined through the sizzle of gunfire, battlefield combatants and screech of gun and cannon fire.Patches of blue and gray combatants engaged in furious hand-to-hand combat; knives, sabers, pistols, and rifle butts found flesh whenever and wherever it lay. The sun slipped westward, hiding its tears behind the cover of veils of clouds. Its now defrocked morning virginity lost, its oranges and reds made a brownish, maroon as it sought solace behind the horizon. The ground was soaked with blood. Bright white teeth clenched around an indomitable will to prevail on both sides; skin color melted men into the darkness of death. The syncopations of the drums of USCT 14th melted into the fury of attack. Syncope thumped in upbeats and careened in crisp counterpoints as the morning mist became a musty dirge.

NASHVILLE

"Move out. Roche. You are in support of the 14th!"

Later Thomas would say to General Wilson, "The question is settled; the blacks will indeed fight!"

"'Slave castle.' That's what Bama had called Negley. 'Slave Castle' built piece by piece using black refugee labor. He had not seen the fort built from the ground up, but he had witnessed its refinement into the largest Union fort south of the Mason Dixon line. He had seen the ranks of teamsters swelled by African Americans sporting a multiplicity of mutilations of hand, back, feet, body, and face. Feets readjusted the Whitworth wrapped over his shoulder, pocketed his field map, inspected his piece, rechecked the load in his revolver, and snapped the reins of his wagon over the head of a solitary mule.

"Roche! Watch for those fieldstones on your left and the reload signal!" barked the signal officer. The screechy command startled the mixed team of horses and mules. They twitched and stutter-stepped against the tightly held reins. Feets double wrapped the reins in his fist.

FEETS

Cannons perched on the state capitol steps, once wrapped in canvas as ice shields, belched deep into the foggy enclaves developing Hood's position. The music of "Eternal Father" was replaced by combat unction, "Ugh, damn it, shit, ah, oh God, kill them damn it" and the dull thuds of minie balls.

"Foller the colors, foller de colors!" The screams chased his wagon into its logistical position. Layers of battle actions dissonated chaotically while cannons and minie balls whistled, whined and moaned. The screams of men and horses shrieked in agony, metal met metal at ruthless angles, and waves of blue and gray crashed in crests.

The battle accelerated with actions of punching muscles, gun and cannon fire, tearing flesh, cracking skulls, and ripping kneecaps while searing through the brisk daylight skies. Sudden soft puffs of smoke like little pillows rose, raising souls of soldiers, colorblind to ethnicity, heavenward. The mayhem did not confuse his thoughts but the boom, perhaps of cannons or was it the cargo he ferried, jolted him off the earthy trail. Sprung upward, the wagon juggernauts as cheers of onrushing troops sailed out through the crisp morning air.

Clubbing, stabbing, pistol shots, and rollicking taunts scarred the shrouded haze of smoke before it lifted upward. Feets quick-scanned his battle movement. Astonishment crept across his face, accompanied by a searing pain in his left arm. The acrobatics of his wagon mesmerized not only him, but also the gazes of his surprised comrades in arms. He astonished himself while he aimed, targeted, and squeezed off a single shot. Feets flipped the inside of his telescope while he calmly reloaded and waited for the signal to come closer to the troops.

"Not too close," said the signal officer.

The den was now a kitchen of hell as the clatter banged and screamed while missiles were screeching overhead. The wagon lurched, and the gun shifted, buoying across his body.

"This way, boys," pointed the signal officer as the waves of attack gathered more momentum. The earth thundered beneath him but never zigzagged like now. He raised his arm and bloody flakes washed toward him.

"I can't hold my direction, *can't hold...*"

The donkey squealed and the wheel wobbled sideways as the wagon bumped frantically as boxes of ammunition were thrown airborne. The taste, unfamiliar at first, reminded him ... *blood, blood!* The wheel of Ezekiel rolled hapless past bluecoats surprised to be attacked by objects freed from the rear.

Airborne in its flip, the explosion blew off the front seat of the munitions wagon, throwing Feets clear of the concatenation of its cargo.

"Take him to the medic. Double-time, double-time it on the stretcher!"

Those comments vaguely floated past his consciousness. The critter team galloped ferociously to the medic. The billowing hammer pinched at both ends by flagpoles while sunlight draped over the drenched altered shadows. The 59th veered recklessly, swarming as it charged over the hill. A hurricane of arms and legs, limbs of smoked

NASHVILLE

Yankees crested Overton Hill, some cracked, some splintered, some whole and others severely wounded. All participants engaged in the push for freedom and personal sovereignty. Cheers mingled with moans and groans. The ammo erupted over a furious maze of unnerved horses. Curses cruised the air freely abandoned in the blood-rinsed mud. The losses of the 59th USCT outdistanced those of any regiment during the two-day contest. Fierce drumming spit crisp counterpoints urging grimy black faces to march on after their color bearers were struck downward. The flag never lay grounded for more than seconds, as it was borne by fifteen different color bearers on the march up that hill!

Feets instinctively bent his body and quarter-turned his head as the bullet ripped the muscle in his left arm. The flesh was torn badly and exposed a reddened bone. The hind quarter of one mule splattered across the reins, rendering them slippery and unmanageable. In seconds, boxes of ammunition lay strewn across the sloped terrain. The rear axle broke, and the forearm was dragged thirty yards literally parallel to a forward trench. "Ambulance, get an ambulance!" shrieked the rear guard as Feets was raced to the nearby hospital half conscious.

XXXIX

Nashville

From the letter penned at the colored hospital:

The wounded of the first colored brigade were faithfully cared for by Surgeon Clements, 17th US Colored Infantry, Surgeon Strong, 44th US Colored Infantry and Assistant Surgeon Olson, 14th US Colored Infantry.

Feets scribed:

Dear Mother,

The papers say that we have a won great victory. President Lincoln and General Thomas congratulated me yesterday and thanked me for my service in the battle of Nashville.

FEETS

I am wounded, but well, on December 25, 1864, at the colored hospital in Nashville. My wagon broke an axle after the mule pulling it stumbled while throwing me clear of scattering ammunition boxes. I ferried ammunition for the assault made upon Overton Hill. I tried to lift my left arm and found that it had been amputated. Otherwise, I am fine and free. I am a fine, free right-arm black man. As soon as I find a mirror, I will send you a drawing of my smile.

Merry Christmas,
Private Feets Roche

After writing his letter, his right arm and fingers cramped a bit; the writing used muscles that he had perhaps overused in recent days. He used his convalescent time in the hospital, pitiful and forlorn place that it was, to walk and draw a picture of the battlefield terrain as its image formed in his mind at the time of the shooting.

"Maybe you got shot first!" one of his hospital mates had advised. "Let it go! That signal officer had no business trying to charge you with disobeying orders. If you got shot first, then you couldn't obey any orders, especially if you was damn near dead! You jus' lucky to be alive, so take that and run with it! The damn charges been dropped. They were stupid in the first place!"

"Attenshun on deck," barked the sailor standing guard duty at the main entrance of the hospital. General George strode in the large, open room. Most of the blacks in that room could not stand. Those that could, did.

"Good morning men. I have a telegram I wish to share with you from our president," he read aloud: "To George H. Thomas, Office U.S. Military Telegraph, War Department, Nashville, Tennessee, Washington, D.C. December 16, 1864. 'Please accept for yourself, officers, and men, the nation's thanks for your good work of yesterday. You made a magnificent beginning. A grand consummation is within your easy reach. Do not let it slip." A. Lincoln."

The men cheered several loud huzzahs, and the general smiled at Feets, taking a seat next to his bed.

"Private Roche, I understand that you lost your father at Fort Pillow. Is that correct?"

"Yes, sir. We found his remains there," Feets thought

the words would come out easily, but his voice choked ever so slightly.

"Well young man, I want to thank you for your efforts in this victory. You saw the battlefield, you know your people fought bravely. It will not end here. Your people will have need of education and support. They have just begun to help the country polish the apple of democracy. I have two words I want you to remember, *spiritus disciplinarius*!"

He wrote those words for Feets beneath the drawing he had constructed, "Keep drawing. This is good! My adjutants have compared the statistics of our losses. Those killed, wounded, and taken prisoner at Pillow and here at Nashville. You witnessed at Fort Pillow the number of black prisoners taken there was awesomely negligible. The losses here at Nashville, our percentages of blacks lost, was much, much less. None of you was taken prisoner. We owe that to young men such as yourself, who read the tactical manuals to your peers, schooled them in the way of warfare, and sweated over hot flames to shod horses necessary for tactical advantage. Your father would have been proud. Thank you, Feets!" and he saluted, donned his homburg, and exited.

NASHVILLE

Feets watched as "Slow Trot" faded into the distance, standing in the corner near his hospital bed.

"Man," voiced another of his hospital mates, "They gone have to write a story 'bout you; call it The Feats of Feets! Read, teach, and sweat!" A stream of laughter followed that comment and he curled up in the cover of his hospital bed. He took a long deep breath and inhaled once more before drifting off to sleep. Later, his eyes opened partially as if he was almost breast-stroking upward and gradually detecting penetrating light from beneath a watery surface. Teeth were in motion, framed by familiar lips that moved slowly and then came closer to meet his face to kiss him on the cheek. Outside warbled the tentative notes of a cornet powered by cold lips, lungs, and fingers, "Taps." It was accompanied by a long melismatic cadence and descended gradually to a fermata.

Mother Roche's and Penny's faces came into focus and behind them stood Eggplant with round jaws smiling. At first, his heart fluttered with caprice, its irregularity frightening him until it evened out somewhat. Their words came to him as if in slow motion. "Feets, we got here yesterday and talked with your doctor. Mom changed your bandages and made you some soup." In fact, she had taken on the entire floor and the men spoke with her warmly about their hometowns and she helped pass out their mail.

Mother Roche glanced at the window. She espied the sharp lift off of a red-tail hawk. Quickly, she rose from her seat and went outside, only to find one of Feets' brogans missing.

"That hawk, that hawk stole one of your shoes! All I could see of it when I got outside was the slow flapping of its huge wings and its talons wrapped around one of your brogans. How strange!"

Feets smiled, murmuring, "It's so good to see you, Ma."

Mother Roche took out the scissors that were always at her side. Scissors were always close by for pruning hair or cutting loose swab bandages. Penny, tears in her eyes, came up to him with paper, pencil, and game lines already drawn.

"Mom says these nurses can't take care of you like she can. She quit that job in Memphis soon as she heard you'd been shot. She done spoke to General Thomas and he said she was welcomed to help the nursing staff. Says you been a real asset to the Union cause." Penny pouted a bit, then broke into tears adding, "Oh, Feets, you really did your part here in Nashville, but you came just too close to dying. You'd best be more careful next time you volunteer for battlefield work!"

Mother Roche cast a quick glance at Eggplant, and they both chuckled.

The telegram that General Thomas had not read to the convalescents read as follows:

Washington, D.C.
December 15, 1864

Major General Thomas
Nashville, Tennessee

I was just on my way to Nashville, but receiving a dispatch from Van Duzer detailing your splendid success of today, I shall go no further. Push the enemy now and give him no rest until he is entirely destroyed. Your army will cheerfully suffer many privations to break up Hood's army and render

FEETS

it useless for future operations. Do not stop for trains or supplies, but take them from the country as the enemy has done. Much is now expected.

Grant

After putting on her glasses, Mother Roche started to read articles to Feets from both the *New York Times* and *Harper's* magazine.

"The practical question of arming the slaves is interesting. What would be the effect of the movement, even if the mere proposal did not cast an apple of discord into the happy family of 'free, sovereign, and independent States of the Southern Confederacy?' Would it prolong the war? Would the slaves fight for the slave drivers? It is obvious that the large mass of slaves are so ignorant that they might easily believe their masters when told that the Yankees would sell them to Cuba. But the truth is, as told by slaveholders themselves and confirmed by universal testimony, that the slaves perfectly understand the war. They have never doubted, according to the most trusty testimony, any more than the laboring classes of Europe, that the cause of the Union and Government was their cause." (*Harper's*, December 31, 1886)

A faint smile decked the face of Private Anthony Roche as he quick-scanned the feet of the convalescents. He had ducked the need for a tombstone; he had mastered the trade of blacksmithing; his trusty Whitworth gleamed and winked from the corner next to his bed; and his feet would be covered with new Union issued brogans to cover his feet, just in case he had to walk out of Tennessee.

LaVergne, TN USA
11 October 2010
200006LV00010B/2/P